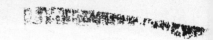

THE WOMAN WHO WORE A BADGE

THE WOMAN WHO: BOOK THREE

C.K. CRIGGER

WOLFPACK
PUBLISHING
— EST 2013 —

The Woman Who Wore a Badge
C.K. Crigger

Paperback Edition
© Copyright 2021 C.K. Crigger

Wolfpack Publishing
5130 S. Fort Apache Road 215-380
Las Vegas, NV 89148

Paperback ISBN: 978-1-63977-045-8
eBook ISBN: 978-1-63977-044-1
Library of Congress Control Number: 2021946540

THE WOMAN WHO
WORE A BADGE

CHAPTER 1

SHERIFF HANK SCHLINGER SIGNED HIS NAME TO THE LETTER AND stuffed it into an envelope. He hadn't addressed the envelope yet as he didn't want Deputy Dabney—the name a joke around the county—to spot it and start talk. Dabney was notorious for shooting off his mouth at inappropriate times.

Schlinger preferred to keep his business private until the end of the month when the news became known.

As usual, Dabney's mouth flapped without cease as he went back and forth to the back, cleaning the single jail cell where a drunk had spent the previous night. The man chattered like a girl with not much sense between her ears, but the sheriff wasn't really listening. Couldn't have repeated back a word, truth to tell. Every once in a while, to keep the deputy happy, he'd mutter, "uh-huh" or "I'll be."

It was something of a relief when the door opened on a gust of chilled wind. Schlinger slipped the envelope into his desk drawer and eyed the man who used his back to shut the door. "Can I help you?" the sheriff said.

"Hope so." The man, a stranger to Schlinger, peered around the small, dark room. Usually, it was crowded with the sheriff, his deputy, and the city marshal, who all shared the space. Right now, the marshal was out doing his rounds. Or more probably, chewing the fat with T.T. Thurston down at the general mercantile.

In order to give his visitor a more precise once over, Schlinger figured instead of just the lamp above his desk, it wouldn't hurt to light all the lamps.

"Take a seat," he told the man. "Be right with you." Rising with some difficulty, still a little stove up after a shot coming at him from ambush last fall—over six months and still laid low—he lit the wall sconce nearest the desk. The brighter light allowed him to observe the stranger.

What he saw was a youngish fellow with a hard face. Dark of eye and hair, dark of demeanor, and dark of complexion, though that may've been due to a chin full of whiskers. He looked a little scruffy, as if he'd been on the road a day or two without the opportunity to clean up. Schlinger thought maybe if he had said opportunity, he'd be a well-enough looking man, one the ladies would give a second look. Average height, lean, but broad shouldered and muscular.

What did unsettle Schlinger just a bit was the way he wore a big pistol in a shoulder rig that lay half across his chest. The gun was one of those newfangled ones like he'd seen in a magazine advertisement, a 'Broomhandle' Mauser he thought they were called, imported all the way from Germany. It looked uncomfortable as all get out, especially as the fellow had to shift his coat out of the way to get comfortable.

Schlinger resumed his seat and opened the desk drawer, easing his own piece forward into reach. "Now then, what can I do for you? I'm Hank Schlinger, sheriff of this county."

"I know who you are. I'm Pasco. I bought out Winkler from over north of here about a month ago."

The sheriff nodded. "I knew he'd put his place up for sale. Lock, stock, and barrel, so I'm told. Heard his wife is sick and wants to go back east to her family. Be a shame to lose him, but I understand his motivation. Didn't know the place'd sold, though."

"The sale went through the first of last week. And yes, that's what he told me about his wife." A muscle in Pasco's jaw flexed. "Too bad the rest of his family haven't gotten on board with the idea."

"What do you mean?"

"I mean the lock, stock, and barrel idea met with a loose interpretation according to some of the family." Pasco had a wry sort of half-smile on his face.

Schlinger leaned forward. "What happened?"

"Turns out I'm missing a horse." That wayward jaw muscle flexed again.

"A horse?" Schlinger's face changed as realization dawned. "Well, hell. Don't tell me one of Winkler's boys made off with that stallion of his. See here, more'n likely, the horse got loose and ran off during all the moving up-heaval. Windswept, that's the horse's name. Fancy kind of name for a horse, but he's well-known hereabouts. Or..." Another thought struck him. "Unless Noonan from down on the Palouse has started indulging in horse stealing activities. I know he's been after Winkler to sell the animal to him f'ever since last spring. Still, Noonan ain't known as a thief, far as I know. But he drinks and has a reputation of tilting a little off kilter when he's on a bender. Although he has a son who tries to keep him on the straight and narrow."

Pasco appeared puzzled by all this information being heaped on him. "First I've heard of anybody named Noonan. I don't think that's what happened and, from the looks of things, neither does Winkler."

"He doesn't? What does he have to say, if you don't mind me asking?"

"I don't know what he's saying to others. I only know what he's saying to me. But—"

He started to say something else, but the sheriff interrupted. "Then how do you know what he thinks?" Schlinger had always liked Winkler and didn't want any fuss with him now. Not when the man was on the verge of quitting the country.

Although, and here he took a closer look at Pasco—and whether Pasco was first name, last name, or a 'known as' name, he couldn't tell—he wasn't any too sure he wanted to tangle with him, either.

In answer to the sheriff's question, Pasco reached into his coat's inside pocket, drew out a folded piece of paper, and handed it to Schlinger. "This might give a hint."

Taking the paper, Schlinger unfolded what turned into a small poster and began to read just as Dabney, who'd slunk into the room like a shy coyote, joined the conversation. Nothing would do but Dabney lean over his shoulder and read along with him.

"Say, Hank," Dabney said, "I heard something about this. My girl..."

Holding his hand palm out to stop the deputy, Schlinger said, "Let me read and study on this. I don't need you telling me what you heard."

Pasco sent each of them a narrow-eyed look, as if maybe wondering if either had any intention of being helpful. A question the sheriff himself couldn't answer at the moment.

"It's straightforward enough," Pasco said. "Shouldn't take much—"

The sheriff made another of those palm-out gestures again, surprised when the man raised an eyebrow and complied.

As Pasco said, the paper was straightforward. *Missing girl*, it said. *Left home Wednesday morning, last seen riding a dark brown stallion of 15½ hands. Very fast horse, so don't bother to give chase. If spotted, inform Norman Winkler, Box 31, The Falls, WA, or the sheriff of Stevens County with the location. $10 reward.*

Schlinger set the poster flat on the desk in front of him. "Well."

"Anything strike you about the wording?" Pasco said. "Winkler's offering a reward. Not a real generous one either," he added as an afterthought. "Not likely to draw much interest."

"I expect he'll hear something soon. Funny he hasn't let me know. I shouldn't have to find out from a poster passed around by a stranger." The sheriff spun his chair, eyes boring into Dabney. "You heard about this, you say? Didn't occur to you to mention anything to me?"

"Got one of those posters right here." Dabney shuffled through the pile of papers Schlinger had in a box on his desk. The pile included some with "Wanted, Dead or Alive" printed as a headline. "A youngster brought it in a day or two ago. I put it right on top. Figured you'd seen it. But my girl..."

Schlinger stopped him again when Dabney triumphantly held up the poster.

Pasco, watching them with a frown, shook his head. "Now you know. The papers are signed. That horse is mine and not being real acquainted hereabouts, I need help finding him. And the girl. She needs located, too. Bad as the weather is right now, if she hasn't found shelter, she and the horse could be in trouble."

"She's in trouble, all right," Schlinger said. "Apt to wind up in a home for wayward girls when her pa gets done paddling her behind."

Pasco shifted in his chair, his odd-appearing gun banging against his side. "Wasn't what I meant. I meant she could be in danger."

"You ain't planning on shooting her, are you?" Dabney's eyes bugged. "My girl..."

This time, Pasco cut in over him. "So, Sheriff, how about arranging for some men to start up a search party. There's plenty of rough country up near the falls. And she's been gone going on three days."

"Rough ground for sure. Some rough customers, too. But, son, maybe you haven't heard, but I was shot up pretty bad this past fall. I still ain't up to riding rough country."

"Not even to look for a missing girl?"

Regret oozing out his pores, Schlinger shook his head. "Afraid not. I'd hold the searchers back."

Pasco fixed on Dabney. "What about you? You're the deputy, aren't you?"

But now Dabney seemed doubtful, too. "Well, yeah, but I just serve papers and talk to folks. Oh, and hold down the desk when the sheriff is out."

"You can ride a horse, can't you? And spot a girl on a horse when you see one, can't you?" He turned to the sheriff. "Are you two the only law in this county?"

A flush colored Pasco's cheekbones in what Schlinger suspected was a show of temper. Not that he blamed him, exactly. Once again, Schlinger opened the drawer where his pistol lay. "Dabney is apt to get lost himself, Mr. Pasco. Hang on and I'll see if I can't round up some fellers to help."

"Too bad that Deputy U.S. Marshal Ford Tervo ain't back in town hanging around you know who," Dabney said.

It was, Schlinger decided, the smartest thing he'd ever heard his deputy say, and it brought an idea to his mind. A little underhanded, maybe, but the best he could think of. "Come to think of it, we do have someone else we can call on."

"We do?" Dabney's mouth dropped open, giving him a strong resemblance to the traditional village idiot.

"Sure. We got Deputy Billings." The sheriff's narrowed gaze warned Dabney to shut his mouth for once. And surprising him, the message got through. Dabney didn't say a word. No, but his eyes got big and round.

"Billings?" Pasco shot them each suspicious looks. "Why didn't you say so before?"

Schlinger hesitated a beat. "Well, see, Billings lives on a ranch out off the mountain road northeast of here, and isn't on the regular county payroll. But we had a spot of trouble in the fall and Billings was instrumental in helping clear up a murder."

"Yeah, but—" Dabney started.

"I never got around to the *UN-deputizing* process," Schlinger said, no more than the truth. He kept telling himself he was doing the right thing. Clearing his conscience about not riding out and not letting Dabney either. Either of them, or more likely both, were apt to become liabilities to the search rather than an asset. Himself, because he hadn't been well after the shooting, and the deputy because Schlinger had told Pasco nothing less than the truth. Dabney had no sense of direction and his job as a deputy was more of a joke than anything.

But Deputy Billings. He smothered a wicked smile. Deputy January Billings, newly widowed, well, she was as tough and as able as they come. And considering there was a missing girl, well, wouldn't a woman do better with a young girl—provided they found her alive—than a gaggle of men? The justification soothed the sheriff with its logic.

Might be a bit of a surprise to this Pasco feller, however. Might be a surprise to young Mrs. January Billings, too. *Deputy* Mrs. January Billings. Or should it be, Mrs. Deputy January Billings?

Sheriff Schlinger blinked and came back to the conversation.

Pasco stood up and buttoned the top two buttons on his coat. "If you'll give me directions, I'll head out to the Billings ranch." He even took a step toward the door before turning back to Dabney, his brow puckering. "You kept saying this, 'my girl' like you had something to tell us. What is it? Anything that might help find the Winkler girl?"

Dabney beamed. "Just that my girl goes to school with Zora Winkler. That's the girl's name, you know. And she told me her friend has been crying and talking about running off ever since she learned her pa sold out. Most of all, she's upset about her pa selling Windswept. Zora Winkler and that horse have a special bond, see, or so the girl says."

"Your girl say if the Winkler girl mentioned where she'd go? Some spot she'd found to hide out? Somebody to stay with?"

Dabney nodded. "Canada. Maybe to Fort Steele. My girl said Zora talked some about going there. They run a lot of horse races up at Steele, you know, so she's been there before. They're not racing now but will be later in the spring and there's a big meet during the summer."

"I do know. It's where I first saw the horse." Pasco frowned. "But Fort Steele is a long ride for a girl alone. Doesn't seem likely she'd try it. Oh," and here he turned to bring Schlinger under his cool dark gaze. "It appears you haven't noticed, Sheriff, but the only description on that poster is of the horse. Pretty much worthless when looking for the girl. You'd almost think nobody, including her family, cared about anything but the horse."

The sheriff had a dizzy wave come over him. By damn, the man was right. And now Pasco had more questions for Dabney.

"This girl, Zora, how old is she?"

"Twelve, maybe thirteen. Thereabouts."

"Blonde? Brunette? Eye color? Skinny, plump, tall, short, pretty or ugly as sin?"

Not being the most observant of men, particularly when it came to his youngest daughter's friends, Dabney had a hard time with all that. Finally, he stuttered out some kind of description, the more accurate one being precise directions to the Billings ranch.

Sheriff Schlinger and Deputy Dabney both felt as though a weight had lifted when Pasco went back out into the cold where a few flakes of snow drifted down and stuck.

Once alone, the two looked at each other.

"Hated to sic him on to the widow," Schlinger said, although if he'd meant what he said he wouldn't have been chortling inside. "But if anybody can get the job done, she can." His biggest worry was what Rebecca Inman would say about him shifting the responsibility for the lost girl off onto Mrs. Billings. He and Rebecca were getting married next week, and as he'd learned in these past months, she always had plenty to say about everything.

Dabney, who appeared drained after answering all of Pasco's questions, simply nodded.

* * *

ELI PASCO, THE NEW OWNER OF THE WINKLER RANCH WAS, IN retrospect, less than pleased with his purchase and grew more so every minute. In the first place, it was a small outfit, smaller than he'd wanted. He'd settled for it due to one single reason. Windswept. He'd wanted the stud and the property came as part of the deal.

Consequently, his mood had taken a downturn from the moment he walked into the sheriff's office, and it hadn't been any too high from the start. He'd heard a thing or two about Sheriff Schlinger. Oh, not that he was dishonest, but comments saying the shooting had pretty much knocked the stuffing out of him. This visit proved the comments correct.

The deputy hadn't struck Eli as the sharpest axe on the chopping block either, and even as he mounted Henry, his steady brown gelding, his hopes weren't high regarding this other deputy. The one who lived on a ranch a couple hours' ride on the other side of town. He swore under his breath, even as he patted Henry's neck. More miles to cover before day's end.

Another day that would be gone before he—they, if this deputy could be persuaded to take up the chase—got on the trail of the missing girl and his stolen horse.

Eli looked up at the leaden sky, blinking away an errant snowflake melting on his eyelashes. March had turned into April. Late for heavy snow, but you never knew. And if he had to follow this trail into Canada, there were mountains to cross. It just didn't strike him as feasible. Bad enough for him, but for a twelve-year-old girl? What had Dabney called her? Zora?

And his missing horse? Did Zora even know anything about Windswept's care?

Between one thing and another, mainly pondering a route to Fort Steele should it prove necessary, the sound of Henry's hooves thudding across a wooden bridge, awoke him to realization they'd nearly reached their destination. He took note of a half-built house sitting sheltered on a nearby hillside, dark in the falling snow. Twenty minutes more brought him to the turn-off to some ranch buildings.

A tidy outfit, he admitted, pausing to look it over. Well-sited, with a good barn, a meadow spreading down to the river, and a house only a little bigger than a cabin, partially built of logs. All in better shape than the place he'd purchased. Several horses came trotting up, hanging their heads over a board fence to examine the newcomer. Eli stopped, examining them with a connoisseur's eye, especially a long-legged silver-grey yearling. After a minute or so, he rode on.

Chickens, their muttering indicative of dissatisfaction with the weather greeted him in the dooryard. A big black dog ambled around the corner of the house and observed the process as Eli stopped to toss a canvas over Henry and his saddle. Smiling a little, he stepped up onto a recently swept, well-made porch and knocked.

Footsteps sounded from within, and the door opened. A woman dressed in a man's shirt belted over an ankle length split skirt stood there. A fine-looking woman. Slim, with a mess of mahogany colored hair piled on top of her head and eyes of a shade somewhere between brown and green. Then his gaze dropped lower and as she turned her face he saw the scar on one cheek. Shiny white, a perfectly shaped S marred her smooth skin cheekbone to jawline.

"Yes?" she said, only a slight tightening of her lips

showing she noticed that he noticed the scar. "Can I help you?"

Eli blinked. "I'm looking for Deputy Billings."

"*Deputy* Billings?"

She appeared a little blank, which changed to a little startled, so Eli wondered if he'd met up with yet another of the not too swift characters who seemed to inhabit the area. Until she flashed a wicked half-smile.

"You're looking at her," the woman said.

CHAPTER 2

WHAT JANUARY BILLINGS HOPED WOULD BE THE LAST SNOW OF THE
season had begun falling in the early afternoon. By the
time she and her helpers, Rand (the only name she knew
for him) and Johnny Johnson, had climbed down from
the roof of the new house and detached themselves from
the ropes they'd tied around themselves, it was already
too slick for safety. Cold, too.

Relieved beyond words to have a top over the building's framework, January paid Rand for his work and
told him to skedaddle on home before dark. Johnny, her
regular hand now that Bo Cobb, her good neighbor, had
said the kid should divide his time between ranches,
took it on himself to say he'd see her tomorrow and went
on his way, as well.

That just left Pen, January's big black dog, to accom-
pany her back to the old ranch house. The new house
under construction was sited near the bridge she'd
built over the river at Kindred Crossing. Sometimes she
wondered why she went on with the house now Shay
was dead. Murdered, after they'd only been married

four months. She'd been without him longer now than with him. Longer than she'd even known him, in fact. Her heart still hurt something fierce, even though she'd avenged him. But revenge didn't bring him back, no matter how much she wished it could.

As had become a habit in these last six months, when she got back to the ranch, she checked the barn for anything out of kilter before unsaddling Mollie and giving her a bit of grain. All being well there, she visited the chicken house, the woodshed, the lean-to where Shay kept the threshing machine and other farm implements, and went to the edge of the orchard and listened, hearing only the wind brushing the still leafless trees. She even looked under the front porch before entering the house. A house that ached in its emptiness.

But no intruders appeared, which happenstance hadn't always been the case. And anyway, Pen would've warned her if there'd been danger. It's just that some habits refused to die.

January built up the fire in the kitchen stove and pumped water to heat. Chilled to her core, she didn't know if it was the loneliness in her heart or the actual drop in temperature, but a hot bath sounded just the thing after the hard day—half-day, at least—of work clinging to a slick rooftop and nailing the decking to the rafters. Reaching down the galvanized wash tub from its hook on the back porch, she brought it in and set it in front of the stove.

Once settled in the tub, drowsy from warmth and work, she almost went to sleep, right up until Pen, who'd been lying next to the tub, scrambled to her feet and went to the door. She uttered a series of short barks.

January stood up, water sheeting from her body and, heart racing, reached for the towel.

"What is it? Is someone coming?" Just her luck, vulnerable, buck-naked, and taking a bath. In the middle of the afternoon, no less. She didn't like being vulnerable. Not one bit.

"Hush, Pen."

The dog quieted although she scratched at the door, wanting outside to guard her territory.

Scrambling out of the tub, January did a quick job of drying off and flung on some clothes. A short skirt, reaching only to her boot tops, and a shirt cut down from one of Shay's. Only then did she go to the window.

A single rider on a brown horse had paused by the pasture fence and sat surveying the horses. As she watched, he patted his own horse's neck and continued on toward the house.

Somebody wanting to buy one of Shay's horses, January figured, who'd unfortunately arrived at the most inappropriate time.

"Come on, Pen," she told the fretting dog, taking her to the back and letting her go. She waited then, for the knock, and refused to hurry when it came.

"Can I help you?" she asked the man standing on the stoop.

"I'm looking for Deputy Billings," the man said.

The "Deputy Billings" part of the stranger's answer gave her quite a start, just as her answer noticeably gave him. A wry smile tugged at her scar. At least Pen, standing between the man and the door, appeared unworried. Her tail wagged.

"Who sent you here?" January asked.

"Sheriff Schlinger." The answer seemed almost to stick on his tongue, and she saw his attempt to keep from lashing out when he said, "A joke of some kind, I guess. Sorry to bother you, ma'am. He seems to have taken against me." He turned to go, every move a little slow, a lot weary. He had fathomless dark eyes and wore a long, but thin duster bulging around the firearm beneath. He gave a shiver. The coat wasn't warm enough for the day.

"Oh, most probably not you. Me."

"Ma'am?" At her reply, he stopped and faced her.

"He's taken against me, although once I thought of him as a friend." Even now, these months later, she felt sad. He'd been good to her when Shay first died, but it hadn't taken much to turn him when she complained that he didn't do enough to put away the killer. Not even after she proved the culprit guilty. Finally, she'd taken care of the matter herself—with the help of true friends. But the sheriff had lost respect in the community, and he blamed her.

Still, he'd sent this man here. Why?

"I take it Sheriff Schlinger didn't tell you Deputy Billings is a woman," she said. To his back, as it happened, as he resumed his...what should she call it? Flight? It looked like one to her. "Even so, for him to have sent you all the way out here, you must have an important problem. One he doesn't feel up to handling."

He continued down the steps and paused beside his horse to remove the tarp over the saddle. "No, he didn't mention a woman deputy. He did say he got shot last fall and is slow recovering. And the deputy I met..." He trailed off, mouth twisting.

No more than she'd expected. January made a throw-away motion. "Yes, Deputy Dabney. He means well. Mostly. As for Schlinger, I'd say it's less of the bother from his old wound than the fact he's getting married in a week or so. I doubt he wants to take on anything in the meantime. Especially anything strenuous." She shivered a little as, following him onto the porch, the wind blew a flurry of snow to swirl around her.

"Or dangerous." He spoke so low it was hard to hear.

"Dangerous?" Intrigued now, she surprised herself by offering an invitation. "You look cold. Why don't you come in and warm up? Tell me what's happened. There's fresh coffee on the stove," she added as further temptation, "and you can put your horse in the barn out of the wind for a bit."

He added to the surprise when he agreed. Kind of spoiled it though when he said something along the lines of not knowing what a woman could do. His problem called for action and know-how.

She only compressed her lips. After all, she'd been hearing the same sort of thing all her life whether it concerned building a bridge or taking care of bad people, and didn't see any need to prove her abilities to a stranger.

One thing about it, the time it took this particular stranger to take his horse to shelter gave her a few minutes to get rid of the bathtub and wipe the splashes from the floor.

January only realized she'd neglected to ask his name when he knocked on the back door and waited for her answer before he entered. A courtesy she appreciated. He also removed his hat and attempted to finger-comb his hair before unbuttoning his coat and sitting at the kitchen table. He found it necessary to first shift his long-barreled firearm—of a kind she'd never seen—forward over his chest. He could also, she decided, have used a shave. Her eyes narrowed.

Whatever had caused him to seek help from the sheriff, she surmised he'd been using his own resources for a spell. She brought coffee for them both, piled some oatmeal cookies on a plate, and settled across from him. Here, where the light was better, she watched his gaze move to her scarred face.

"Now," she said, as if she hadn't noticed, "what's your name. I like to know who is sitting at my kitchen table."

For the first time, a smile flicked across his grim mien. "I'm Pasco."

Her smooth brow puckered.

"Eli Pasco. I bought Norman Winkler out a couple weeks ago and have been staying at the hotel ever since." His eyes shifted from her cheek as he picked up his cup. "I've already run into trouble with the deal."

"What kind of trouble?"

"The kind I've since been told somebody should've warned me about."

"That sounds ominous." She tilted her head. "Why come to me? What brings you here asking for Deputy Billings? Deputy January Schutt Billings, if you want my complete identification."

For answer, he drew out the poster Winkler had been circulating and shoved it across the table to her.

A paper with more about the horse than the missing girl. At least now it contained a description of the girl as well as the horse. The best Dabney had been able to remember, anyway, which Pasco had copied down across the document's bottom.

A very fine, artistic handwriting January noted with some surprise although she concentrated on the message rather than the delivery. "A missing girl? Who is she and what has she to do with you?"

Pasco flicked her a dark glance. "Doesn't it say? Sorry." He drew the paper to him and took the stub of a pencil from an inside pocket of his coat. *Zora Winkler,* he wrote in the same neat handwriting.

"Zora Winkler. Missing girl, missing horse, father sold the ranch." January reread the document, summed it up, and sat back in her chair with a faraway look in her eyes. "You own the ranch and I'm betting, you own the missing horse. I'm also betting the girl, Zora, has run off with the horse."

Pasco's eyes widened a little. Snorting, he had a single correction. "Stole the horse. And God knows where the two of them are now. If they're still alive, or unharmed. Could've been eaten by a grizzly for all I can discover."

"We're not troubled much by grizzlies around here, I'm happy to say." Still, January read more into this than he, or any other man, might have thought. His concern seemed as much about the girl as about the horse, a little surprising, considering. "I suppose you've spoken to her father and mother. Or siblings? Did they have any ideas?"

He took a gulp of his coffee, hot and strong enough to make him cough and sputter. She'd put a smidgeon of

Old Crow in it, same as Shay'd liked when he got chilled. She stared at him blandly as he took another, smaller sip.

"I talked to her father. According to him, the mother is too sickly to be worried about the girl. He says the woman's health is why he sold out. There were a couple older brothers sitting around with their ears hanging out when the old man and I talked. They acted like it's all a joke. Not a one of them appear to be worried about her. Only about the horse and even then, because they're afraid I'll blame them. Maybe prosecute or demand my money back. They know Windswept is why I bought the place, and they don't want accused of hiding him away somewhere. They're using the girl as an excuse."

Bitter words. Mr. Pasco clearly didn't see this as any kind of joke.

"Ah, Windswept. I see. But girls of this age, Mr. Pasco, often become a little silly over horses. I did myself. And for this girl and a horse like Windswept? I'm not surprised."

He only grunted.

She'd had her Mollie horse since she turned thirteen and loved her dearly. Then and now. Almost as much as she loved her dog Pen, short for Penelope.

She patted the dog's head where it rested on her knee.

"Where did you get this added information." She tapped the paper.

"Dabney. Turns out his daughter is friendly with Zora. He says she chatters a lot and he doesn't always listen, but he's pretty sure about what he told me."

January smiled. Her feathery eyebrows lifted. "*She* chatters a lot?"

His mouth turned down although his eyes sparked. "Might take after her pa."

The moment of levity passed.

"So tell me, Mr. Pasco," January leaned forward, "where have you been searching? What have you discovered? When did you learn the girl and the horse had gone missing? Tell me what you've done so far."

The sharpness of her questions made him blink, then stand and jam his hat onto his head. "Not enough from the look of things, since she's not been found. And she won't be with me sitting here drinking spiked coffee. I'd best be going."

"Sit down, sir. We're not done."

"Yes, ma'am. We are." He not only remained on his feet but made a move toward the door—until she stood and blocked his way. The dog stood too, tail no longer wagging. Given her size, she suddenly appeared menacing.

"Sit down," January repeated, "while I explain something to you."

He was stubborn, she gave him that. He didn't move to sit, but didn't try plowing through her, either. Which, had Mr. Eli Pasco only known it, was a very good thing as she had her little derringer, hidden by a fold of her riding skirt, ready to point at him.

The tableau lasted for a good many seconds. Long enough for January's galloping heartbeat to ease down. She wasn't so sure about Pasco's. His face had gone from pale brown to having spots of color on his high cheekbones. Of course, that could've been the effect of the whiskey in the coffee, but she didn't think so.

After a bit, he stepped back and sat. "I'm listening."

"Thank you." She tucked the pistol under her thigh, within easy grasp. "From the moment you contacted the sheriff this became law enforcement's job—as it should have been from the very start. When he sent you to me, the problem became mine. It's official. Instead of you running the business, since the sheriff has placed the investigation into my hands, it's the other way around. I'm in charge."

January had read up on "law enforcement responsibilities" over the winter, just to pass the time. She hadn't actually figured to ever have the need, but she'd been lonely and bored. What she'd learned might just come in useful in this situation.

Still, Eli Pasco wasn't giving up his preconceived notions about women easily, as she soon found.

"Women aren't deputies," he said, mouth twisting. "Not ones that go out looking for horse thieves and lost girls, at least. Matrons in a woman's jail maybe."

His argument fell on deaf ears. All she really heard was the last part, when he added, "You're a woman."

"Indeed, I am," she said, drawing herself up. A twinkle gleamed in her eye.

Which is when he realized what he'd said, but with a different sort of meaning.

January saw it flash in his eyes and she felt it, too, for the first time in months. Since Shay's murder, in plain fact. *I am a woman.*

CHAPTER 3

THE LADY DEPUTY POURED HIM MORE COFFEE, THIS TIME WITHOUT the whiskey, even as she smiled ruefully. "I'm sorry to disappoint you as to my gender, Mr. Pasco, but I assure you, I know the countryside well and am capable of riding into the mountains without getting myself lost. I take it that's what you're worried about."

Eli figured it wiser not to say anything. He looked at the dog. "Good to know," he said. Besides, he wasn't disappointed in her gender, per se, but in what she conceived as her occupation.

"Yes." She sat with her hands clasped on the table.

Capable hands, Eli noticed, with a few scars and at least one fresh scab. He wondered what she'd been doing, to mark herself up so. And her face—what story lay behind that?

"Now tell me, how long has Zora been gone?" Deputy Billings had no hesitation in starting with her questions. "Did she let anyone know where she meant to go? Where has her family looked? Are they even sure she took the horse and ran away or might someone have kidnapped her?"

Her questions tumbled out, one right after another. A couple he hadn't even thought about and his heartbeat quickened.

"Yesterday morning Winkler, evidently not up to doing it himself, finally sent one of his boys to the hotel where I'm staying and told me Windswept is missing. The kid indicated they, the girl and the horse, might've been gone a day or so before that." He'd thought it mighty careless of the family not to notice before and had told them so at the time.

Missus, or make that, Deputy Billings' fine dark brows drew together. "Might've been? Three days?" Her astonishment came through clearly. "And nobody said anything? Good Lord. Yet *you* waited until today before telling the sheriff."

He hoped she wouldn't get emotional, as in his experience women were prone to do. "It didn't seem my place. I figured it oughta be up to her father. Anyhow, Winkler and I went out looking for them yesterday morning after his son finally gave me the news. In the afternoon he sent the elder of his boys with me. This morning I went alone. He said his wife was poorly and needed him with her."

"And what did you find?"

"Nothing that led to the girl or the horse."

She didn't appear impressed. "I'll have to talk to her family, including the mother."

"I doubt Winkler will allow it."

"Oh, he'll allow it." Her gaze was so steady he believed her.

"Where have you looked?" she asked then. "Where

has her family looked?"

Eli shifted uncomfortably, aware of the wasted time. "Winkler's boys said they'd been over the foothills and around the ranch. Said they figured she camped out and would be back soon."

"Camped out? Why?" she broke in. "Why did they think that?"

He huffed. "Probably because it's the way they wanted it to be. But they said they found no sign of her, so when I took up the search, I went further out. I found some tracks in the snow on the north side of Baldy, but it's hard telling if they belong to her and the horse."

Deputy Billings—he had a hard time getting his head around the deputy business—had a faraway look on her face. "You said Dabney's girl told him about the girl talking wild about running off to Canada with the horse. What do you think?"

"I don't know what to think. I don't know her. Don't know if she might've been showing off for her friend. Fort Steele is a far piece for a girl on horseback. Might depend on how well prepared she is."

Her face, the pretty side turned toward him, puckered in thought. "I'll need to speak with the Dabney girl, as well as Mrs. Winkler."

She rose, startling him with the decisiveness of her movements. "So, Mr. Pasco, I'll meet you in town first thing in the morning and we'll head out. Please be ready."

Pasco almost laughed. "Yes, ma'am, first thing in the morning." Plans were forming in his head, one he had to admit wasn't polite. Just expedient. First thing in the morning? The women he knew considered first thing in the morning to generally mean around eight o'clock at best. He'd be well away, by then, while she wasted time chatting up the Dabney girl and fighting Winkler over the need to talk to the mother. He thought she might follow along behind him for a few hours, but figured she'd soon give up the chase. He'd done his duty in reporting this. From now on, he'd handle the situation his own way.

* * *

AS MUCH AS SHE DREADED GOING OUT INTO THE SWIRLING SNOW, an inch of which already covered the ground, January bundled up in her winter gear and went to the barn to saddle Mollie. She stopped at the stall where Shay's silvery grey gelding, having heard her approach, hung his head over the gate.

"How do you feel about a trek over the mountain, Hoot?" She rubbed the gray's velvety nose. "Sound good? We've been missing any excitement lately. It might be good for both of us." Smiling a wicked smile, she huffed a breath into his nostrils. "And it might give you a chance to meet your archrival. Wouldn't it be fun to have run-off?"

Hoot against Windswept? She'd bet on Hoot every time.

Hoot tossed his head as if he knew what she'd said. And maybe he had. January often gave him credit for being smarter than most of the men she knew.

The idea made her full-on laugh. "All right. Save your energy tonight then. Tomorrow we'll set out."

But for now, her buckskin mare Mollie carried her to

town. She arrived about four. A good time, she thought as she rode down the middle of the street where the snow had melted and made a loblolly underfoot. Deliberately avoiding the sheriff's office, she cut around the block to an area of small houses. Smoke rose from chimneys where it hid amidst the gray skies. Most of the porches had been swept clean. The Dabney house, she found, was no exception. She stopped outside, dismounted, and hitched Mollie to the porch rail.

"This won't take long," she told the horse. Once invited inside, she repeated the words to the Dabney girl. Dora Dabney perched on a worn footstool while January, at Mrs. Dabney's insistence, sat in the room's best chair. Mrs. Dabney fluttered about, first to the kitchen to stir something, back to the parlor to offer tea, then to a chair from which she bounced back up and went to the kitchen yet again.

January took the opportunity to smile at the girl. "Your name is Dora, correct?" It would've been easy to get that mixed up.

"Yes," the girl mumbled.

"You know who I am, don't you?"

"Sure. You're the woman who built a bridge across Kindred Creek, killed Mr. Hammel, then shot Mrs. Hammel after she killed your husband." Dora's eyes lit, most certainly enjoying the heroics of the story and eager to talk.

"Harrumph." January most definitely did not enjoy the story, the latter three acts anyway, or the notoriety that came with them. "Then you know Sheriff Schlinger made me a deputy."

If possible, Dora brightened even more. "Oh yes, ma'am. Everybody knows. I'd like to be a deputy just like you."

But not like her father? January turned a snort into a cough.

"Good," she said. "Then—"

She cut off when Mrs. Dabney appeared again. "Are you here about Zora? Dora and Zora." She smiled fondly at her daughter. "Their names are so alike I think it's why they became friends."

Dora blushed.

More chit chat followed. January fretted at the waste of time, bearing with the delay until she got her question asked. The only one she considered necessary. "Fort Steele." She fixed Dora with her most compelling gaze. "What, exactly, did Zora say about Fort Steele? Did she plan to go there?"

Dora squirmed on her footstool. "I thought she meant later. In spring after school is out. But then her daddy said they were moving back east after he'd sold the ranch to some stranger. And he sold him Windswept, too. Mr. Winkler always laughed and said Zora owned him, owned Windswept, so how could he sell him?"

January could imagine how the girl had felt. Sad, mad and betrayed. But Dora still hadn't answered her question. "Did she set out on Windswept for Fort Steele?"

Biting her bottom lip, Dora nodded. "I think so. Maybe. She said she knew the way. She's probably in Canada by now. She must be. It's been three days. Maybe even three and a half if she set out after school on Tuesday."

As much as the girl tried to sound confident, January

heard worry in her statement. Another thought occurred. "Was she supposed to let you know when she got there?"

Dora nodded. "She has some money she saved up. She promised she'd send me a telegram when she arrived."

A lead weight seemed to plummet into January's stomach. *Three and a half days?* "One thing more," she said. "Does Zora usually keep her promises?"

The girl nodded; her mouth turned down. "Yes. Always. Because nobody ever keeps the ones they make to her."

Leaving the Dabney house, January's next stop was the rooming house where the Winklers had taken up residence while they prepared for their move back east. She suspected Winkler would be in the Barefoot Saloon, passing time with the menfolk and having a drink or two while the girl's brothers swanned around town seeing what mischief they could get into. Which, if January had timed things just right, should leave Mrs. Winkler on her own and, fingers crossed, ready to talk about her missing daughter.

Fifteen minutes later, she mounted Mollie and headed home. Not because her conclusions as to the family's activities was off. Just her expectations. Turns out Mrs. Winkler, who didn't look in the least indisposed regardless of what she told her husband, was primping for dinner. She hardly seemed to notice her daughter was missing and to January's questions, had only a rather severe reaction.

"I'm prepared to leave her behind if she isn't here by the time we have to catch the train." Mrs. Winkler smoothed an eyebrow obviously colored to appear darker. "She's been warned. Imagine gallivanting all over the country-side on that horse. It doesn't even belong to us anymore. For shame." And added. "Fort Steele? How should I know? I can't imagine why she'd want to go there."

Not a woman who cared for horses. Or girl children.

Eli stabled Henry at the livery, but instead of leaving his horse to the hostler, took care of the animal himself. Feet and shoes were thoroughly checked, brown coat brushed to a shine, fed, watered, saddle blanket dried and the saddle searched for stickers. He even spread a blanket over Henry's back because a cold wind blew down the center aisle of the barn and raised an acrid dust.

At the general store he stocked up on ammunition, some food for himself—jerky, a couple cans of peaches, some beans and crackers, added a five-pound bag of grain for Henry—and declared himself ready for a trek over the mountains. He bought a sheepskin-lined vest to wear under his duster, too. The calendar might say spring, but winter hadn't been paying attention.

He found a café and had supper, then stopped in at the saloon for a postprandial drink. He spotted Winkler there, drinking and playing cards at a table with three other men oblivious to anything going on around him. You'd have thought he didn't have a care in the world, let alone a daughter who hadn't been seen for going on four days. Or for a horse stolen out from under the buyer of his property.

Eli wondered if it was too late to stop the sale. Demand his money back since he hadn't gotten what he paid for. All this? It hardly seemed worth his time or money. There'd be other land, other horses. Maybe something more on the order of Mrs. Billings' place.

Even so, he knew he'd be out searching for the horse and the girl in the morning.

Turns out the hour or so he spent in the saloon filled his head with new information. Nothing about the missing girl or his missing horse, to his regret, but plenty about Deputy Billings.

"The woman built a bridge over Kindred Creek all by herself," one fellow told him, another standing near nodding agreement.

"Did a fine job of it, too," this one said. "Don't know a man around who could've done better."

Eli took a sip of his whiskey and inwardly snorted, until, with some astonishment, he remembered the bridge he'd crossed going out the Billings ranch. That one? For true?

"She saved Shay Billings' life and almost lost her own, but by gory, the two of them brought Marvin Hammel and his gang of gunslingers down," another said. "Them and that Ford Tervo fellow and a couple other ranchers. They prevented Hammel from damming the whole river for his single use. And when Shay was murdered, she found his killer and got revenge."

"So, she's a widow."

"Yup. Tough as they come though. Managed to clear the shysters out of this county, by gum. Haven't had any trouble since."

She hadn't been entirely successful in that, Eli thought, even as he nodded. He guessed they didn't realize Winkler ran pretty near the edge.

"It's why she got deputized." The first man looked around and spoke in a low tone. "Schlinger wouldn't take charge, and somebody had to. She stepped up. Dunno what the county is gonna do for a sheriff when his term runs out. Dabney sure ain't cut out for it."

"Her scar..." Eli said, thinking one of the men would take up that topic. After all, it wasn't every day you saw a good-looking woman with an S-shaped scar on her cheek. Carved or burned, he couldn't tell which.

But none of them had a word to say regarding her scar and later, as he tossed on the lumpy hotel bed, his curiosity went begging.

At five o'clock in the morning, Eli was the only person stirring as he left the hotel. Unless a dog sniffing in the narrow way between the hotel and the hardware store counted. Other than that, main street was silent and empty. The aroma of coffee cooking somewhere showed at least one other person was awake. He was happy to see it was the hostler, who offered him a freshly brewed cup.

Eli appreciated it, finding time to risk scalding his mouth as he packed his few items in saddlebags and latched them on behind his saddle.

The hostler, "Call me Squirt," he'd said, "on account of I ain't very tall," had informed Eli that while the snow had stopped down here in the valleys, higher ground was apt to find it piled up on the north slopes. "It don't usually melt until June. Wouldn't hurt was you to carry a shovel and a hatchet if you're traveling through the mountains."

No doubt a good plan but Eli figured he'd manage without.

Thanking Squirt for the coffee and the advice, he led Henry out of the barn. The ghost gray horse and rider who stood waiting in the street were a considerable surprise, enough he had to smother a curse. The black dog sat between them and a buckskin packhorse.

"Morning, Missus Billings," Squirt called from within the barn. "A fine day for a ride in the mountains."

"Morning, Squirt," the deputy called back. "I don't know about fine, but I'm looking for successful."

The handle of a shovel stuck up from the neat pack on the buckskin's back. A hatchet was clipped alongside. The deputy had prepared for some serious traveling.

"Mount up, Mr. Pasco," she said, crisp as a new dollar bill. "Time is wasting. That girl has been missing for four days."

"The girl and my horse," he corrected her, his voice scraping.

But what else could he do? Eli swung onto Henry's back and shook out the reins. "After you, Mrs. Deputy," he said.

CHAPTER 4

IF MR. ELI PASCO THOUGHT HE'D HIDDEN HIS REACTION FROM HER, he had another think coming. January could plainly see he resented her for taking charge. Even for being on time and being female. Not that she hadn't seen it all before and become used to it—almost. The attitude made her laugh, when she was in a good mood. If it hadn't been for her dad who'd taught her women were capable of most everything men were and that everyone ought to know how to fend for themselves, she might even have taken the attitude for granted. Shay had been different too. He'd accepted and respected her talents and loved her unabashedly, scars and all.

She'd had clues that maybe Deputy U.S. Marshal Ford Tervo was learning, too, although he had a tendency to look upon her as an outlier to be admired if not quite understood. A woman who'd killed in the name of justice and law? Not exactly a feminine trait and she knew Ford preferred a refined, womanly female. *But he'd liked her, warts and all.* She'd been aware of that, as well. A lot aware, some of the time.

This Eli Pasco. What kind of man would he turn out to be?

Sighing a little because she hadn't had enough sleep, January supposed she'd soon find out. Cooperation between was the only reason it mattered anyhow.

January gestured for Pasco to keep up. He'd had enough time to get over his pique at not escaping town fast enough. It tickled her funny bone, having accurately surmised he'd try to get on Zora and Windswept's trail without her. Forgivable, she supposed, and predictable as the actions of a man accustomed to being the one to give orders.

If she'd been asked what sort of background this man came from, she would've said the only son in a well-to-do family. She thought his acquaintance with women—decent women, she meant—was most likely with young women of the debutante type, concerned with dancing, parties, and finding a suitable husband. Somewhere along the line he'd abandoned the life planned for him. Why or how, she had no idea, but there was something about him that fogged the picture.

For now, she pretended not to notice.

"We'll start another search spreading out from the Winkler ranch." Then, shaking her head, she corrected herself. "No. Sorry. I mean we'll begin at the Pasco ranch. I imagine you've already done an extensive search of the area, have you not? Please, tell me what you found so we don't have to go over the whole thing again."

She saw catching and acknowledging his ownership gave him some gratification. Good. If they were to spend hours together, she'd rather they were on speaking terms. With Shay, she'd found reticence the opposite of helpful. He'd taught her not to hide behind a blanket of silence and evasion.

Take her scars, for instance. Not speaking of them didn't make them go away and from Shay, she'd finally learned the shame of them was not hers to bear. Which didn't mean she planned on telling Mr. Eli Pasco her life history. Not even if he asked.

Pasco chirped to the brown horse who pricked his ears and picked up the pace. "I've been looking around the place these last couple days. Winkler seemed to think a few shouts into the woods enough to serve. And unless he was hiding it, he didn't act all that disturbed when he didn't get an answer. Had plenty of excuses for the lack."

"Such as?"

"Said maybe she'd gone off to stay with one of her friends. Or took the train ahead of time to stay with her grandparents until the rest of them arrived. He came close to saying she eloped with some yahoo but stopped a scant inch short. Maybe he remembered she is still a very young girl."

January heard a wealth of disgust as he recited the list. "Was he specific about the friend?"

"Doubt he could tell you the name of any one of her friends." Pasco stared straight ahead.

Although she'd never met the man, she had to agree. "I wonder why he'd mention elope. That doesn't even make sense."

Now he did look at her full on. "Didn't to me either. I got the impression there may've been a good-looking young feller hanging around, but that doesn't hold water either. What man with a lick of sense is going to seduce a twelve-year-old?"

If he was trying to make her blush, he failed.

"It's not unheard of, I believe." True. "But not around these parts. And according to the Dabney girl, her friend Zora had no interest in boys beyond whether they were potentially good horsemen." This was the conclusion that led to her next question.

"So what are you suggesting, Mr. Pasco?"

"I'm not suggesting anything."

But January wasn't ready to give up on an idea she'd gotten from what he'd said. "I'd like to stop by the ranch buildings, if you don't mind. I noticed when I spoke to Mrs. Winkler yesterday that the room was crowded with boxes of their things. I imagine the house is cleared and ready for you to move in, but I'd prefer to leave nothing to chance. I want to check, especially in Zora's room."

Pasco shrugged. "Fine with me. I've never been through the place."

"You bought it sight unseen?"

"Pretty much." He hesitated. "I was buying a horse I'd seen run, not a ranch."

"Looks like you got more than you bargained for." She tossed her head. "As well as less."

They rode on another hundred yards, Pen trotting alongside Hoot, before she spoke again. "I think she may have been kidnapped."

His expression went from surprised to hard. "The thought crossed my mind. The question I'm asking is, whoever did it, was he after her or after the horse?"

"Excellent question. But if that's the case, why hasn't

the family been asked for ransom money? And why do neither of her parents seem concerned?"

Their eyes met before shifting aside. January didn't want to say what she'd been thinking. She thought Pasco didn't either, but she'd bet they were alike.

Were they looking for a live girl or a dead one?

THE RANCH YARD STRUCK PASCO AS A DIFFERENT KIND OF PLACE now the Winklers had cleared out. Lock, stock and barrel meant Eli had taken over everything but the family's personal possessions. A few scraggly chickens still scratched in a pen where any halfway determined coyote could sneak through any time he took a notion. A thin black-and-white cat, abandoned without a second thought, sat at the entrance to the barn. Deputy Billings' black dog ignored her hisses as less than worthy of expended energy. A few of what Winkler had assured him were a hundred head of Hereford cattle grazed on the hill rising above the buildings, and seven horses stood about in the pasture.

Seven. He'd paid for ten and he knew just which ones were missing. The best ones.

Having seen the Billings place, Eli was more dissatisfied with his purchase than ever. Even the house displeased him. Mrs. Deputy Billings might have a much smaller, less grand house, but a great deal more comfortable one. Prettier too. Hers had touches as though talented artisans had been at work.

He had the key he'd been given in his hand when they dismounted at the front. Mrs. Deputy got ahead of him and tried the knob. It turned under her hand, proving the Winklers hadn't bothered to lock up after they closed the door for the last time. Eli wished he could think it was because in case Zora returned she'd have a place to go, but frankly, he doubted either of the parents had as much consideration.

The door swung open onto a foyer with wood paneling on the bottom half of the walls. What should've been elegant failed its mission. Dirty, the only halfway clean patch of floor was where a rug had been taken up.

Deputy Billings' nose wrinkled. "Are you a married man, Mr. Pasco?"

"No."

"Then I suspect you may need to hire a housekeeper." She turned to her dog. "Stay, Pen."

The thought of a housekeeper had already crossed Eli's mind. The Winklers had simply packed what they wanted and left. Eli couldn't help resenting the lack of respect they showed. A disreputable family, no matter how hard they pretended otherwise. Little wonder the girl had run off with his horse. *If that's what had happened.* If so, she probably didn't know any other way to act.

He soon found the previous owners had considered most everything of value *personal possessions.* The scant furniture remaining was mostly old and rickety. Pots and pans were the ones with scorch marks and dents. He minded that less than the evidence of poor housekeeping.

Zora's room was the only one different. Mostly just as empty as the rest of the house, it was the only one without cobwebs hanging from the ceiling or dust collected on windowsills and baseboards. An old dresser with a shim under one leg was wedged between two windows. It still contained clothes.

The deputy pounced on a diary she discovered buried under a layer of small frilly nightgowns.

"They didn't pack her clothes." Eli had to clear his throat. "As if they figured there'd be no need."

Deputy Billings shook out a nightgown and inspected it. "These may be things she's outgrown. They seem small for a girl of twelve." She replaced the frilly and turned to the final page in the diary. "Zora last wrote in here the day before she rode off."

Sometimes Eli wondered if Zora had actually ridden off, or if something else had happened to her. He strode over to the deputy. "What does she have to say?"

The woman's pretty, dark hazel eyes flashed to his, then away. "One thing I won't repeat as I think it only counts in an accidental way. But here's another passage: *Dad lied to me. Mother lied. They all did. What if this man who bought Windswept is mean to him? What if he never feeds him carrots or apples? What if he beats him?*"

"Carrots or apples?" Eli blinked. "Where in the world would she get the idea I'd beat him? For God's sake! I bought him because he's a fine horse. A fast horse. Good stock. A beaten horse is no good to anyone."

He saw how she bit back a smile.

"Could be she read *Black Beauty,* an old English novel," she offered as an excuse. "It's a showcase for the mistreatment of animals."

"I know about Black Beauty."

She read off another bit. "*Willy told me he heard this Pasco man is an outlaw and that an outlaw's spurs have rowels that would cut hay. Think what it'll do to Windswept! It will cut him to pieces.*"

He drew a sharp breath. "Cut hay, like... Who is this Willy? Sounds to me like he needs switched."

Another of those half-smiles curled her lip. "She has older brothers. I expect this is one of them."

Eli hadn't heard the younger of the two brother's name but guessed she was right.

"You know what this means, don't you?" she said.

He suspected but didn't know enough about young girls to say with exactitude. "What?"

"I'd say she thinks she is saving the horse. She's frightened for him." She stared at him, frowning and worried, and shook her head. "But still, she wouldn't have left without taking her diary. Not on purpose." When he didn't say anything, she added, "I don't think Zora ran away. If she'd meant to, she would have taken her diary. It's what girls that age do."

"What happened to her then? Where'd she go? Where's my horse?"

"That's what we're here to find out."

They poked around the house a while longer but found nothing more. The deputy, Pasco noticed, brought along the diary for further investigation, tucking it into one of her saddlebags to read later. "There may be something more that'll give us a hint."

He nodded. *Us.* At least she intended to search longer than a couple hours. And she asked no questions regarding the outlaw silliness. Besides, wherever this Willy had gotten a crazy idea about outlaws and spurs, the boy was wrong. He could vouch for that.

They rode out, Eli taking the lead as he showed her where he and the Winklers had looked. They halted at a split in the road.

"I see no point in going over where you've already been," she said, looking around. "I trust you to have been thorough. What we have to do is find some evidence of the direction she took. If Zora was simply getting in one last ride before she had to give the horse up, I'm sure she wouldn't have gone toward town. She would've opted for quiet, for peace and privacy so she could cry her heart out by herself. Our best bet is either toward the mountain or along the river."

"Makes sense," he said.

Missus Billings was a woman of decision. "Since I know the country better than you do, I'll take the mountain trail. You take the river. Any tracks you find along there will have come from this ranch, as long as the wet snow yesterday didn't wipe them out. There's a deep gully in about four miles that completely cuts off the trail. The terrain becomes more rugged then and I doubt she went beyond that. She wouldn't want to chance her horse's legs. I'll start up the mountain. If I don't find anything within that distance, we'll meet back here and head for the road over the pass to Canada. At that point, I'm afraid it'll be our only choice."

Eli nodded. The deputy's plan sounded good. "Fire off a couple shots if you find anything."

"Yes. You, too."

There wasn't anything else to say. He chirped to

Henry, branching off toward where he could hear the rush of the river burbling over rocks. He looked back once to see the silver-colored horse she rode already stepping out and making good time toward the mountain. The pack horse, the buckskin he'd previously seen her riding, followed a few steps behind, and farther back, the dog.

The woman had good horseflesh. He'd seen that from his first glance into the pasture at her ranch. If he never retrieved Windswept, he'd try to talk her into selling him the gray. Nah. She'd never sell that one. But maybe the yearling he'd seen running loose in the pasture.

After the previous day's storm, the morning had dawned clear. The sun, shining out of a true-blue sky had melted the snow, and although it wasn't warm enough to give up his duster, he shed the sheepskin vest. If he've been on a different task, Eli would've enjoyed the ride. Maybe even reveled in learning his way about his newly acquired property.

The house needed some care, although the outbuildings were in decent shape. Everything needed to be cleaned and repaired, but that was about the size of it. The location, situated away from town—but not too far—allowed for privacy. He wouldn't be plagued by many visitors. He'd be king of his domain.

Without much guidance, Henry trotted along the narrow river trail. A pretty ride, where stands of cottonwoods edged the riverbank. Birds of different colors, blue, yellow, some mottled almost like leopards, sang their little hearts out. Evergreens, fir, spruce, a few cedars, provided a cool canopy overhead with their dappled shade. At one point, Eli found where cattle had beaten a path to the river to drink at a low spot where water pooled. He found a marker there: the end of his ranch.

He'd bet there was good fishing in the stream. Maybe he'd purchase some gear and give it a go. A mess of trout fried in cornmeal and bacon grease beckoned.

But when he came to the gully the deputy had mentioned, he'd discovered nothing to show the girl and his horse had been this way. The only tracks belonged to the cattle, which Winkler hadn't bothered to keep on his own land, instead using the gully as the border. Eli had turned and started back to the meeting place when he heard the shots. Two of them. Deputy Billings had found something. He shook out his reins.

"C'mon, Henry, move." He thumped the horse's sides with the heels of his boots. His spurless boots.

CHAPTER 5

JANUARY, ALMOST CERTAIN ELI PASCO WOULDN'T FIND ANYTHING along the river road, had greater hopes for her own route. For one thing, this trail led into the foothills above the home buildings and eventually reached a little-known route into Canada. *Eventually* being the prime word. It wound through some rough country where a few years ago a windstorm had left treacherous deadfalls and washed-out gullies where a horse could sink through to its knees—or worse.

But it was also a route known in the 1870s and 80s for outlaws seeking a hideout. Nowadays it had become favored for bootleggers bringing booze over the border, bypassing the prohibition of sales on the nearby Indian reservation.

It was, she reflected, a dangerous place to be on two accounts. Back at the Winkler house it had occurred to her, aside from the missing horse, that the rum running, or more likely, whiskey running, business might be why Pasco had bought the place sight unseen. Supposedly sight unseen. But when he'd gone off in the opposite direction without protest, the idea faded. Besides, why would he be so adamant about bringing in the sheriff to look for the girl if he rode on the wrong side of the law?

She found tracks. A lot of them, both coming and going. Most, she imagined, belonged to Winkler and his sons from their first day of searching as they had all been made around the same time, and came straight from the ranch. There were others too. Older ones, that had been overlaid by the Winkler clan. Blurred and messy, it was difficult to separate them out, but she kept following. After a bit, she found where the Winklers had stopped and gone back.

She had come to the outer edge of a meadow, the trail meandering through a patch where bunchgrass was greening and bushes beginning to leaf out. From there, the trail narrowed and began climbing as it headed into thicker woods and higher country. Not far from there, she found what she'd been looking for—yet been afraid to find.

Dismounting, she took out the .38 revolver that had once belonged to her dad and aimed at a dead branch hanging from a distant fir. She fired twice, smiling a little at the twig's diminished length as she reloaded. The report echoed as she rode back to the meadow, slipped Hoot's bit to let him and Mollie graze on the new grass, and settled down to wait for Pasco. Besides, a break would do her old dog good. Let her catch her breath and sleep.

It took him more than an hour to reach her, his face clouding when he saw she was alone. "I thought maybe you'd found her."

"My greatest hope." January shook her head. "But I've

found evidence she was here. The hunt is still on."

He looked around. "Evidence? Where?"

"On ahead a way." Gathering up Hoot and Mollie, she mounted, leading off and retracing Hoot's own prints.

Refreshed after a nap with her head resting in January's lap, Pen ran ahead, first casting about with her nose to the ground, then into the air.

At a critical point, January stopped and, seemingly out of the blue, said, "What do you make of this?"

He surveyed the woods, the sky, the trail ahead. Then he dismounted, eyes on the ground and his gaze sweeping from side to side. "I see tracks that most likely came from the ranch. These." He pointed at the ones they'd first seen as they broke from the grass-covered meadow onto the dirt. Smeared from the melted snow, but the direction of travel still discernible. "Can we assume they belong to Windswept and the girl?"

She shrugged. "Maybe."

"But where'd these others come from?"

The others he referred to suggested between three and five shod horses had appeared from out of the woods. It was a little hard telling exactly how many due to the animals milling about. In one place it looked as though the Winkler horse had reared, pulling a dismounted man off his feet. Then more footprints converged on the horse and finally, a set of smaller feet overlay the horses'. Then, spaced out ahead, several sets where those small feet appeared to be running.

Then they weren't.

"She struggled," he said. "Tried to run. But they caught her."

"Yes. That's how I read it."

Eli drew a deep breath. "No blood."

"No," January said softly. "Not yet."

He still stood, his gaze hard as he eyed the trail ahead, the tracks leading north. "Do you think this might be a set-up, Deputy Billings? A way for Winkler to get rid of the property and sell the horse twice. Make it appear as though horse thieves took him?"

"I don't know." She'd been worrying over this piece of the puzzle. "I've seen the man, Winkler, but never spoken to him. Shay—my husband—never spoke of him either, that I can recall. There are indications though..." She trailed off, unsure of what she should say.

Pasco mounted. "Indications that would explain why there hasn't been a ransom demand," he finished the sentence for her. "Could also explain why the poster Winkler sent around only mentions the horse. He might figure it puts him in the clear. If we go back, I'll be out the horse, but it's possible the girl is back with her family by now."

A shiver shook January, felt to her very core. "You want to go back and find out for sure, Mr. Pasco? Because this..." Her forefinger pointed at the trampled ground. "... isn't enough to make me stop until I catch up with them. One way or another. If she's home, she's fine. If not, her chance of being rescued is running out."

A truth burst out, surprising even herself. "You may find I'm not a particularly forgiving woman. I don't appreciate anyone trying to hoodwink me. I dislike wasting my time on wild goose chases and I have a great distaste for liars and thieves. Most of all, I abhor grown men who hurt little girls." Without thinking, she

reached up and touched her scarred cheek, fingers un-
consciously following the curves of the S. Then, aware
of what she'd done, she pulled on Mollie's lead rope,
drawing the packhorse nearer.

"Yes." To her relief, Pasco gathered his reins and
clicked his tongue at his horse. "Well, ma'am, you won't
find me arguing with you. Let's go."

This chase would not, could not, end up with Pasco
and herself catching up with the marauders any time
soon. January knew that. She expected they'd need to
follow a steadily weakening trail for days before they
found Zora. If they ever did.

Besides, she had questions about Pasco. Wished
she knew more about him, about his background. For
instance, if, by some wild chance, they found the horse,
Windswept, but not the girl, would he keep looking after he had his horse back? A question of integrity, and
she had no answer.

The going slowed to a walk. In the past days, compli-
cated by the late snow, the trail had mostly been obliterat-
ed. Only luck kept them moving. Luck and, after January
pointed to the tracks she wanted her dog to follow, Pen's
nose working as she separated out the proper scents.

"You'd think she's a hound, the way she holds to the
trail." Pasco smiled as he watched the old dog.

January warmed, knowing his words for a compliment. "Could be she has hound blood. A mish mash of
parentage, for sure."

It became a game, guessing the dog's antecedents.

"From the look of her, there's some Newfoundland
in the mix," Pasco added.

"Maybe. She does like water. And a tinge of border collie, I think, to bring down her size even though she's a big girl. She's always been energetic and has a good work ethic."

"I can see that."

There'd been a dry stretch during those hours when they all, including the dog, kept to the trail even when all signs vanished. Darkness gathered under the trees as the afternoon drew to a close and January's thoughts turned to finding a place to camp. A final sharp ray of sunlight struck her on the side of the face as she rode under a low-hanging tree branch.

That's when she saw it. Well, felt it really, as she brushed at something soft and light as a spider web that stuck to her face. It clung to her fingers, as well, wrapping around them as she attempted to brush free. And then she really looked.

"Whoa," she told Hoot.

Pasco, unaware, had already ridden past her.

"Mr. Pasco." Her voice came out soft.

He rode on, unaware.

"Pasco."

The second summons worked. He stopped. Turned.

"I may have found something." Or something had found her. Hope rekindled.

He turned, urging Henry toward her. "What is it?"

"This."

Pasco squinted. "Is that...hair? Human hair?"

"I can tell you it's not bear." The strands, no more than a half-dozen of them, fluttered from her fingers, shining pale and bright.

"Where'd you find it?"

"Ran right into it." Her rueful admission admitted to carelessness. "It was hanging from this pine."

The tree limb in question stuck over the trail at a height where a grown man would need to duck. January's face had been at the perfect height to catch the strands on her face.

Pasco found another two tendrils stuck amongst the pine needles. "Hers, do you think?"

Slowly, she nodded. "Maybe. The color is right. Light brown, according to Dora Dabney. Dark blonde according to Mrs. Winkler. She's blonde. I imagine she sees her daughter that way as well."

"Shall we keep on going? Might find some more."

January shook her head. "It's almost dark. We could miss any other markers there might be. We'll camp. Continue on at first light."

He gave her a narrow look. "You're not afraid for your reputation?"

Opening her mouth, January paused. Thought. "No." A little late to worry about something as silly as her reputation, anyhow.

They continued, eyes peeled not only for signs of the girl, but a decently sheltered spot for an overnight camp. As it happened, what they found were the remains of the horse thieves' camp. Pallets made of young, pliable tree branches had kept sleepers off the ground as they surrounded the fire, the ashes of which were wet and clumped to the consistency of cement.

January, grateful to have Pen to cuddle with and keep her warm, figured she'd as soon sleep on rocks as sticks and kicked the branches out of the way. She thought to use the fire ring someone had rigged, however.

Surprisingly, Pasco found where someone had dug a latrine trench. January, examining the area for any sign of Zora, spotted where bark had rubbed off a tree by a rope presumably holding a bag of supplies high out of reach of scavengers.

"This was more than an overnight camp. Looks like several people camped here for a couple days." January paused a beat as Pasco stripped the saddle from Henry's back. "Waiting for the girl and the horse?" Another thought occurred. "Or for you?"

January didn't miss the quick shift of his eyes toward her.

"Me?" he said. "Don't know who'd be waiting for me anywhere, let alone in these woods. Not many people even know I'm here. And if they were here for me, they missed their chance and moved on without making contact."

She regarded him over Mollie's back as she released the pack. Funny he'd said who to her question but didn't ask why. She let it slide and set about gathering dry—or mostly dry—wood for a fire, digging old stuff out from under deadfalls or from debris around piled up rocks.

They slept early and got up the same. At first light they were on their way again, a scant breakfast in their bellies. Pasco, gnawing on a length of his jerky, eyed her bread and cheese with envy, but didn't say anything.

January bit back a smile. She'd warned him to bring supplies. Let his belly growl due to his own ignorance. Feeding him wasn't her responsibility.

Pen, her vitality renewed from a long sleep, ran out

ahead and cast about. The dog seemed to know who to look for. She picked up on the tracks January—and Pasco, too—had determined belonged to Windswept, and forged onward.

The people, not speaking, followed.

A couple miles further on, with the trail steadily climbing, Pasco stopped, barring January's way with an outstretched arm. "There. More hair."

He had keen eyesight, she thought. Three or four brown-to-blonde strands were hooked on the bark of a tree where they looked like fine spider webs, seen only because they got caught in the light. Almost invisible as well as weightless, they fluttered on currents of air.

"Do you suppose she's leaving those for us deliberately? Us or anyone who might be searching for her?" He pushed back his hat, dark eyes questioning and puzzled. "Putting down sign for us to follow?"

"I think she must be. Look at the way the hair has been latched over the rough bark." January pitied the poor girl. "This is probably the only thing she has to leave as a guide. Give her credit. She's smart and she's brave. And using her head."

"Smart for sure." Pasco snorted. "In more ways than one. She's lucky you're the one on her trail. You, me, and your dog. Take her father, the sheriff, Dabney...would any of them have found this?"

"Doubtful." Interesting that his estimate of the three's powers of observation marched beside her own.

"Let's hope those outlaws don't catch her at it."

"Yes, let's."

They rode on a few more yards. "We'll have to watch

extra careful from here on out." January's voice hitched. "We had some luck where there's timber and trees overhanging the trail. It's when they—and we—cross over the top of this hill that the trouble begins."

Pasco thought a moment. "No trees?"

"No trees. At least, not like this. That side has been logged off and the road widened."

"Hope to God the girl don't pull all her hair out before then."

"Yeah," January said. They rode on.

The signage stopped when they reached the top of the hill. They'd spotted a small cabin squatting a hundred yards back from the trail, almost hidden by the thick timber. Pen led them to it, setting off from the main track where evidence of horse thieves or kidnappers or whoever they were had disappeared.

She and Pasco had followed Pen down the barely discernible path more than halfway when the dog sat down square in the middle of a clump of bear grass. January held up a hand to stop Pasco.

"She find something?" His voice was quiet.

"Must have." January kept her voice down, too, because of the way Pen's ears went down and her tail stopped wagging. "And she doesn't like it. Stay here. I'll go ahead on foot." She dismounted, leaving Hoot ground hitched. When she put her hand on Pen's shoulder, she discovered the dog vibrating with tension and her nose twitching.

A few steps took them to an overgrown bush with leaves sprouting in a riot of greenery. An oddity, when others of the same kind growing nearby were still leafless. The sight made her uncomfortable. There were few reasons a single plant could leaf out early and overgrow like this. She could think of only one.

Blood and bone, so she'd heard, made good fertilizer, and decomposition warmed the soil.

Once past the barrier of the bush, a cabin, the logs weather-beaten to a gray color with the chinking between missing, sat with its door open to any wildlife that chanced to enter. A squirrel sat in the doorway washing its face. A crumbling stone chimney stuck up from the patchy roof. No smoke rose from it.

A broken-down pole enclosure reached right out from the side of the cabin. The enclosure was empty now, but it was obvious several horses had occupied it recently, their odor strong on the still mountain air. Beyond the cabin, a small meadow about the size of the horse corral at home, opened up.

January watched for a few minutes, Pen quivering beside her. When January gave permission to proceed, the dog slunk ahead.

Dread rising within her, January slunk too, only to find herself cursing under her breath. At the doorway, the squirrel departing in a rush, she stopped and peered inside. Choked.

"Mr. Pasco," she called after a moment. "Come ahead. Bring my horse, please."

She'd wait for him at the door. They could enter the cabin together.

CHAPTER 6

Eli heard the strain in Mrs. Billings' voice, and even as he gathered Hoot's reins and got him and the buckskin mare moving, he knew she must've walked into a situation. She hadn't drawn the .38 she carried however, so whatever waited there must not pose a shooting problem.

He clucked to the horses and started toward the cabin, walking between them.

Being a cautious man, he took his time going forward, letting Henry plod while his gaze darted from tree line to cabin to corral and beyond. He swept his duster aside, hand hovering near the butt of his Mauser 'Broomhandle'. Just in case, he told himself. Just in case she was in trouble even though he neither heard nor saw anything amiss.

She stood on the single step up into the rundown cabin waiting for him. Her head drooped and her shoulder length, mahogany brown hair slid like a veil to obscure her face. Even from halfway across the little meadow he'd seen the way her shoulders slumped and kind of curled in like a turtle protecting its core. The dog lay at her feet panting. That was the only thing that kept his gun in the holster. If the woman had been in trouble, the dog would've acted differently, tuned to Mrs. Billings the way she was.

But before he reached her, he smelled a powerful stench, the odor carried on a breeze.

The horses caught the smell too, all three of them fidgeting and shaking their heads as if to cast away the reek of blood. Lots of blood. And rot. He stepped down and tied Henry to an old horseshoe driven into a five-foot stump, then Hoot and the buckskin. Ground hitch trained or not, it wouldn't take much to set them off. Not with this smell around them.

He spoke then, breaking into her silence, his apprehension clear.

"Is it her?"

The deputy shook her head, finding her voice at last. "It's a man. I haven't gone in far enough to see who he might be."

"A relief."

"Maybe. But if she saw..." She stopped. "I have to investigate. This is still my county. My jurisdiction. My responsibility."

He could see she was trying to talk herself into it. What had she seen? Lord only knows the stench was enough to put anyone off. His estimation of her rose. She must have a strong stomach to have stood this close to the carnage in the cabin while she waited for him.

He supposed that meant he'd have to go inside with her.

Her throat audibly clicked as she swallowed before taking a shallow breath. Neither of them, he figured, would be taking a deep breath anytime soon.

He stepped over the dog and stopped beside her. "Ready?"

"No," she said, but turned and walked into the cabin anyway.

Eli, close behind, watched her, ready to lend a hand if she showed signs of swooning. He soon found Mrs. Deputy to be made of sterner stuff, although she covered her nose and mouth as if holding back bile. He knew it would be bile as he choked on the scouring burn.

The body lying in the middle of the floor had been butchered. Belly sliced open, neck sliced deeply enough to nearly decapitate the man. One hand mutilated. Blood splattered the walls, the ceiling, the floor.

"God Almighty," he said. He knew it for a prayer.

"Why on earth would anyone do this to a man? To anything?" She choked the words out.

"Don't know." The place, small and old as it was, had been ransacked. A bag of cornmeal emptied out where the squirrel had been having a heyday. The rope springs of a cot had been cut and the straw from the torn mattress scattered. A small chest lay in pieces, a coat was ripped to shreds. Nothing in the cabin remained whole. Even the hard-packed dirt floor had been dug into.

"Looking for something," he added.

"Whatever it was, they thought this man knew where to find it. I wonder if he did. If they found it."

"Don't know," he said again.

"I hope they kept her outside. I hope she didn't see."

But he could tell by the look on her face that she thought the men may not have been so considerate.

"If I can borrow that shovel you brought, I'll bury him." Eli took her arm, to steer her out. Is this why she'd brought it?

She let herself be steered and started to agree, then her expression hardened. "No. Leave him. We'll close this place up to keep the large critters out, but Sheriff Schlinger needs to see this. All of it. First town I get to, I'll wire him. He may think he's too crippled to leave his office, but this is what he signed up for. He and Dabney need to man up. They need know firsthand what those outlaws left here and what we're dealing with. It's their job. They need to earn their pay and take care of the remains. I doubt they'd take my word for the butchery. And the girl's father. He owes on this bill, as well."

Her anger threatened to overwhelm her, and he wondered who she was maddest at. The outlaws, the sheriff, or the family.

Eli stared her. "I won't say you're wrong, ma'am, but—"

She cut him off. "If the father had reported the missing horse and girl in a timely manner, and if the sheriff had attended to business and gone after them the moment the news came in, this might have been prevented. I don't know." She waved a wild salute at the cabin and the contents. "The man in there might've been murdered, anyway. He may already have been dead by then, from the looks of things. But the girl, Zora, she wouldn't have had to see it."

Eli agreed. "Do you want to go back to town? Turn the mess over to the sheriff?" he asked.

"No." She swung the door closed with a decided snap and propped a chunk of wood against it to keep it shut, but that was about all they could do. Untying Hoot, she mounted and when seated, looked at him with big eyes he saw were the color of a dark forest, all the darker because of her colorless face. "I think Zora is still alive—for now. This man is not. There's nothing we can do for him. Maybe we can for her."

They were underway, the dog following a scent only she could discern, when Mrs. Deputy Billings spoke again. "That's a lethal looking weapon you carry, Mr. Pasco. I hope you're prepared to use it. I hope you *can* use it."

Several answers occurred to him. Only one mattered. "I can," he said.

* * *

THEY LOST THE TRAIL LATER THAT AFTERNOON. THERE'D BEEN no more strands of Zora's soft brown hair to serve as guide, although by this time both January and Mr. Eli Pasco could pick the stallion's hoof prints out of the myriad of others and track him directly. There was a bump in the shoe, and although ordinarily January would've been quick to condemn the farrier who'd shod the horse, in this case she was grateful. She figured Pasco was too, because once he'd pointed the faulty shoe out to her—even though she'd already taken note—he said nothing else about it.

But that came to an end when they crossed the ridge and started down the other side of the mountain. They hit the main road at the bottom, at a U-shaped intersection well enough traveled to cause confusion as to the direction the outlaws had taken. One way led north, but if they kept on the way they were headed, they'd be traveling west.

Sitting their horses to give them a breather and paying special attention to poor Mollie with her pack, January saw Pasco's set face darken.

"Fifty-fifty which way they went," he said.

She had no trouble keeping up with the way his thoughts were running. "I'm afraid so."

"Choose one and it's apt to be wrong." He scowled down at the road.

"But there's an equal chance it'll be right." Neither an outright optimist nor a pessimist, she was trying to make a smart decision and finding it difficult.

It earned her a softened look, but not quite a grin. "Are you a lady who likes a wager?"

"Not as a general rule. I prefer to know the facts and weigh my chances before coming to a logical conclusion."

"Where's that leading you now?"

She blew a sigh. "Nowhere in particular, I'm afraid." Her thumb cocked toward the northward route. "One fact is that Canada has been mentioned a time or two. Plus, we all started out headed north. Does it make sense to keep going? I don't know."

"The girl was the one talking of Fort Steele and Canada, wasn't she? It doesn't necessarily follow what she said has any bearing on what this gang is doing."

January knew her shoulders drooped. Here she was, tired already, and Pasco had to use her own logic on her.

"You're right. But that way," her other thumb pointed west, "takes us toward the Columbia. Keep on going far enough and I'm told you eventually reach big coastal cities. It's a fairly well-traveled route. Would men with a kidnapped girl and a stolen horse take a chance and go where they might be seen and recognized?"

The big river wasn't the only landmark of interest in the direction January indicated. Considerably nearer was a town. Some decades in the past a helpful traveler had erected a sign that made clear what lay ahead. The paint on a rough-sawn board they found had faded almost beyond deciphering. Although several letters spelling a place called Claremont were missing entirely, she remembered hearing of it. A temporary village erected to serve the men building the railroad through the area—a hell on wheels town, according to old-timers—it had switched over to serving the timber industry when those constructing the railroad moved on. Much diminished, it was rumored to be the next thing to a ghost town nowadays.

But maybe not. A second rumor called it a neglected robber's roost. A town, what there was of it, given over to the wild and lawless.

Pasco eyed the signpost. "What's in the town of Claremont?"

"Outlaws, from what I've been told. But I don't know. Never been there. It never had the reputation of being anywhere respectable people wanted to visit, let alone live. I don't think there's much left of it."

Their eyes met. "Sounds right up this gang's alley."

"It does, doesn't it?"

He shrugged. "Must be somebody around to question. There's plenty of tracks going in that direction."

She nodded. "A good deal of logging goes on in this area. Miners still search through here, too, as every so often someone comes in with a cache of gold. This is the main road west to the Columbia from this side of the mountain. I just don't know if the town is still active." Marvin Hammel, the man she'd been forced to kill, had been involved in this neck of the woods. Literally. Both in the timber industry and in efforts to divert their tributary river to his own use. It had been said he was planning to build a town. Or rebuild. Maybe this was it. She couldn't help wondering if even after almost a year, his name would come up again.

Pasco studied the sign a few seconds longer. "If I'm not mistaken, this says it's three miles to Claremont. How about we ride on in and ask around, see if those men are there? Maybe there's a telegraph office where you can wire the sheriff about the dead man."

He had a point. What he didn't have is reassurance that he'd back her up if she had to arrest anybody.

"All right." A lucky break if they did find a still active telegraph line there. Schlinger needed to get off his duff and tend to business. Her ire swelled again. Business concerning the dead, anyway, wedding or no wedding.

Daylight lingered as they stopped just outside of the town. Looking down, there didn't seem to be much to it. January figured even in its heyday it hadn't been impressive. The passing years had done no favors to the shabby buildings, built on site and in a hurry when the rails came their way. Bare shelter for the prostitutes, bartenders, hash slingers, and laundry workers who leapt ahead of the tracks to service the track layers. Most gandy dancers hadn't been particular. They worked, they caroused, they spent their pay. Many of them died. As far as she could tell, the most lasting feature of the place was the cemetery they passed on the outskirts of town, and even that was a victim of neglect, overgrown with flourishing weeds and dried grass from last year's crop.

But the dead weren't the only occupants. There were people around still, clinging to the old place. Those who'd been too weak, too lazy, or too broken to move on when this section of the railroad was complete and a new town sprang up ahead of it.

Or, she decided, taking another look at the men who stopped what they were doing to stare as she and Pasco passed down the street. Some of them could very well be holdovers from a more recent past than that. These could be from Hammel's time. If so, they wouldn't be fond of her. Best, perhaps, if she stayed low and had Pasco do the talking.

But then she heard him curse, a whisper under his breath.

January glanced at him, watching as he unbuttoned his duster and pushed it aside to free the Broomhandle Mauser from its folds.

"What's the matter? Did you see someone you know?" She wondered if she should make a show of being armed, then decided to hold that aspect in reserve.

"We should ride on through here. Not stop. This is not a good place."

While the truth, his reply provided no answer to what she'd asked. Ignoring his own advice, they rode down the middle of the street, both trying to see both sides at once. Meanwhile, she could feel tension like a tight wire strung across their path and it came as much from Pasco as it did from the town.

The buildings, most of which looked like a good wind would bring them down, were interspersed with a few comparatively new ones. Of an age to match Hammel's time. A shack built of rough sawn lumber no more than ten feet square housed a post office. It squatted between two old saloons that had been refurbished with a dozen slats of new wood and a few brush strokes of paint. A general store, half new, half old, lay across the street next door to a café pounded into slightly better shape. It had been added to the front of a building that claimed to be a hotel.

Claremont struck her as a last resort kind of town where nobody cared. It made her own little burg look like a metropolis. Still, why hadn't she known of it?

Their horses clopped side by side in unison. Then something else caught her eye. Wires. "Whoa," she told Hoot.

"Did you notice? There's a telegraph office housed inside the post office." She hadn't really expected to find one.

Pasco kept his head down, scanning the area from under the brim of his hat. "So there is. Don't know about using it though. Hard to tell how trustworthy the operator might be."

"The thing is, Mr. Pasco, I'm the law in this county. In case you wondered, I can demand cooperation from folks, and they have to give it." She kept her voice gentle.

"You think so?" He seemed to be growling. "Most

likely they'll shoot you first. Woman or not, it might not matter."

"They might try," she agreed. "I can take care of whoever is in front. I'm depending on you to watch behind."

Even as she spoke, questions rose in her mind. Not questions about the people of this town. She had a pretty good idea about them. It was Eli Pasco who had her puzzled and more than a little worried. Not that she intended on showing her concern. If this man was untrustworthy, she thought it best to keep those doubts to herself—for now.

"Let's take a ride past the livery before we try the telegraph office." Pasco had already turned his horse down a track at the side of a rickety barn where a shed at the back proclaimed itself a blacksmith shop.

January had a moment of irritation over his take-charge order. Until she remembered she wouldn't even be on this chase if he hadn't notified Schlinger about a girl gone missing along with his horse. He'd showed more concern than the girl's own parents, for certain. And maybe he showed more wisdom than she. Chances were, if they found Windswept, they'd find the girl.

The livery was a good place to start a search.

She toed Hoot, urging him to follow the other horse. Mollie and Pen, last in line, trailed. If a dog could look worried, January thought, keeping an eye on Pen, this one did.

Smoke curled from a forge set just outside the shed at the rear of the barn, an anvil on a stand beside it. Given the state of the buildings—of the whole town—a safety precaution hardly looked for. But no one came to ask their business. One thin mule and a couple horses, all standing near a watering trough and switching their tails at flies, occupied the corral. A good-looking bay mare stood near the hot forge, one foot barren of shoe and looking freshly trimmed.

"This doesn't appear very promising," she said, "except it looks like we interrupted whoever is working on this horse and now he's gone."

"Makes you feel downright unwelcome, doesn't it? Kind of curious as to why a farrier would be avoiding us."

She chuffed a sound. "It seems our reputations precede us." She was sure his reputation was every bit as notable as her own. She just didn't know what his was. Yet.

Pasco swung from his horse. "I'm going to look around, see if I can rouse somebody. Keep watch, please, while I crawl through the fence. I'd hate for anyone to put a bullet in my back when I'm not looking."

She shot him a look, surprised at the way his thoughts paralleled her own.

Glancing from side to side, January finally spotted a gate at the farthest end of the corral and nodded toward it. "All right. And I'll see if there are any familiar tracks leading out from there. It might be interesting to discover where that gate leads."

"Best if you don't head out on your own."

"I know. Didn't plan on it. I'm watching out for you, remember?"

He nodded then and crawled through the pole fence. "I'll check inside the barn while I'm at it."

She had expected no less.

Leaving Pasco's horse and Mollie where they'd

stopped, January told Pen to stay. She reined Hoot around and guided him around the corral to the back where she'd have a better view of the site. The gate, she discovered, opened into a cluster of fir trees growing thickly enough to hide anyone either leaving or approaching. The disturbed ground was soft from the earlier fall of snow. Fresh sign abounded, a thick mish-mash of tracks that indicated recent use. The corral had held several horses only a few hours ago. One set in particular drew her attention, pointing outward.

Anger touched her. It appeared they—she and Pasco—were too late. The outlaws had moved on.

Glancing over at the barn, she saw Pasco had finished his examination of the alley from the rear of the barn into the corral and gone inside. Opening her mouth, she started to call to him, then shut it again.

She saw something else, too. Movement in the hay loft overhead where the doors stood open, furtive in that no one came forward or called out. She thought she saw the gleam of sunlight on metal. A gun?

She pulled the old .38 that had belonged to her father from the holster on her hip.

"Pasco. Above you." January shouted the warning, heedless of potential danger to herself.

A shot answered, brushing past and taking a half-inch of corduroy fabric off the wide shoulder of her coat with it. She bailed out of the saddle without stopping to think, flinging herself prone behind a rotted log. Another bullet followed her down, burying itself in the punky wood only inches from her head.

Emboldened by her quick plunge to the ground and

apparently thinking he'd gotten rid of a threat, the shooter stepped nearer the edge of the loft opening. His form clear now, he looked to be pointing his gun, a carbine she thought, downward. He fired, once, twice, before she got him in her sights and pulled the trigger on her .38. The crack of the carbine and the pop of her shot were both drowned out as another gun fired with a louder, sullen roar.

The man jerked and dropped from sight.

CHAPTER 7

JANUARY BURROWED IN BEHIND THE LOG AND WAITED, SECONDS
ticking past. No movement stirred in the barn. Her anxiety grew when no sign of Eli Pasco appeared at the door
he'd entered. More intriguing, no one came running to
see who was shooting at what—or whom. Did that mean
the people of Claremont were so accustomed to gunfire
no one even questioned the source?

Possible.

Another quarter of a minute passed before she got to
her feet and whistled for Hoot. The horse hadn't gone
far. Just put enough distance between them to avoid a
stray bullet.

January patted his cheek when he came at her toot-
le. She mounted, trotting him back to the other horses.
Pen jumped up to lick her hand, whining her distress.
"I'm all right," January whispered soothingly. "Good
girl. I'm all right."

But what about either of those two men in the barn?

The two she knew about. Sliding from Hoot, she set
herself to investigate.

"Come, Pen." January crawled between fence rails, Pen, her tail curled over her back, crouched beneath the lowest. Running side by side, they crossed the corral to the barn. Clutching her .38, January slipped around the wide-open door to where the odor of horses, unshoveled manure, and blood wrinkled her nose. Pen was a black shadow beside her.

Standing motionless, January listened. Movement in the loft overhead made her tense. Not strong movement, but something that sounded like a sack being dragged across the floor, a clump of something heavy. A moan. A gasping breath.

"Pasco? Is that you?" she whispered. "Pasco, where are you?"

No answer.

A ladder stood hooked over a rail attached to the loft floor. The ladder's rungs were rickety, one hanging by a single nail. She'd have to climb the dangerous old thing. January squirmed, dreading the thought of putting her weight on it. But where was Pasco?

"Find him," she told Pen. "Seek."

Oddly disobedient, the dog refused to leave her side and sat at the foot of the ladder, acting as though she'd follow right behind her mistress. January shook her head and, gripping the highest rung she could reach, began the climb, stretching her leg high to miss the ruined rung.

Although taller than the ceilings of most houses, it didn't take long before January cautiously poked her head through the square hole into the loft. Loose hay formed a thin layer over about a third of the floor. An alley between stacked hay led to the drop-down door from which the man had shot at her. About halfway between that door and the hole in the floor, a man lay sprawled, a carbine dropped a few feet from him. He lay face up.

Even before the details registered, she knew it wasn't Pasco. Matter of fact, no one she'd ever seen before. The man was blond, for one thing, with Nordic-pale flaxen hair, a short light brown beard, and fair skin. He'd been a good-looking man. Tall and lithe. Stretched on the floor, he'd left a trail of blood as he dragged himself toward the ladder. Those must've been the sounds she'd heard from below, accentuated by the scrape of the holstered revolver strapped around his waist.

He'd ceased all movement now.

Pistol at the ready, she approached and knelt beside him. He was still alive, air whistling softly in and out of his lungs. Blood bubbled, coating his chest as though he wore a bright red vest. Unconscious, though, which suited her fine. Heaving him onto his side, she saw he'd been hit twice, so both her shot and Pasco's, if that had indeed been Pasco shooting, had been true. The wounded man labored to breathe, his inhalations growing quieter and further and further apart.

There was nothing she could do for him.

Taking up the man's carbine to throw down to the ground, she found the vantage point from the loft's door a good one. Still, no one came running to see what the shooting had been about. The silence struck her as ominous.

Uneasy at the townfolks' lack of curiosity, January made her way down from the loft, sliding the last several feet when a rung gave out from beneath her and the ladder tilted sideways. The clatter as it hit the ground brought no response. She barely kept her feet as she landed.

Pen, having dodged the falling ladder, whined.

"I'm all right." January patted the dog and scratched behind an ear. "Where's Pasco, Pen?"

Reluctant to call out, she followed the dog who ambled, nose lifted as though she didn't like the smells, into an empty stall that had been put into use as a room for whoever tended the livestock. A single glance showed her a tiny cast iron stove, a cot, a shelf with a couple cooking utensils and a coat hanging from a peg. A lidded barrel contained grain smelling richly of molasses. A three-legged table held a ledger type book with a blunt pencil holding a place between pages.

She found Pasco there, too, sprawled on the floor where he lay as if dead. Gasping, she rushed forward. Pen beat her there. The dog dug her snout into his ear, at which his eyelids fluttered, and he lifted a hand to push her away.

Not dead then. Checking for wounds, January leaned over him at the instant his eyes opened, dark and fathomless. Time stopped for unknown seconds.

Then, "Come to wake me with a kiss?" he said.

"What?" Had she really heard what she thought she had? "No."

But then he blinked, and his brow puckered as if he were asking himself what it was he'd just said.

He tried to sit up, reaching halfway before dropping back with a groan. "Ow. Sonofa... Who clobbered me? Did you get him?"

"Clobbered you?" She sat back on her heels. "You're not shot?"

"Don't think so. Am I leaking?"

He must've meant to say *bleeding*. She shook her head. "Not as far as I can see. Where do you hurt?"

He managed to sit up before he spoke again. Passing a hand over the back of his head, his fingers came away smeared with blood. He looked blankly at them. "My head. That's where I hurt."

He had a lump the size of one of her good, raised biscuits above his left ear. Swaying, his eyes glassy, he found his hat flung under the cot and jammed it on his head. Sitting lopsided, the swollen knot cocked the hat to one side.

January stared around, doubts filling her mind. "Who hit you, Mr. Pasco?"

He didn't answer her directly. "My name is Eli."

She blinked. "Yes. I know. What happened here?"

"Happened?"

His question may have sounded like it came from a bewildered man with a headache, but she didn't miss the way, glassy eyes notwithstanding, his gaze at her sharpened.

"Yes. Happened. As in, how did you manage to shoot the man in the hay loft when I find you knocked unconscious in here."

His face took on a reddish tinge. Embarrassed? Thinking up a lie? Pasco settled for shrugging. "I don't know, ma'am. I don't remember being in here in the first place."

She stared at him. "Well, you most certainly are now. Who else is here? Where is he now? Or she?" An explanation of his curious comment when he first awakened occurred to her. Had he expected a kiss? Not from her, obviously, but from a different woman? But if so, how did he come to be cold-cocked? How had anyone managed to sneak up on a man as wary as Eli Pasco?

He looked around. "There's nobody here but us, Mrs. Billings."

Her lips, her whole jaw, tightened. Those doubts rose in her mind like a recurring winter fog. "No, not now." Pen would've told her had there been. "But there was. I doubt you knocked yourself out, after all. You should tell me who?"

He eyed her blandly. "Got me. I didn't see anybody. Or just the guy in the loft."

There appeared to be a lot he didn't know. Or wouldn't say.

Mr. Eli Pasco was lying. January knew it. But nothing she said shook him from his story.

"We should get out of town," he muttered. "This is an unfriendly place."

As if she couldn't judge that for herself.

Since he seemed bound to stick with what he'd told her, she gave in and helped him to his feet, leading him out of the barn to where the horses waited. Pasco managed to mount, mostly by himself although she stood by holding the stirrup.

The streets were empty. The only signs of life came from lamps being lit behind the filthy windows of a saloon.

January led the way through the deserted town, her dog trotting at Hoot's side. Although she saw no one, she knew people were holed up behind doors. Why? Because of them? Or because of whoever had buffaloed Eli Pasco?

She stopped outside the telegraph office. Drawing to a halt, she stepped from Hoot and flipped the reins over a rail.

"You can wait here if you like," she said to Pasco. "Maybe you can see that nobody steals my horses and gear." If she sounded a bit frosty, she figured she had due cause. And just because she was leaving him in charge of her horses didn't mean she trusted him.

"Yes, ma'am. I'll do that." A bit steadier now, he dismounted, letting Henry's reins go slack as he leaned against the rail, his attention fixed on the street. A street as quiet as ever, where no one stirred.

But where people watched, hidden behind windows and around corners, with gazes that felt like insects crawling on her skin.

Pushing the telegraph office door open, she went inside, swiftly moving to the right where she had an open field to survey the small room.

A simple counter nailed together with pieces of planed wood separated the back half of the rectangular room from the front. A two-by-four set on edge divided the counter in half and a sign declared one of the halves the Claremont post office. The other half served the telegraph. At her entrance, a man, a shrunken fellow with a face like a wizened brown apple, appeared from a curtained alcove at the back of the room. He clumped forward to stand behind the post office side with a stack of six or eight envelopes laid in front of him. He reminded January of a card dealer at a gambling table.

January waited for him to greet her, but after one shifty-eyed look, he busied himself sorting through the envelopes. Envelopes that appeared well-worn, the writing smudged as if they'd already been handled more than once. Maybe more than a dozen times, like objects at the end of their usefulness, discards bound for the trash burner. Even so, without a word, he turned his back and poked the envelopes into slots on a board on the wall behind him.

January had the impression that while the post office was never a real lively place, the little man would like her to think him too busy to attend to whatever brought her there.

What, did he think she'd disappear if he didn't look at her? She smiled to herself. He was going to discover differently.

But amusement died and impatience flared at the silliness. "I wish to send a telegram," she said, her voice loud against the bare wood walls of the room.

He pretended not to hear, but she caught the movement of his eyes as his attention wavered. Behind thin lids they darted from side to side.

"Make that, I *need* to send a telegram. Now."

Even had he been deaf, he had no excuse or reason to ignore her. Unless he'd received orders from someone to do so. She came forward and set her finger on an envelope as he reached for it.

He tugged at the envelope under her finger. "Telegraph is down," he muttered. His two front teeth were missing, and he spoke with a lisp.

Proving him a liar, the apparatus sitting next to him

on a desk clattered to life. He jumped as though poked by the pointy end of a knitting needle.

"Well. Look at that." January smiled. "How fortunate. Guess it's back up."

He scowled, increasing the dried apple effect. "Too late. I'm closed for the night. Going home."

Actually, she rather doubted he had any home besides this shack. It was possible to see beyond the curtained-off doorway behind him. Inside the alcove, the corner of a dresser and the head of a narrow cot with a greasy pillow was on view. A crooked stovepipe poked through a hole in the ceiling, its flange drooping.

Her smile faded, rather like the Cheshire Cat's in the Lewis Carroll novel. Very slowly, making certain she had his attention, she turned the lapel of her coat to reveal the badge Schlinger had given her last fall. The little man's gaze wavered as he glanced at it.

"This is official business." she said. "I'll write the message out for you, and you'll send it. The sooner you get it off, the sooner I can leave, and you can *go* home. Or not. It makes no difference to me."

"You're a woman and a liar. Women can't carry a badge. Not a real one." The little man's mouth set in a stubborn line and finally, he looked directly at her. "You get on out of here before I..." But then his eyes fixed on her scarred cheek. He stopped talking and his feet moved in a nervous, birdlike dance.

"I see you've remembered at least one woman in this county has indeed been known to carry a badge." Her lips tightened into a thin line. A small silence added menace. She leaned on the counter, inches from his wrinkled face.

"And a gun. You may even have heard she has used the gun to good advantage when it comes to putting criminals in their place." Pressing forward, she added softly, "Which is in the ground. Are you a criminal?"

He blanched, backing up until he was stopped by the wall and the letter slots. "No, ma'am. Not me."

January, not particularly proud of using either her formidable reputation or threats as persuasion, eased backward, out of the reach of the stench of his sweat. "Good to hear. Because there is a man at the livery stable right now who needs the services of an undertaker. I suggest you do your duty like every good citizen should."

"Yes, ma'am." His eyes bugged out and his hands shaking, the telegraph operator slid a pad and pencil to her. "Who do I send the telegram to and what do you want to say?"

"It goes to Sheriff Schlinger over at the county seat." In as few words as possible, she laid out the murder and the cabin's location and what she expected the sheriff to do. Prudent to a fault, she said nothing of her own plans. She pushed the telegram toward the little man, then on a whim drew it back and added another line. *Who is Eli Pasco?*

"Send it. I'll wait for a reply."

His wizened scowl didn't lift until she left the office twenty minutes later. By this time full dark had fallen. Outside the office, she found Pasco hunkered with his back against the wall, his dark coat gathered around him until he was almost invisible. If it hadn't been for Henry standing patiently alongside Hoot and Mollie, she might have thought him gone.

A little unsteady, he rose to his feet and spoke softly. "We'd best leave, Mrs. Billings. This don't seem like friendly town."

As if she couldn't figure that out for herself. January made a sound midway between a laugh and a chuff and left him to get himself in the saddle.

"We passed a decent camping spot not far out of town," she replied. "It'll be more comfortable than this filthy place."

CHAPTER 8

LAST EVENING, DEPUTY SHERIFF BILLINGS' SUSPICION OF HIM MAK-
ing her less than sympathetic at first, had warmed some
when they stopped a mile outside of town and made their
camp at an abandoned cabin badly overrun with various
types of small vermin. They'd chosen to stay outdoors
rather than compete with the critters.

With an efficiency he'd come to realize was as much
a part of her as her scars, she took care of her horses,
leaving Henry to him, gathered wood for a fire, and
laid out the sleeping arrangements. She'd done that
last night, too, as if from long practice. His place, Eli
noticed, on one side of the fire, hers on the other. He
had no quarrel with that.

When she insisted on examining his noggin, the
size of the lump helped her decide he hadn't been lying
about being unconscious and confused. Upon which,
digging through the impressive array of supplies she'd
packed on her buckskin horse, she produced a balm of
some sort, a length of gauze to wrap around his head,
and a measure of a headache powder made up of mead-

owsweet and willow bark that when ingested put a dent in the pain. Her ministrations felt good, her touch soft and light. And cool.

Finished playing doctor, she stepped away and tossed a bloody bit of gauze into the fire. "You should lie back," she said crisply. "I can see you're worn out and in pain. You probably have a concussion."

"Wouldn't be the first time." Her advice sounded tempting.

She caught some of the bitterness in his tone. "The concussion or the aches and pains?"

"Both." Lying back, he stretched out and closed his eyes. Turned out, she wasn't done with him.

Sitting and resting her back against a stump, she poked at the fire.

"Why the Winkler place, Mr. Pasco? Why this horse? Why not demand reparations from Winkler instead of this frantic chase? It's clear he fudged the conditions of the sale. Any court would uphold your claim."

"Would they?" He shrugged. "Do I appear a fool to you? Can't say as I'd blame you for thinking me one. You don't really think I'd get anything out of Winkler, do you? As far as he's concerned, it's all up to me now."

She made a strange whooshing sound. "Even his daughter?"

"It's beginning to look like it." He flapped a hand. "I should've listened to his neighbors. One of them, fellow by the name of Langley, told me Winkler wasn't particularly honest or trustworthy. His wife, she didn't say much, but she rolled her eyes when we were talking about the Winklers. I heard her whisper something about Mrs.

84 C.K. CRIGGER

Winkler being friends with somebody named Elvira. She said it like it was shameful."

"Bent Langley?" The deputy sounded surprised.

"Yeah. You know him? I met him and his missus on the road from the ranch on the day I signed the papers."

"Appears you should've heeded his warning." She paused. "The Winker ranch isn't in the best part of the valley, you know. Not the best land for growing crops, or even hay for livestock. It does have a lot of timber. In view of what's happened, I hope you didn't overpay."

Eli smiled to himself. Subtle. There were questions there. Restatements of her first ones. She wanted answers.

"I wanted the horse. The rest didn't matter so much," he said. It seemed the easiest.

Until she said, "There are better horses." She looked toward her gray. "For instance, Hoot. And his little brother will be another like him. Windswept is fast, but is he sound? I've heard there's some question."

"Beginning to look like I'll never know." He sounded almost resigned.

They spent the night huddled around a fire barely big enough to warm a small meal of beans and bread and a couple rather shriveled, though still tasty, Wealthy apples from last fall's crop.

The apples came from her late husband Shay's orchard, Mrs. Billings told him, her expression sad and withdrawn. Unexpectedly generous, she handed him a portion of the warmed food without further comment. Fifty/fifty, a fair split, considering he hadn't prepared for the necessity of a prolonged camp-out.

He fell asleep with an apple core still in his hand.

They returned to Claremont in the morning. Although the goose egg and a headache still plagued him, Eli's vision had cleared, and his surroundings stopped whirling. The person who'd tapped him had struck hard.

Between her generosity in sharing her meal and the nursing of his head, he felt bad about lying to the deputy.

Oh, he hadn't actually seen who wielded the pistol butt, but he sure enough knew who enabled the deal. His own fault for having even a pinch of trust.

And now, here he was, following Mrs. Billings on her fine silver gelding toward what she called 'the scene of the crime', She called a halt while they were still sheltered amongst the trees. From this angle, all looked just as they'd left it yesterday evening. The loft door still open, ditto the broad back doors. Even the two old horses and the mule, although the half-shod horse were gone, and someone had moved the forge and anvil to cover. After watching and listening for a few minutes, she urged her horse forward and dismounted at the back of the barn.

"Do you feel up to looking around, Mr. Pasco? Maybe there'll be something to say who the dead man is and why you were attacked. Or—" her face lit, "—maybe you'll be able to remember."

The way she sounded, she wasn't exactly counting on that happening. She had pressed him for those answers last night, while the fire she built smoldered, and she fussed over his head.

He'd had no answer for her then, and still didn't. Even so, he said, "Could be."

He wished he hadn't said what he had to her, when he'd first woke up and found her looking down at him, concern on her face. About the kiss. And yes, he remembered those words coming out of his mouth just fine. But she was quick. It had put the idea of a woman in her sights. And that had been a mistake.

No. He shouldn't have said it, but he'd been just woozy enough to first, have thought it, and second, to allow the words to escape. The deputy, same as he'd thought the first time he saw her, was an interesting contrast. Almost beautiful and delicate on one side; scarred and tough as a well-worn boot on the other. His curiosity ran rampant. He wanted to know more about her, and about her murdered husband.

Pasco hadn't gotten far into this adventure before he started wishing he hadn't gone to the law over his stolen horse. It would've been better, easier, to handle the situation on his own from the first. And if that meant handling it with a gun, so be it. Not much of a rarity considering his line of work. His previous line of work, he meant. He suspected he'd've been better off to have sucked up the monetary loss and let it all, land, house, horse, go. Except for the missing girl. That needed action. Too late now, he figured. He was in for it, come what may.

Following the deputy's lead, Eli swung his leg over the saddle and slid from Henry's back, landing lightly so as not to jar his head.

Even with the barn door open, cross currents of air couldn't quell the odor of fresh manure and urine-soaked straw bedding that needed a change. A couple horses, loose in their stalls, stood with heads hanging over the gates. They nickered anxiously at the sight of humans. One nosed an empty water bucket.

The ladder to the loft appeared just the same, with the two broken rungs and the ladder lying helter skelter in the middle of the aisle. Something about the ladder's position seemed different though. Maybe as if it had been moved, then put back not quite the same. Under the loft overhang, a small, congealed puddle showed where the dead man's blood had seeped through cracks in the loft floor above to splash on the floor below.

"Ugh," Mrs. Billings said.

Before he could take a hand, she studied the ladder a moment before lifting and propping it against the loft opening. Jumping for the lowest whole rung, she climbed up. Eli, despite his aching head, admitted to himself that he admired the view of a lady wearing britches.

She disappeared into the loft. A moment later, she called down to him. "You'd better come up, Mr. Pasco."

No choice. Reluctantly, he climbed the ladder, dreading what he'd find there.

* * *

THE BLOND MAN'S BODY LAY ALMOST, BUT NOT QUITE, AS SHE'D LEFT it yesterday. Rigor mortis had come and gone, but January didn't think that accounted for the difference. An arm slightly twisted, body turned a couple inches or so to the side, boot heel resting now outside the trail scuffed into the dust. Someone had been up here and seen what there was to see. Now, paying stricter attention, she saw where footprints in dust from the hay showed, though they'd been purposely smudged. Two separate sets, one as small as her own, the other set larger. A man's.

"He's been moved," she told Pasco when he stood beside her. "And searched."

He stared down at the man, a flicker of recognition showing.

"You know him?" she said.

"Know of him," he admitted. "I expect if you looked through the wanted posters on the sheriff's desk, you'd find his picture there."

She bent to examine the body more closely, clamping her mouth and recoiling some at the proximity. The corpse had begun to smell of putrefaction. Only faintly so far, but it seemed to her the man's features had sunken in on themselves during the night, diminishing his once good looks. Thrusting her hand into the back pocket of his britches, she withdrew a thin wallet and opened it and found the sum of two dollars. Nothing else. His front pockets were empty, one turned inside out. The tag from a small bag of tobacco hung from the right side of his shirt, with the papers tucked in behind it. Blood had soaked into the smoke supplies.

Pasco's shot had taken him in the upper chest. Her own a little lower. Or maybe the other way around, but it was a toss-up whose shot had killed him. It would take a real autopsy to differentiate between her .38-caliber and Pasco's Mauser, and that, she knew, wouldn't be happening.

"Do you have a name for him?" Her narrowed gaze at Pasco watched for a reaction.

"Not for sure," he said, but January thought that might not be the whole truth. She held him in a steady gaze.

"Could be an outlaw named Bill Lawton," he added when she didn't say anything. "A horse thief noted for his skills, or so I've been told."

"Told? By whom?"

He shrugged. "People. Men talk when they're in a saloon, especially horse people. Can't always rely on what you hear, but sometimes there's truth to what they're saying. I think this may be one of those times."

"Why?"

"Why?"

January watched his face redden. Not a lot. Just a little. Embarrassment? Now she had two whys. Why did he think there was truth to the horse thief story and why the embarrassment? She pushed for an answer.

"Are you disturbed by his reputation, Mr. Pasco? Where, exactly, did you hear about this Bill Lawton?"

"I told you. In a saloon."

His answer, she noted, was cool and unconcerned. Maybe overly so because her tone had been a little aggressive, a little argumentative. She wouldn't be surprised if he took offense.

Unclasping the man's gun belt, she yanked it from beneath his body and stood up. "You know what I'm asking. What saloon? What town? Why the reluctance to tell me what you know?"

If anything, Eli Pasco reddened another shade darker. "Well then, not that it gets us any further in finding either my horse or the Winkler girl, but I heard of him at a little dive some miles south of Spokane. Not much more than a crossroad along the main route to Lewiston."

"And does this crossroad have a name?"

"Redbone."

January's brows drew down. "Redbone?" If Pasco believed the place wouldn't mean anything to her he was mistaken. She hadn't lived in this county all her life, one of those people who died without stirring more than ten miles from home. She and her dad had moved every few months right up until he passed on, what with her Grandad Schutt's killing hanging over them and putting them on the run. Or so he'd thought. Turns out that for more than ten years he'd been wrong.

Anyway, while they hadn't stopped long at Redbone, she hadn't forgotten the place. Even remembered the saloon. Mostly, she remembered her dad wouldn't allow her to walk past the boisterous place unless he was with her.

Granted, not much of a town, its claim to fame being a hang-out for ruffians. As Pasco said, a little dive. Not a place respectable people favored.

A good many wealthy farmers lived in that part of the country, though. An amazing number, who took great pride not only in their acres of wheat, but in raising blooded horses and purebred cattle, all of which went for big prices. A lot of rustlers congregated there, too, or so she'd heard. Or more likely they dashed in and out on rustling forays. Had Pasco come from there? And if so, was he one of the rich horse breeders, or one of the rustlers? At this point, she didn't know what to make of him.

But maybe she wouldn't mention knowing anything about Redbone.

He eyed the gun belt January had confiscated. "Windswept has gotten quite a reputation. Enough, I figure, to draw the likes of Lawton this way. Most likely because word got around about me buying the horse."

Him specifically? Did that mean he was a target just as much as the horse?

January's curiosity soared though she banked it down. "A possibility, I suppose. My question is, why has this man's body been abandoned here?"

"Abandoned?"

"After trying to gun us down, I mean." She carried on as if he hadn't spoken. "Why has he been left here like this when they must know he'll be identified? Wouldn't you think they'd bury him? Or at least pay to have him buried, quickly, maybe hoping we wouldn't figure out who he is. Because once identified, it's an easy thing to discover who his cronies are. Is this whole deal a simple rustling scheme gone wrong? Was he deliberately left behind to get rid of us or was he supposed to turn our search in a different direction? Or was he, perhaps, being punished for protesting the killing of the man we found? Do you suppose his death is the result the gang hoped for?" She was almost breathless by the time she finished.

Pasco stared at her. "That's a lot of questions with interesting possibilities. All without answers."

"It is a lot. I hope we can find somebody who's willing to talk to us." If she knew the answer to any of the afore-mentioned questions, more might fall into place.

Dark brows puckered as if the light shining into the loft hurt his eyes, he remained silent as she turned the belt over and examined the underside. A few seconds later, she made an exclamation and, drawing a folding knife from her coat pocket, picked apart the two layers of

leather making up the pockets holding a dozen .45-cali-
ber cartridges. A slip of paper fell out from the opening.

"Hah," she said again, and picked it up before Pasco
could lay a hand on it.

"What does it say?"

She looked up at him. "It says 'We'll meet in Steel on
the 25th. Don't do anything until then. R'." She handed
it to him. "Recognize the handwriting?"

"No," he said as if surprised she should ask, but only
after a hastily muffled inhalation that led January to
think maybe he was lying again. But if he were, he
didn't like doing it.

"She misspelled Steele," January said, watching him.
"If she even means Fort Steele."

"Seems likely." But then Pasco's fingers tightened,
and the paper crumpled. "She? What makes you think
a woman wrote this?"

"Don't you?"

"I asked you first."

January crooked a smile. "How many men do you
know would make giant capital letters and finish them
off with fancy curlicues?"

He had nothing more to say as she turned and started back down the rickety ladder to where Pen waited at
the bottom. "I suppose this poor excuse of a town has a
mayor and a boot hill. Somebody who can take charge
of the body, and see it gets properly buried."

"Not you?" He followed her down, wincing when
forced to let go and jumping the final four feet to the barn
floor. Back in the stalls, one of the horses neighed. Pen let
out a short "whuff".

"No, indeed. Not my problem." She gentled Pen with a scratch behind an ear and looked around. "But maybe these poor horses are. We'll turn them into the corral where they can get water and hay. I imagine somebody will claim them soon if the hostler doesn't come back. Unless that..." her finger pointed upward, "...is the hostler."

He nodded and took over moving the two horses, while January stowed the holster in the pack on Mollie's back.

They drew plenty of attention as they rode out of the barn into the street. A couple women with shawls draped around their shoulders lifted tattered skirts out of the mud as they openly stared. Another, her features and clothing too fine for the surroundings, flashed them a look and turned her head before whirling about with a swish of a teal blue skirt. She disappeared inside the tinsmith shop. Hard-faced men fixed them with cockeyed looks. Nobody nodded or spoke. Neither did she nor Pasco. They stopped in front of the mercantile.

"Whoever owns this will know who is in charge," January said, slipping from Hoot's back. She looked up at Pasco, still mounted. "Will you keep an eye on things? You and Pen?"

"Sure." He dismounted and prepared to keep watch.

Did her imagination go too far, January wondered, or did he appear relieved to be left outside? Intuition goading a portion of her brain, she wished she'd gotten a better look at the woman wearing the blue skirt.

The store contained little in the way of stock. Small stacks of canned goods. A few half-bolts of plain cloth, gray, a blue, and a faded red; a barrel of strong-smelling

vinegary pickles; some dusty crockery. A loaf of bread
that already appeared stale and dry. More interesting,
she spotted guns and ammunition. A lot of them. Oh,
and various kinds of tobacco, bags of Bull Durham and
Mail Pouch. There were no customers, only a tiny woman
almost hidden by the brass and oak cash register sitting
on the battered wood counter.

Beady dark eyes watched January as she wound a
way down the center aisle, careful to dodge a stack of
mismatched pots and pans.

"Ma'am," she said to the woman upon safe arrival.

"Do for you?" the woman replied. Her whisper
matched her diminutive form. Her eyes shifted sideways as thought trying to see behind her where a drape
closed off another room. The drape moved as though
struck by an errant waft of air.

Half-turning, January bent the lapel of her coat
to show the badge. "I could use some information, if
you'd be so kind."

The woman didn't speak. Her eyes flicked from the
badge to the right then the left and back again. Settled
on January's scarred cheek.

"I'm looking for the mayor of this town," January
continued.

The woman nodded, pointing a finger as though
directing her somewhere off to the left. "The...hole,"
she said, so low January asked her to repeat it.

The woman shivered and spoke again.

Pursing her lips, January said, "Perhaps you could
show me?"

At this, the little woman puffed out a sigh, stepped

down from the box she'd been standing on, and led the way toward the front of the store. They both peered through the dirt-grimed window.

"The dead man?" the woman asked. If January hadn't been standing right next to her, she'd never have heard. The woman's lips didn't even move.

"Yes. So you know about him."

"Some. His name is Lawton. He showed up in town a few days ago. Him and a woman. The mayor has been waiting for someone to make a report. He don't want trouble." Her finger was pointing again, so January nodded, glad to have verification of the dead man's name. Pasco had been right. No surprise.

"The mayor?"

"Yes. There's some men been around. The kind that make trouble."

"I understand. Well, I'm afraid the town will need to see the dead man buried."

The woman's lips twisted, wrinkles around her mouth showing a path often taken. "A hole. Somebody will dig it. Stop the stink. You..."

The woman's eyes finally met January's full on. "You better watch out for her, the woman. Her name is Ruby. That was her man."

With that, she marched back toward the counter and the box she stood on. She didn't even acknowledge January's *thank you*.

They had been looking out the window at the street. January's hand was on the door when she realized that while Pen and the horses had been in plain sight, one of her party had gone missing. Where was Pasco?

She let herself out, the harness bells on the door tin-
kling. Looked right, looked left and spotted him at the
gap between buildings from which he'd just emerged.
His hat set cocked sideways on his head, the knot still
visible even at a distance. But that wasn't what drew her
attention. No indeed. Credit that to the flip of a blue skirt
she spotted just within the gap.

He turned and headed toward her, and if that wasn't anger she saw on his face, she planned to take off her badge.

"Find the mayor?" he asked, erasing the angry expression fast enough January wondered if she'd imagined it.

"Yes. He's at The Watering Hole. The saloon across
the street," she elaborated. "That's its name." She waited
for him to say something about the woman, but he didn't.

"Who was that in the alley?" she finally asked.

"No one. Just some woman I asked about Lawton, but
she said she didn't know him."

He said nothing more as they led the horses across
the street, but she saw the way his mouth set. It put her
off from demanding more of an explanation. For now.

Inside the saloon, through open doors, a bartender,
although whether or not he was the mayor was an open
question, could be seen wiping glasses with a towel well
past its prime. He apparently kept a sharp eye on potential customers. As January, leading the way, started in he
dropped the towel, seized a revolver from under the bar
and shouted angrily at her. "No Women Allowed."

January heard the capital letters but disregarded
them. Pen at her side, she stepped across the threshold
only to have Pasco, his attention on the gun, grab her arm
and yank her backward.

The barkeep was yelling something along the lines of blankety-blank hussies who'd better keep their blankety-blank, cheap chippy behinds out of his saloon. A bullet whistled bare inches over their heads as punctuation.

Pen set up a caterwauling fit to wake the dead. At least it covered January's barely contained scream.

"Holy—" Pasco bit off the imprecation as he jerked her outside. None too gentle about it, either.

January, to her surprise, felt quite light-headed. It had been a while since anybody tried to kill her and she wasn't used to it. "Why is he trying to shoot us?" She blinked. "Shoot me? I guess you're not the one he's yelling at."

Pasco, his face turned three or four shades lighter, stood in front of her. He pushed her out of view of the doorway and drew in a breath. "I think this conversation is one I'd better tend to. What do you want me to say?"

Doubtful though she might be, January didn't think she had any choice but to trust him. With this, at least. She wasn't so sure about anything else. "Tell him I'm turning the body at the livery over to him. Frankly, it doesn't matter to me if he likes it or not. Ask him about the rustlers, about the young girl and the horse, about the woman whose name begins with an R. See if there's been talk about that murdered man. Ask him which way the rustlers went when they left here. If he heard where they're going. Ask him everything. But be careful. He's crazy."

Oh, she saw him blanch at the mention of the woman with the initial R, all right. Although, on second thought, she supposed it could've been over consulting a crazy man. But January didn't think so. Her eyes narrowed as she thought.

Ruby.

Who was she and what did she have to do with Eli Pasco?

CHAPTER 9

ELI'S THOUGHTS WERE ON WOMEN AS HE STEPPED INTO THE SA-loon. On Deputy January Billings, first of all, who didn't trouble to hide every thought that came to her mind. Her distrust of him had just taken a leap forward. He knew she'd seen enough of him there at the alley to rouse her suspicions. Seen enough to know he'd been talking to a woman.

Then there was Ruby. Mrs. Deputy had seen through that, too.

Damn Ruby to her wicked core. And damn his father, too, who, unable to contain his late in life desires, had forced this predicament on him. He should've let the old man answer to his own mistakes. This was none of his doing.

Jamming his hat over the lump on the side of his head, when Eli's cautious entrance resulted in being greeted by a simple glare rather than a shot, he strode into the saloon signaling a bravado he didn't feel. This entire situation was something he hadn't counted on. As of now, if it weren't for the Winkler girl, he'd write off the loss of the stolen horse, maybe of the whole danged ranch, and say good riddance. He wasn't so old he couldn't start over. This time he'd choose a different profession—if he could.

Gazing around, he tried to see everything at once. The saloon took up a single room, was dark, and smelled to the high heavens. Vomit, spilled hootch, piss, sweat. He figured nobody had mopped in here since the building's inception. As if that weren't enough, a miasma of stale smoke hung over all, a permanent fixture embedded in the rough plank walls. In the lower order of saloons, this one was a cesspit.

The room, Eli discovered, appeared at first glance to be empty of everyone but the barkeep and himself. He went up to the bar with his hand under his coat where it hovered an inch from the butt of his Mauser. No fine mahogany bar here, to wipe and polish with a clean cloth. Only a rough slab of red fir. He figured what smoothing it'd had came only from railroader and outlaw elbows.

All embellished with a whole lot of splinters, he'd bet.

The thought brought forth a twitchy grin. Spinning a silver dollar onto the slab, he stopped the bartender's motion to pour from a squat brown bottle. Drink out of that glass? He'd as soon sip from a porcelain toilet.

"You the mayor?" he asked.

The barkeep's beefy forefinger lifted to point into a corner. Following the motion, Eli squinted into the darkness, enabled, as his eyes adjusted, to make out the figure of man seated at a table littered with bottles and empty glasses. The man was slumped over with his forehead resting on the table.

"Middleton," the barkeep boomed out. "Hey, Mayor.

Somebody to see you."

The mayor never stirred.

"Is he dead?" Eli studied the figure, noticing the way one arm hung slack with fingers almost touching the floor.

The bartender shrugged. "Dunno. Go look." He glanced at the door. "But don't you let that woman in."

January was peeking through the open doorway. Motioning her back before she got shot at again, Eli went over to the mayor's table and stood over the man. Although hesitant to lay hands on him, he touched the mayor's neck, feeling for a pulse.

"He dead?" the barkeep called with mild curiosity.

"No."

His touch did nothing to awaken the mayor. Neither did rattling the glasses or scooting the chair. Finally, Eli decided the man was more likely unconscious than asleep and gave up. He went back to the bar.

"He do this often?" he asked.

"Pert near every night."

Eli shook his head. "Well, you might tell him there's a dead man in the livery's loft when he wakes up. He might want to take care of that."

A death in their midst didn't appear to come as any surprise to the barkeep. Just as nobody had appeared curious about the shots that killed the man in the loft, the one at Mrs. Billings just now drew even less.

"He knows," the barkeep said. "We all do. A stranger in town. Been hoping the dead man's friends will come back and haul him away. Beginning to look like that ain't going to happen."

"His friends, huh? Got any names of who they might be?"

"Nothing what ain't a lie."

Aliases. Eli had expected no less. "You said come back. Do you think they will?"

A slight lift of the shoulders indicated unconcern.

"Did you see which way they went when they left?"

The bartender sniffed and shook his head. "When their money is gone, I don't care where they go. To hell with all of them."

"Well then, did you hear anybody talking about where they might be headed?"

"Say, mister, I think you done used up that dollar." The man, checking the doorway again as though to make sure it was clear of women, shut his mouth and went back to scrubbing glasses.

Sighing, Eli spun another coin onto the bar. The barkeep snatched it up with fingers as dirty as the towel.

"They rode out west," the barkeep admitted. "But that don't necessarily mean anything. Road splits a few miles down the road. I did hear some mention of Canada but that don't mean nothing either. We ain't that far from the border here."

Just what Eli had been afraid of. "I notice you keep a close watch on the door," he said. "You've got a view right out onto the street. Those men might have a young, brown-haired girl and a fine brown horse with them. Did you see anyone like that? You could probably tell the girl is unhappy."

The bartender, not much to his surprise, shrugged and shook his head.

Eli lowered his voice. "What about the woman?"

Ruby, who'd married his father purely for what she could get. The first time she ran off, it was with a gambling man. The elder Pasco sent his son after her, and she'd made a play for Eli on their way back. The next time she left, she cleaned the old man of his ready cash, an amount of around three thousand dollars. Eli refused to chase after her, that time. Not long after, his father caught a bullet and was left a cripple. Who'd fired it had never been caught, although Eli had his own ideas. If Pasco senior knew who shot him, he wasn't telling. Ashamed, most likely, at being hornswoggled by a beautiful tramp.

And Ruby, well, Ruby could be icy cold—when she wasn't being fiery hot.

The barkeep shrugged. "Don't know about any women. Don't want to."

The man was in danger of throwing his shoulders out of joint. "Don't know nothing about girls, neither," he added. "Can't trust 'em even when they're young. Won't catch me consorting with any females."

Eli had already gotten that impression, when the man shot at January.

"Do you know where the dead man's friends have been staying?" Although Eli figured asking was a waste of time, it couldn't hurt to try for the information.

Turned out he was right about the reply. Or did he mean the lack of one?

Laconic to the end, the barkeep shrugged again. "Not here," he said.

Not having expected anything different, Eli turned to leave. "If I were you, I'd get that man buried before he stinks so bad he ruins the hay."

The advice earned him a grunt. It made a change.

He found January pacing back and forth outside, kicking through the inches deep manure layered outside the bar where patrons tied their horses. Didn't look as if anyone had shoveled it in years. Or ever. The dog paced close to the woman's side. Their horses waited patiently, drowsing in the warming sun.

"Well?" She came to a stop in front of him, looking up with worry in her eyes. Pretty eyes, he noted, and not for the first time. They were of an odd color that sometimes looked brown and sometimes green, surrounded by thick black lashes like a shaded pool in the woods.

Fanciful.

Eli removed his hat and gently rubbed his sore head. The swelling was finally abating, although it still hurt like the dickens. "The mayor is a drunk, dead to the world. I figure he's a lost cause. Turns out I paid two dollars for the bartender to tell me the whole town already knows about Lawton. He also says he knows nothing about a woman, about my horse or the girl, or about any of the men except that they're all using aliases. What he knew for certain is that he doesn't like females."

His dry observation, he was relieved to see, brought a tiny smile to her lips.

"I'll ask the county to reimburse your two dollars," she said. "As for the rest, another dead end?"

"Looks as if, except for one little thing." Eli stepped over to Henry and checked his cinch. "What next, Mrs. Billings? All we've got is guesswork to go on, and that too hazy to count for much."

"What little thing?"

She jumped on that fast enough, no surprise. He'd counted on it. The only thing he didn't plan on telling her was where the information came from. God only knows if there was any truth to it.

"Something vague. Probably not reliable. According to the story, the race meet started out to be the intention, but then when the Winkler girl got taken with the horse, they figured holding her for ransom was a surer bet."

January stared at him doubtfully. "Huh. Then why has there been no ransom demand?"

"Good question. When we catch up with them, you can ask."

She didn't like that. Not a bit. "What about the man they killed at the cabin? Anybody have a say about that?"

"Can't tell you that either. Could be a personal vendetta. Doesn't appear to be connected with Windswept or Zora Winkler."

He saw the question in her eyes. The doubt.

"Who were you talking to? The gun-happy bartender?" she said. "Sounds to me like it might be a trick, meant to throw us off the trail. Something meant to be told and retold and not a word of it true."

Eli had known she was smart. "You may be right. I told you it was vague, but if true, they need to stay close around here. Here or somewhere with a telegraph. They can't go running off to Canada with the girl and expect to be paid the ransom. And for the record, I wouldn't bet my last dollar on it being the truth."

"If I were those outlaws, I'd be wondering if that easy money is ever going to arrive. Because it's been days now, with Winkler sitting around the saloon and his wife only worrying about transporting all of her expensive possessions to wherever they're headed."

"You think the outlaws have moved on?"

"I think they may have somebody telling them what's going on with Zora's family. They'll have guessed by now there won't ever be any money. What do you suppose they'll do with Zora when they finally give up?"

Eli had been hoping this hadn't occurred to her. Should've known though. "It's apt to be too late already. Nobody says they've seen her." He watched her face turn white, the scar standing out like a signpost. He hesitated before coming out with a harsh truth. "But they probably wouldn't kill her. They'd probably try to sell her."

"Poor girl. My father..." she stopped, and he watched her hand come up and trace the scar on her cheek. "My father," she said then, "would've gone to the ends of the earth to save me. Nobody seems to care about her. But there is one thing in her favor—"

"What's that?"

"We haven't found a body."

Eli smiled, faint but there. "So we go on."

"We do." Calling to her dog, January climbed aboard her silver horse.

WHAT WASN'T ELI PASCO TELLING HER? WHAT HAD HE TOLD HER that was true, and what a lie? Even more to the point, why lie? If she were required to go along with this chase, shouldn't she be privy to all the facts? Especially if people were going to shoot at her.

Anger surged. She'd been a fool to become involved in this chase. Was it because Schlinger was too lazy, too wrapped up in fear and his own affairs to bother? Or because Dabney was too inadequate to do anything for the county but putter? Or because this man had come looking for her? Most of all, she was angry at herself. Anybody with a brain would've told him no. A resounding *no*.

After she'd brought justice to Shay's killer, she vowed she was done with this sort of thing. Clearly, she should've stuck with her previous decision.

January rode ahead on the way out of Claremont, glad to leave the place behind. Pasco kept a horse length to her rear, careful to watch their backs, the buildings, the windows. But nothing threatened. She suspected the town folk, especially the Watering Hole's bartender, were as happy to see them leave as they were to be gone.

They stopped once at the telegraph office, where the operator, looking at her with shifty eyes, handed her a flimsy with six words on it. *On our way. Find the girl.*

Wondering what kind of reception Schlinger would get if he rode into the town proper, a wry smile twisted her lips.

"Like it or not, the sheriff is on his way," she told Pasco, and he nodded.

Abreast now, they rode west, relying on the bartender to have told the truth, but not trusting he had.

"He didn't seem the kind of man to have friends he cares about," Pasco told her. "Not the loyal type, either.

So I don't figure he had any reason to lie."

"You believe two bucks paid enough to buy an honest report?"

"Let's hope so."

January looked behind her to where Claremont was rapidly fading into the distance. She'd done that several times already, watching their back trail as her dad always warned her to do. There had been no quickening of activity, the street remaining empty of people. Nobody followed them.

"Any stir?" Pasco asked, even though he'd just looked for himself.

She shook her head. "Doesn't appear to have raised any alarms."

"A good omen."

"Maybe. The one thing we know is that the gang didn't backtrack. Wherever they are, they're ahead of us and on the move."

Questions still nagged at January. Pasco had met with a woman in Claremont, remaining out of sight in an alley while they talked. She'd spotted only the hem of the woman's dress. What had they talked about? Was Pasco part of the gang, meant to lead her astray. If so, why? Where had the woman gone? Did she run with the outlaw gang? Did Pasco even know? If he did, and if he was on the up and up, why didn't he tell her?

The questions plagued January enough to cause her to miss the bird calls, the warm freshening breeze, and the sun rising higher in the sky. For more than two hours her mind floundered between all those baffling questions and the fact she had no answers.

And no real hope of recovering the girl. Or Pasco's horse, for that matter.

But Pen remained on the job. She stopped in the middle of the narrow, rutted road and refused to budge out of Hoot's way. A loud "woof" drew January's wandering attention as Pasco pulled up beside her.

"What is it, Pen?" She looked down at her dog.

"I think she's trying to tell you something." Pasco's amused comment broke the prolonged silence between them.

Pen's black nose had lifted, pointing toward a particularly large old fir overhanging the trail, whose branches hung low enough to be a hindrance. January, who knew better than to ignore the dog, followed the point to where, at just about shoulder height of a small person, a scrap of cloth fluttered.

"Well then! Good girl." Reining Hoot closer to the tree, she plucked the bit of fabric and held it up for Pasco to see. Blue, with small pink and yellow flowers, the colors bright and fresh.

"The girl's?" Pasco asked. He dismounted, pushed Hoot a little to the side and eyed the ground under the tree.

"I think so. Looks like she may be back to trying to leave sign. Something must've happened. Something to make her brave again. I wonder if she knows we're following the outlaws."

Pasco's dark eyes shot her a glance and moved as quickly away. "Maybe so." Hunkering over the mess of tracks, he traced one that showed more clearly than the others. "Here he is. Windswept. Looks like these signs were made this morning, Mrs. Billings. The edges are sharp. And there," he indicated a pile of horse manure, "those are fresh."

She nodded. "So we're headed the right direction and we're not far behind. A relief. I'd hate to be wasting all this time on a false lead."

"We aren't." He sounded positive as he stepped up on Henry again, they rode on.

Eventually they came to where the road split. Dismounting, January on one side, Pasco on the other, they strode on foot, examining the roadbed for tracks. Presently, Pasco called out, "Here, Deputy Billings. They went this way."

The tracks headed west, not north to Canada.

CHAPTER 10

THE TROUBLE WITH ASKING FOR INFORMATION ABOUT PEOPLE WHO did business outside the law was that word soon got around. In which case, those folks were likely to get defensive. Particularly when their freedom depended on working in secret. Or at least staying ahead of the law. Because the whole situation could unravel at any time, meaning trouble with a capital T.

Eli could guess at what was coming, but he didn't figure he'd had a choice. Talking to Ruby had been a risk, one he felt he had to take. Whether the risk paid off remained to be seen.

He—and January—discovered the answer when they rode into a trap only a few miles down the road. Close enough to the town of Claremont for the outlaws to take their rest there, if they felt like it. The close proximity of a telegraph had most likely had something to do with the way they'd stayed around, as well.

When he thought about it, he figured the gang had left the town only minutes before he and the deputy rode out. Possibly while he'd been wasting time with the deranged bartender.

As far as the trap goes, Eli had no doubt he and January both were meant to be caught in it at once, but she inadvertently became the first victim.

It happened that Eli, being a polite gentleman, had gestured her to ride on while he paused to step into the bushes and Pen, intrigued by his action, stayed to keep a watchful eye on him. The dull thump of what sounded like a minor explosion up ahead stopped both of them mid-stream, so to speak. Then silence.

Eli's mind blanked, then he swore.

Fingers flying to button his britches, he got a hand on Pen before she could run off to find January. "No. Not if you don't want to be killed."

That's what he said out loud to the dog, anyhow. What he believed ran along the lines of, "She'll shoot me herself if I let anything happen to this dog."

What he...they...had been worried about had come to pass, and he suspected Zora Winkler's kidnappers had been waiting along the trail for just this sort of chance. Separate him and the deputy and take them out one at a time. If she were killed right off, they'd expect him to give up. He figured that's what they wanted. When he lagged behind just now, it made the whole plan easier.

But what had they been told about Mrs. Billings? It depended, he supposed, on who had done the telling. What had they done to her? His gut squeezed, the vision of the dead man they'd found at the cabin filling his mind.

Still hanging on to Pen, he found a rope and tied it around the dog's neck, which he then tethered around the base of a shrub. "You stay here," he said. "I'll go see what's happened. You get in sight of somebody's gun and you're apt to be a dead dog." He doubted his orders did any good. The deputy's dog was almost as smart as a person. He just hoped he could get to January before the dog got loose.

"And don't you chew on that rope," he added, for all the good it would do.

Swinging aboard Henry and urging the horse into a lope, Eli checked his Mauser. The weapon held ten rounds. They'd be expecting a regular six-shot weapon. Six at best. One small advantage for him.

A curve in the trail hid the view ahead from him. He heard voices though, shouting back and forth and huzzahing like they'd won a battle. Then the drum of horses' hooves. Several of them. He figured the gang, whatever had happened to Mrs. Billings, were making a getaway.

Even so, he kept to the verge and in the shadow of the trees lining this section of road, where he made less of a target. Setting a heel to Henry, they broke into a gallop until, sweeping around the curve, he found... not what he'd expected.

No blood, no crumpled, destroyed body.

Only the deputy's packhorse, Mollie, standing immobile in the middle of the road with the pack on her back half-on, half-off. Her ears were twitching back and forth, making Eli wondered if the detonation had deafened her. A twelve-inch-deep crater in the middle of the road attested to the explosion he'd heard.

Eli checked again. More thoroughly, this time. No body of a pretty woman with a scar; no sign of her silver-gray gelding. No trace of blood, which to Eli's mind meant both Mrs. Billings and her gray horse were still in one piece.

Why had they taken her? His guts squeezed. And where were they going?

Everyone was gone. No January Billings, no Zora Winkler, no gang of cutthroat outlaws or their leader. Just Mollie the packhorse and Pen, who even now came galloping around the bend in the road, a three-foot length of rope trailing out behind her. It had, Eli noted ruefully, taken the dog even less time than he'd thought possible to gnaw her way through it. It had been a good hemp rope, too.

The dog stopped beside the packhorse and looked at Eli.

"I think she's okay," Eli said, though he felt a little foolish talking to the dog. "There's no sign of blood. Only this hole in the road. Looks like they set off the charge somehow from a distance and she missed the worst of it. They must've taken her with them, but we'll get her back. Don't worry. We're only a couple minutes behind them."

By the sudden shake Pen gave herself, the big black dog didn't seem impressed by his reassurances. Maybe she realized he was only one man and the outlaws were... he counted the tracks. Counting Ruby, they were five, plus Zora on Windswept.

But when had long odds ever stopped him?

"Damn her," he added fiercely, and the dog cocked her head as if asking an offended question.

"No. I'm not talking about your deputy. The other one. Ruby."

Eli got Mollie's packsaddle straightened and a new

lead shank fashioned, the one dangling from the chin strap having been cut short. Pen stayed beside him without a struggle, something of a surprise, and within a few minutes they were following the fresh tracks. Not that Pen couldn't have tracked them anywhere, visible sign or no visible sign. Eli just hoped she could sense ambushes well in advance, because he intended on going fast.

Maybe too fast, because not five minutes later a land mine planted in the middle of the trail knocked Pen tumbling and sent Henry spinning onto his back. The blast also had an unfortunate effect on Eli. Crushed beneath the horse's weight, the collision between his head and a boulder flung up by the explosion had a detrimental effect. With a severe knock on the head twice in as many days, the injury overcame his senses. The only good thing was that having been hurriedly laid, the detonation had more sound than smash.

Smart of them, stupid of him. Eli's vision wavered, his senses going back and forth, in and out. He hadn't been expecting a double trap. Although, considering the result, he should have.

Groaning, he pushed himself to sit up and called for the dog. Her black fur covered with dust, she appeared beside him like a wraith. At least she didn't seem to be hurt. He couldn't even imagine the trouble he'd be in if something happened to the deputy's dog. She was one fierce female.

He didn't mean the dog.

* * *

"You go on ahead," January remembered Pasco saying. "I'll be along in a minute or two."

She had turned to face him, starting to ask what had claimed his attention, but a look at his red face gave a hint. She turned back to the road. "Take your time," she said, hiding a smile. Seemed to her it was the first time Pasco had loosened up enough to act halfway human. And Pen, always curious, decided to stay with him.

So January kept riding. She hadn't gone far when, up ahead, she spotted a bit of cloth dangling from a small dead tree that had been uprooted and was leaning out over the road. The cloth fluttered like a flag in the breeze. Angling Hoot toward the cloth, she was already reaching out to grab it when a thought lit up her mind as though caught in the headlamp on the late Elvira Hammel's fancy Pierce-Stanhope automobile.

Too obvious. Don't touch it.

But it was already too late by then. A chest deadening "whoomp" went off close enough to Mollie's feet to startle the mare into jumping straight up in the air. Then, humping her back, the packhorse bucked like she hadn't done since her yearling days, yanking on the lead rope and jerking January, who was woefully unprepared, backwards off Hoot. Hoot, startled as much by his stablemate's antics as by the blast, crow hopped a dozen or so yards down the road, even as January, still attached to Mollie by the lead-rope, slammed to the ground flat on her back. The wind whooshed from her lungs, leaving her helpless.

Helpless, but with her hearing intact. A couple of the men who ran up leaned over her and guffawed as they watched her struggle to breathe.

"See? It worked just fine," one man bragged to another who stood beyond her field of vision. "Told you one stick would do the trick." He grinned, adding as an afterthought, "Hey. I'm a poet."

"Worked just fine, my blind eye," a person who stood farther away said. "You should've let her pass. She isn't the one we're after."

"Well, how was I gonna stop her? When she reached for the flag, it was too late. Anyways, they was supposed to be together. Get both at one crack."

"Yeah. Where is Pasco? He's the one we want. What good is she to us? A scarred up woman? What's she even doin', ridin' along with Pasco?" So said one of the men closest to January in a whiny kind of voice. Then, in a harsh whisper, "Is Dent blind?"

The other man pushed the first aside and leaned closer. Unshaved and unwashed for days from the looks him, he tee-heed like a girl. "That's easy. This one's prolly his woman."

Which is when, as January's diaphragm finally released tension, a woman speaking nearly put it into spasm again. She seemed angry. "She is not his woman. She's a deputy of some sort. She even killed somebody a while back. Somebody important."

If anything, this drew even more laughter, until Dent's stronger voice overrode the merriment. "In that case, somebody take her gun. First thing one of you yahoos should've done anyhow."

"Then load her onto the gray," the woman said. "We'll take her with us. She might prove valuable. And

hurry up about it. Pasco will have heard the racket and
he'll come running."

"That's what we want, ain't it? Why load her up?
Let's take care of him right here. Take care of them
both at once."

"He'll be ready for that," the woman said. "Which
one of you wants to die today?" She paused and got no
answer. "No volunteers? To kill him, we need to take
him by surprise. And that's not going to be easy. Not
after this failure."

"Well then," said the one proud of the trap he'd made,
"let me at him. I got just the thing. It's sure to kill him."

"He won't fall for your trick a second time, Ike, if that's
what you're thinking," the woman said.

"Yeah? Bet he will."

January, still panting, couldn't help thinking Pasco
hadn't fallen for the trick a first time. But she had.

"Who knows," Dent put in. He sounded snide to January's ears as he added, "Although the woman doesn't
appear to be much damaged. Or only by falling off her
horse. But maybe we'll get lucky, and Ike's charge will kill
him. Or tell me, Ruby, is that what you're trying to avoid?"

Ruby.

January missed the woman's reply. Her head might
still be in a whirl, but it appeared her first suspicions of
Eli Pasco were right. He did know this Ruby woman, and
she was part of the gang. What was their connection to
each other? That's what she wanted to know. Most certainly something Pasco didn't want to tell her about.

On that note, one of the men yanked January's .38
from her holster while another heaved her upright.

Happy to be on her feet, she lashed out at the one who groped at her breasts, surprising him by dealing a blow that knocked him off balance. She should probably have expected the clout she received in turn. Staggered, she landed in the dirt yet again.

"You, Ike, stop playing around. We need to get going. Get that woman loaded up," Dent, the boss, shouted at the man. Quelled, between them, the men got Hoot to stand still long enough to get January, still protesting, on his back.

"Dang! He's coming. I can hear it in my bones," the one called Shandy said.

The *he* meant Pasco, January thought, fighting past the renewed dizziness the slap had dealt her.

The others laughed at Shandy, telling him their bones didn't have ears, but the woman called out, "Hurry. Mount up. Let's get out of here. Go, go."

And then, with January hanging on to the saddle horn for dear life while one of the men led Hoot, they sped down the road. She couldn't hear a thing over her own gasping breaths as her lungs labored to breathe, not to mention the way her head still spun. Time felt like it had crunched down, and everything was happening in a vortex.

In less than a handful of minutes, once they rounded a switchback in the road, they all drew up again.

"This'll do," said the self-proclaimed explosives expert.

Dent, the fellow who'd been giving orders, agreed. "The rest of us'll keep moving. Ike, follow us as soon as you set your dynamite. And try not to blow yourself to bloody chunks."

"Yessir." Ike, smiling with a show of snaggly teeth, slid from his horse and got to work with a spade digging a shallow hole. The rest of them shook out their reins and kept going.

The pause had let January recover—mostly. Also gave her time to look over the gang who'd taken her...well, captive, for lack of a better word. Her attention centered on the two other females in the group.

One, she knew, was Zora Winkler. The girl looked scared. Tears had left tracks down a very dirty face. She also looked cold as she wore only a light jacket over what had been a pretty, blue blouse printed with pink and yellow flowers.

January wondered how Zora had managed to tear off the strips she'd left to mark the trail and not get caught. Or had it even been Zora who left the one that set off the blast? The idea grew as January began to doubt Zora's fault in the process. The more likely possibility was that the slender woman who rode knee to knee with the Winkler girl had taken it on herself.

Ah, yes, January thought as she took her first hard look at Ruby. The woman rode astride a sorrel with the teal blue skirt rucked up over her knees. She and Pasco had had a conversation back in Claremont, but what were her intentions now? They didn't appear to be friends, that much was for certain. Or had the attitude been for show in case someone had been watching? As she had.

And then there was the horse. What had to be Pasco's horse. Since it was the only whole male in the lot, January knew the long-legged, deep-chested brown horse

Zora Winkler rode must be Windswept. She found it odd that one of the men hadn't taken the animal over, most likely the one called Dent who seemed to be in charge. *Seemed.*

January cast a wary glance around, her gaze again settling on the woman. On Ruby. If January had been told to point out the boss, the lovely Ruby is who she would've chosen to fill the role.

Using the word lovely to describe Ruby was no more than the truth, January admitted to herself. Pale alabaster skin, lots of dark curls, eyes so vivid a blue they almost glowed. One of those much-admired hour-glass figures that appeared to be shaped by nature rather than artifice. Mostly, anyhow. Sharp tongued, though, and harsh voiced.

The argument she was having with Dent stung like lye splashing from a soap pot.

"You don't know what you're talking about," she was saying to him. "I know him, I tell you. We need him alive. For a while, at least. As soon as he signs the papers, you can do whatever you like."

Dent made a sound that January couldn't decide whether denoted admiration or disgust. "You're a greedy wench, aren't you, Ruby? And cold. What did he do to get on your bad side?"

Ruby's coo grated on January's nerves as though they'd been scraped by a wire brush. "Why, Dent," she said. "I have no bad side."

The man burst out with a boisterous laugh. It was just fading when another of those *whomps* split the air.

"Oh, sorry," Dent said, a false apology overriding

Ruby's exclamation. "Sounds as if Ike didn't get the message."

Ruby cussed like a wild woman, as crude as anything January had ever heard—and she'd heard plenty in her life, dating back to when she and her dad were on the run.

That's when she began to really worry.

CHAPTER 11

E<small>LI</small>, <small>EXPECTING A BULLET AT ANY MOMENT</small>, <small>CLOSED HIS EYES AND</small> groaned at the pain gathering in his head. This getting knocked down and thrown around was on its way to forming a habit. But then he heard hoofbeats riding away and managed to sit up. Seemed as if whoever had set the charge figured the job had finished him off.

One thing sure, he wasn't in any shape to mount up and go after a gang of outlaws determined to blow him to bits. Or if not that, to use him for target practice. Not just yet. Maybe never. It all depended on if Henry had come through the fall without damage.

After a while, when nothing further happened, he forced his eyes open. He spotted his horse standing off at one side. While he knew horses had only four feet, he managed to see eight on this one. At least eight. Blinking, he examined Deputy Billings' packhorse next. The mare, too, was on her feet, of which he counted only six. Maybe that meant he was getting better. At least this animal seemed fine as well, too many feet or not, and had wandered off to put her nose down and graze. Pure luck.

As for him, trying not to move too much, he remained sitting on the ground where he'd fallen and allowed January Billings' dog to crawl into his lap. She was a big dog and all of her didn't quite fit, but they made do. He ran his hand over her legs, each in turn.

"Fine kettle of fish, ain't it? Dog, our record doesn't show much in the way of success."

Pen whined. Eli heard agreement.

"Nope. Isn't your fault. I'm not blaming you. Not blaming her, either. Not your girl, that is. The other one? Yep. I figure it's all on her. Her and whatever man she's taken up with this time."

Pen growled.

"You can say that in doubles. I feel the same." He gave the dog a final pat and, easing her aside, struggled to his feet. In seconds, it became clear that if he'd thought the Broomhandle Mauser an uncomfortable fit against his ribs when riding, it was nothing compared to the bruise accrued when fallen upon. The worst seemed to be that he'd had no chance to use it against these horse thieves. Not yet anyhow. A hot burn of anger let him know the lack of action wouldn't last much longer. He just had to catch up with the gang and get the job done. Rescue Mrs. Billings and young Zora, provided the outlaws didn't kill them first, and to finish the job, recover his horse. A horse that grew more expensive every minute.

Calling to the dog, he set out to follow.

Slowly. As it happened, Henry had come up lame after all. But not, perhaps, as lame as Eli himself. Between the two of them, it meant a delay.

* * *

JANUARY FOUND HERSELF RIDING BESIDE ZORA WHEN RUBY WENT ahead to talk with Dent. Talk? More another argument.

The man, Shandy, leading Hoot on a lead like a dog, seemed to be dozing as he rode, and behind them, Ike. He was serenading the group with a song not fit for a youngster like Zora to hear. Between the two of them, they formed a bubble of privacy.

A piece of luck. With everybody occupied with their own concerns, it left free. She was anxious to put her questions to the girl.

January reached over and touched the girl's leg. Zora startled, her eyes as wide as though the touch had been hot, but at least she became aware.

"Are you all right?" January whispered.

The girl's lower lip trembled. "No. Yes. No." Tears filled her eyes. Green eyes, though more the green of old grass rather than new.

January tried a smile. "Which is it?"

"I...I'm not hurt."

An answer of sorts. January knew there were ways of being hurt that didn't require the letting of blood. Scars formed on the inside instead of out.

"That's good," she said. "I'm a deputy sheriff. Deputy January Billings. I'm sort of like Dora's father, only I hope more capable. I'm here to help you."

This drew an astonished flash of those green eyes. "But now you're a prisoner, too."

"Um." Unfortunately, the girl had a point. The outlaws

hadn't bound her, and they'd overlooked her boot gun. Careless of them, a form of neglect they might soon rue. "Not so much a prisoner as they think," she said. "And my dog is free. So is Mr. Pasco. He's been helping to find you."

"Him." Zora huffed, a show of disdain. "He just wants to take my horse. And my home."

"I don't think you should blame Mr. Pasco, Zora. Your father put the ranch and the horse up for sale and Mr. Pasco bought both in good faith. How was he to know you considered Windswept yours?" She eyed the horse in question. "He is very fine, I see. Anyone would be proud to own him."

What on earth was she doing, defending the enigmatic Eli Pasco? Didn't she have her own doubts about him?

"Anyone but my father," she heard Zora say bitterly. "He doesn't care about anything but money."

January's lips tightened. She couldn't blame the girl for the lack of respect. According to her own father, respect is not a right. It must be earned, and obviously, Winkler had failed the test.

The serenade stopped. "Hey," Ike called out. "Little girl. Give that horse a kick. You don't want to talk to the woman. She ain't gonna do nothing for you."

Dora was still looking at her. January winked. "We'll talk more later," she said as the girl, glaring over her shoulder at Ike, moved on.

Eli Pasco is not the villain. January didn't know when the realization first sank into her brain. One minute she was still worrying about his intentions, the next she felt sure he'd be coming along soon to help out.

As long as that second explosion hadn't killed him.

Apparently, even Ike didn't think it had. "Slowed him down some, Ruby," January heard him say to the woman. "That's about all. You can quit worrying." He cast a sideways look at Dent that the boss either ignored or didn't see. "Until he catches up, at least." He laughed. "If he does."

* * *

HIS FOOT IN THE STIRRUP, ELI WAS PREPARING TO MOUNT WHEN a sensation like lightning bolts and spiraling whirlpools came together, overwhelming him. He dropped onto his backside like he'd been shot. The jolt to his head, never mind his abused tailbone, turned the world black and for the third—or was it the fourth?—time in two days, he passed out.

When he came to himself, he still held onto Henry's reins. The horse hadn't budged, and Eli saw why. Henry stood with one foot cocked up and, considering that Eli sprawled on the ground with his face within inches of the foot, even through blurred eyesight it was easy to spot the swelling at the fetlock.

Eli swore.

Pen, sitting beside Mollie, drew his attention with her whimper. Eli didn't think he'd been out more than a minute or two, as that's where both horse and dog had been before he went down. But if dogs worried, he thought this one was. He lurched to his feet, sickness roiling in his stomach and with such a pain in his head he knew he couldn't go on. Not until his innards settled and the pounding in his head eased.

And not with Henry lamed. He leaned against the horse.

"Rattled my chain but good," he informed the air at large, the sound so huge it made his eardrums vibrate. Not only that, but when he reached out to tether Henry to a bush, he discovered the limb was six inches farther beyond what he'd thought. All he touched was air.

At this rate, he'd be no more help to January Billings or Zora Winkler than the lunatic bartender at the Watering Hole. Maybe less. He tried not to think of Windswept's recovery, most surely becoming less likely every minute.

He knew only one thing to do. Stretching out at the side of the road, he closed his eyes, willing the blackness to fade, willing the whirling vision and rushing noise in his ears to recede. Pen crawled up and lay beside him, a comforting warmth even if she did smell of dog and dust. He slept.

The afternoon had advanced some hours when he awoke. The horses, to his shame and embarrassment—and gratitude, stood patiently, drowsing the time away. Mollie with her unwieldy pack askew, Henry with the leaves from the bush devoured. The horse could've simply walked away if he'd felt like it. Same with Mollie. And the dog. But the dog hadn't, and Eli thought he knew why.

Mrs. Billings hadn't come back for her dog, to Eli, that meant only one thing. The deputy had been taken, just like Zora. Which, those thoughts digging deeper, meant he was responsible for finding and freeing all of them. Mrs. Billings, Zora, and his horse, Windswept.

That's if he didn't come across the deputy's body along

the trail. That strong, bright, and strangely beautiful woman? He thought not.

Slowly, Eli stood, relieved to find the dizziness, if not gone, then much improved. His hearing seemed normal, a bird's song and the crunch of Mollie chomping on grass a relief from the previous roar. Only one black dog rose to stand beside him, stretch, and shake away the debris clinging to her fur. No more double vision to plague him, though stuff blurred if he looked at it too hard.

"She'll be wondering if we're dead," he said to the dog, whose soulful brown eyes stared at him. "As long as she's not dead and her body dumped in shallow grave somewhere. That, or left beside the road."

Pen whuffed, making Eli wish he could take those words back.

They had to go on.

An examination showed the swelling in Henry's fetlock improved, though not enough for Eli to consider riding him. Eyeing the deputy's mare, he remembered Mrs. Billings riding her into town, meaning the buckskin wasn't just a packhorse.

Within minutes he'd switched the saddle and pack between horses, climbed onto Mollie and clicked his tongue to get them all moving. Slowly now, though anxiety rode him, as much for the sake of his head as for Henry's leg and Mollie's years, as Eli knew the mare had some age on her.

Pen leading the way, they were soon following the trail, leaving the divot in the road behind.

They didn't stop until twilight overtook them, and it grew too dark for him with his blurred vision to see.

Eli, muttering his frustration, had been relying on Pen's nose for the last couple miles when he noticed a clear spot a few yards off the road. He whistled to the dog. "This'll do. Hold up, Pen. We'll stay the night here."

The dog turned to look back at him, eager to persist her tracking. Eli figured he'd have to find a way to tie her so she didn't leave during the night without him. He'd need her in the morning, the moment the sun broke over the treetops.

"We haven't found her body," he murmured to the dog. "That's good. She's a tough lady. And smart. Believe it." He wasn't sure he did. The mutilated dead man at the cabin kept coming to mind.

Rummaging through January's carefully packed medical supplies, he found her headache powders and mixed some in the coffee he made. Afterward, he shared his beef jerky and some stale biscuits with Pen and, though there was still light in the sky, wrapped himself in a blanket and went to sleep.

The old dog, also worn out, slept heavily and stayed by him, even though he'd forgotten to tie her.

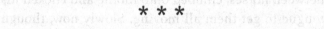

NOT MUCH TO JANUARY'S SURPRISE, RUBY AVOIDED RIDING NEAR her as the outlaw band followed a shadowed trail around a hill thick with big timber. The sun had already slipped behind the tallest trees, and it was growing dark. So was January's patience—growing dark, that is.

Suspecting the woman didn't want to discuss her

meeting back in Claremont with Pasco where the outlaws might overhear, January decided to wait. A time would come. Unless, of course, they killed her first.

Meekly, she followed every directive. As long as they thought they had her cowed, they'd leave her alone and unbound, she had a chance.

The trail they followed appeared to lead toward the river. Upon occasion January even glimpsed the water, but in an odd twist, it never seemed to get any nearer. At least she was in charge of Hoot's reins by now, due in equal part to the narrow road and Shandy's displeasure at being elected to, as he put it, "nursemaid her". Dent had gotten tired of listening to him complain and rescinded the order.

Ruby avoided Zora, too, rather to January's amusement, whether from guilt or a dislike of children in general was unclear.

To January, Zora didn't seem childlike at all. Although, upon reflection, she'd never had much to do with youngsters of any age. Her own childhood had been filled with pain, terror, and constant moving from place to place without the opportunity to make friends. So what, when you came right down to it, did she know? Just that Zora wasn't like most girls of the same age. More like a young-looking grown-up woman, who'd already faced hardship and sadness. When comparing Zora Winkler with Dora Dabney, the talkative deputy's daughter, Dora struck January as much the younger of the two. Childlike.

Once, when they came to a wide spot and Ike dropped back to make a trip into the woods, Zora took the opportunity to speak with January again.

"That woman, Ruby, she didn't act like this when they first took me." Zora's glance swiveled toward Ruby who was chatting with Dent, batting her eyes like a flirtatious miss in an 1840's romantic novel. She'd look up at him through her lashes, then moisten her lips. January couldn't help but smirk. Somebody should tell Ruby she didn't have the mouth for it. Lips too thin, too set, and too hard.

Or maybe, she decided, taking another look, it was the missing sincerity or sense of fun. Which is when the memory of Lawton reared its head. Lawton, who'd tried to kill her and Pasco but ended up with the short end of the stick. Hadn't someone said he'd been Ruby's man? If so, her feelings must not have run deep to have switched so rapidly—or pretended to switch. January gave the couple a closer look.

"Do you mean flirting with Dent? She didn't?" January raised an eyebrow. "When did she start? Before or after Lawton got killed?" She felt quite certain Zora knew about the man's death. And who'd done it.

"Yes. Ruby and him were together then. And she kept the others away from me. How can she have switched to Dent so fast? Anyway, what kind of name is Dent? He doesn't even answer to it half the time. I don't think it's his real name."

"Really? How do you know?"

"Because I heard her say something."

"What?"

Zora's voice took on a note as if parroting the individuals. "She said, 'If they knew who you really are, they wouldn't be following you.' And he said, 'Then you'd better not tell, had you? Not if you know what's good for you.' And she said, 'I won't. I promise.'"

She sounded genuinely puzzled—almost hurt by the change in Ruby's behavior. "Dent didn't pay her any mind, before. Not much, anyhow. But after that..." She made a gesture. "Look at them now."

Oddly enough, January didn't think Dent was all that enthralled with Ruby's antics. It turned out Zora, wise beyond her years and with a wisdom born of observing older, malicious brothers, didn't either.

"Those two," the girl muttered. "Seeing them is like watching a play with terrible actors. They go through the motions and say the words, but neither puts the right feeling into them."

January, who'd never seen a play in her life having avoided any spectacle liable to draw a crowd, couldn't disagree. Her imagination filled in the plot.

"Why do you suppose they do it?" she asked, smiling at the girl's perspicuity. "Why put on an act?"

Zora studied them. "I think to test each other. See who comes out on top."

January shot her a look, surprised at her insight. "Who do you think is winning?"

"Sometimes Dent and sometimes Ruby. But Ruby doesn't know it. She thinks *she* is. All the time."

From what January had seen, she had to agree. Not that it made the slightest difference to her. Her only concern lay in freeing Zora and herself from them both and getting away with Windswept. She had to put him in the equation as well. That first. When they were safe, she looked forward to coming back and arresting the whole lot of them.

"Who is their act for, Zora? Do you know?"

"I thought at first it was for that man, the one..." The girl choked, then started again, her facing turning paste white. Tears welled in her eyes and she blinked before saying, "The one Ike killed. He did awful things to him. Did you know that?"

Ike. Narrow-eyed, January stole another look at him, dozing in his saddle with his head bobbing to the horse's movement. "Yes. Mr. Pasco and I found him. What did Ruby say about it?"

"She yelled at him. So did Lawton. She said Dent should've stopped Ike, and Lawton backed her. Mostly, I think it scared her. She came outside and puked." The way she said the last part showed satisfaction. To January's mind, the way she spoke proved the girl had not, at least, been in the same room while they—Ike—tortured the man. And thank God for that.

January cocked her head. "Are you sure Ruby is winning their battle?" It didn't strike her that way.

"Like I said. Sometimes. Otherwise, I think Mr. Pasco would be dead. She didn't want him killed. Or not yet. So she said."

Ike, glowering like a picture book gargoyle, returned just then and Zora, watching him as if expecting a blow, urged Windswept forward, out of Ike's reach. Out of January's too, no matter that Zora's information raised a whole raft more of questions in her mind. One being that Lawton may have been the leader up to then. Events didn't add up.

They rode as it turned dusk, until in what struck

January as a prearranged time, they came to a small house nestled a half-mile from the road in a cluster of poplar trees. They stopped there. Hidden completely by a bluff and the half-grown trees, she concluded finding the place was no accident as even the overgrown path leading to it was hidden.

Ruby rode over and whispered something to Shandy before they pulled up. Something that caused Shandy to dismount and come to stand beside Hoot.

"You keep your mouth shut when we get inside." His whisper fierce, he added. "You let out one peep and that little girl is dead. Ike don't like her see, and he's only keeping her because of the money he can get for her. He don't like you, either, if you ask me. But this place, well, you just do as you're told. You listening to me, woman?"

Someone had guessed a threat to Zora would have more meaning than one just to herself. Ruby, no doubt. All due, January thought bitterly, to Pasco's talk with Ruby back in Claremont, even if he hadn't said as much in so many words.

But then Shandy's words sunk in, worrying her anew. *Ike,* Shandy said. Why did what Ike, who struck her as an uncouth moron, thought matter so much?

"I hear you," she said.

Everyone dismounted and milled around as Ike stepped onto the house's porch and opened the door.

CHAPTER 12

Squeeze four average-sized outlaws, two full-grown women, and one youngish, smallish girl into the tiny, crooked house belonging to the Wicked Witch of the Woods, and bad things are bound to happen. A catastrophe, most likely, considering the witch did indeed turn out to be an elderly and totally evil old lady Deputy January Billings decided must have lost her mind.

Or had she? Chances were, she'd plain been born wicked.

By this time, January had concluded that Eli Pasco had nothing to do with the predicament confronting Zora and herself. Was he still alive? The thought of him being blown up by Ike's booby trap back on the trail haunted her. What had happened to Mollie? And where was Pen? That her dog hadn't come to find her indicated one of two things. Either Pasco was alive and well, and wisely had Pen on a leash, *or they all were dead.*

She shook the thought aside before she broke down and bawled, an act that would terrify Zora even more.

What's more, January figured Ruby, while part of the

gang, was in as much danger and almost as frightened as she, the point being neither of them were women who scared easily.

But first, they had to meet the witch.

Pausing in the open doorway before entering the house, Ruby had leaned toward Dent and whispered, "What is this place? Where are we?"

Shrugging, Dent spoke softly, "Ike's place. We'll hole up here a day or so. I've got plans. Believe it or not, Ike gave me the idea back in Claremont."

"Plans? What plans? Is that why we were hanging around that dump?"

"You'll see. Just keep quiet and don't pay any attention to—"

"Well, I don't like it here. It stinks." Ruby's complaint echoed what all of them must be thinking.

"Get used to it," Dent said, and with an audible indrawn breath, walked inside, dragging Ruby with him. Willy-nilly, the rest of them followed.

January could almost swear the marrow in her bones began melting from the moment she walked through the door, a heavy door that creaked on its hinges as it thunked shut behind them, enclosing everyone in Stygian darkness.

Ike acted the host. Under the guise of a hearty welcome, he gestured everyone inside, into a dark front room. It appeared to be mostly empty, although the inky blackness made it hard to tell. "Ma," he called. "I'm home. I've brought some folks with me."

Shandy, who still stood behind January as if to hide in her shade, was muttering under his breath. "Oh,

Lord God. Please, Jesus, help us all."

It struck her that he truly was praying. She turned to peer at him, a question on her lips, but he made a sound like, "*Sssssst*," and she knew he meant it as a warning for her to be quiet. The less notice she drew, the better off they'd all be.

More than Ike, the creaking door and the lack of light convinced her to obey Shandy's *Sssst*. As for Zora, ahead of January and already halfway into the small front room, well, a soft whimper escaped the hand the most silent of the outlaws held over her mouth. Even Dent had nothing more to say. His former confidence seemed shaken.

Then a drag of slow feet across the floor sounded, and a shape appeared out of the darkness like a gray ghost.

"Ike?" A harsh whisper of sound formed the man's name. "Son, is that you?"

"I'm back, Ma," Ike said. "I did what you said."

"Did you get the treasure?"

"No, Ma. He didn't have it. I looked all over. He would've told if he'd known where it was. I made sure of that."

A screech like the death cry of a witch's pet crow raised all the hair on January's head and turned her hands ice cold. Shandy clutched at her as if seeking her protection. Zora cried out and so did Ruby. January refrained, but only by stuffing her fist in her mouth.

Ma? Ike called the woman Ma? And treasure? What he did he mean?

An answer came to her, along with the memory of the holes she and Pasco had seen inside and outside the death cabin. *Oh.*

She shuddered and Shandy, still gripping her arm with force sure to leave bruises, shuddered right along with her.

Whatever Ike's intention, the others got the reference. As her eyes adjusted to the dimness, she saw Dent nodding right along with the man no one had ever put a name to. Even Zora. None could seem to stop until the old woman said, "That's too bad. I reckon my dream told me wrong. Dreams lie too, sometimes. You should remember that." Another of those witchy cackles escaped her. "Well then, no matter. I'll figure out something else. Someone *here* knows where the treasure is. They'll tell. They always do."

A man horribly tortured and murdered and she brushed his death off as if it were nothing.

Gray garments fluttered around the crone. "Come in," she croaked, gesturing with her pointer finger at the group. "Come in where I can see you. I'm Ike's ma. I be Mabel Wilson." She said her name as if they should know her.

Maybe a couple of them did, but if so, the knowledge didn't reassure them. The tension gripping the room didn't let up. Grew stronger, if anything.

January had no idea who took the first step forward. Not Shandy, she knew. Not Dent or Ruby. So it must've been the silent man, and he took Zora with him. The others, with Ike harrying them along, perforce followed him into a filthy kitchen where the back door stood open. Night-flying insects flew in unimpeded to gather around a couple kerosene lamps with soot-covered shades hung in wall sconces thick with cobwebs.

A rough deal table sat in the middle of the room. Three or four cobbled together stools were pushed around it. There was a cook stove in sad need of a good cleaning and blackening. Some pots encrusted with burned-on food sat atop it. A couple nearby shelves held a few dishes and a small store of canned goods and covered tins. A once-yellow rag did service as a curtain at a window. It looked toward the road they'd come in on, so the woman had surely known they were coming. This scene was an act, performed to frighten them into compliance.

It worked, January admitted.

The old woman must've been accustomed to the weak light as without comment, she squinted and walked up close to Zora. Presently, she nodded satisfaction. "This one will do." She whirled and pointed at Ruby. "And this one."

Dent's face puckered, grew hard.

"What does she mean, I'll do?" Ruby whispered.

Dent shook his head.

After a mere fifteen minutes of Mabel Wilson's hospitality, January had doubts any of them would get out of the situation alive. Law-abiding or outlaw. Men or women, but especially the females.

January's turn for inspection followed. The finger with a sharpened claw on the end pointed at her in a sort of accusation. "But not this one. She's got a scar. She's dangerous and I don't like her."

Her feelings intact, January hated to admit how relieved she felt. She didn't want liked. Neither by Ike's mother, nor by Ike himself.

Ruby, ignoring Dent's advice, spoke up. "Do for what?"

The old woman's smile showed surprisingly good teeth. "Why, for what I have planned."

"And just what is that?" Ruby persisted.

"You'll see, m'dear, when the time comes." Mabel cackled with hair-raising glee.

Dent, still appearing more than a little gobsmacked by Ike and this whole unexpected situation, straightened, placing his hand on the butt of his holstered pistol. "Ike, what in hell is going on, here? You said we were meeting the buyer. You said it's all arranged."

Mabel sniffed disdain. "He fooled you. My son is *smart*."

"You lied to me?" Anger caused Dent to sputter. His face turned a strange puce color.

"Naw, it *is* all arranged," Ike said. "Just the facts is fudged a little. The buyer for the horse is coming, all right. He'll be here tomorrow. There's one coming for the girls, too. That's the fudge part." He appeared delighted by the idea. "See, there ain't two buyers bidding for the horse. That one is a done deal. It's the feller who wants the girls who's had us waiting in Claremont for him. His boat was late getting in. Thought that telegram was never gonna show up."

He grinned at his ma. "I kept telling Dent here we had to wait. Told him a bidding war would give us a better price."

"That'll learn you to fool with a Wilson," Mabel said, chortling at Dent's expression. She slapped her son on the back.

Ike hung his head and grinned at his mother's praise. "See, Ma, I told you I could do it."

"You're a such a good boy," she cooed.

January thought she might be sick. But not as sick as Dent. And Shandy, still behind her and still whispering "ssst" under his breath. What did he know about the Wilsons? She meant to have a word with him and find out.

Before she could set this plan into action, the "girls" were herded into a room opening off the first room they'd entered. January thought it might have been where Mabel had concealed herself until she mysteriously appeared at her son's call. The door was almost invisible from where they'd stood and curiously, it didn't creak.

Was the whole of this queer old house a stage setting meant to unsettle anyone who entered?

The earlier talk with Zora drew the thought to mind. January had to admit that as part of a plot, it worked quite well.

Again, January might not know much about the theater, but this strange and mysterious old woman struck her as someone acting a part from a gothic horror script. One that begged the question, was Mabel Wilson as dangerous as she let on? Or was she, like her son, really so good an actor?

The murdered man—he had not been a stage prop. He'd been all too real.

"Mrs. Deputy?" Zora's soft whisper broke through January's harried mind muddle.

"I'm here, Zora." January didn't whisper, but she did speak softly. She sensed the girl reaching out, shifting around the room trying to find her. "Here," she said again to give Zora's search a proper direction. "My name is Mrs. Billings. You may call me that."

"It's awfully dark in here." Ruby made a curious moaning sound. "I hate the dark."

"I wonder if the Mabel Wilson we see is real," January said, "or if it's all part of her act."

"Act?" Ruby and Zora spoke together. "Real?"

"Do you believe this is her real life? The costume? This awful house? The tone of her voice and the grating laugh? Don't you think she's acting out the part of the witch in Hansel and Gretel?"

"Who is that?" Zora asked.

"An old German fairy tale. You know fairy tales, don't you?" Ruby jumped in with the explanation. "Scary ones?"

"No." Zora considered. "And if this is what they're like, I don't want to."

"Wise of you. I don't want to either," Ruby said, "but it's too late for me."

By this time, Zora had found January. She thrust her small cold hand into January's equally cold one and held on. "I'm scared enough already. Mrs. Deputy...I mean... Mrs. Billings, what was Ike talking about when he said someone was coming for the girls? He meant us, didn't he? A buyer? But nobody can buy us. And nobody better think they can buy Windswept, either. He's mine!" Her voice had risen and ended on a hiccup.

January hoped nobody was listening. She wanted Zora to maintain the courage she'd been showing all along.

Ruby raged. She paced back and forth across a curiously hollow sounding floor, boot heels clomping. Once she grunted as she ran into something.

Taking heed, January went behind her and swept another of those raggedy curtains away from a small, filthy window. The curtain shook down a cloud of dust, smelled though not seen. She sneezed and used the rag to dust the windowpane.

"That helps," she said. "At least we can see where we are."

Zora's small voice whispered, "Where is that?"

"Up the creek, kid. Purely up the creek," Ruby answered before January could.

ELI STARTLED AWAKE AND LAY STILL, LISTENING. MOVEMENT FROM over where he'd picketed the horses indicated they had stirred, as well, although it didn't go beyond a little shuffling of their hooves. Nothing to worry about, he decided, and couldn't think what had awakened him. But then Mrs. Billings' dog lifted her head and, stiff with the effort, rose to her feet. Eli clamped his fingers onto her ruff and said in a low voice, "Hush, Pen. Good girl."

As though she understood, the dog stilled as the sound of horses' hooves and men's voices rose from only a few yards distance. Two men, Eli thought, and neither of them happy with traveling at night on an unknown road.

"How do you know we're even on the right road? His directions were muddled," the first speaker said. "The fool struck me as more or less illiterate."

Listening, Eli figured the man to be in an irate state of mind.

"Not that muddled," a second man said. "And seeing as how there's only one road going this way, I doubt we'll get lost."

"I didn't say we was lost. I just wondered if his directions were good. Seems we should've got there by now."

"We can't be far off. Nine miles, he said. I think we've ridden about that far." The second man hesitated. "I'm used to traveling by sea. Land miles are different. The only thing is, he said the trail to the house isn't clear. Could be we should stop somewhere along here and wait for daylight. A few hours' sleep won't hurt." An inflection came into his voice that made Eli's ears stretch. "Those girls. They might not want to cooperate when they learn where they're going. Waiting will make them more docile."

"Not my problem," the other said. "Just as well I'm not here for females. I'll stick to horses. The wildest bronc is better than a docile female. Anyways, there should be tracks to follow. Which would be a whole lot easier seen in daylight."

The second man snorted. "Truth. We'll look for an open spot."

They rode out of hearing without saying more.

Eli didn't ponder on their talk for long, his head aching too much to concentrate. He slept again, and though he didn't know it, left Pen on guard. The rest of the night passed undisturbed.

Fingers of pink and red were spreading across a pale sky when Eli sat up a second time. A wave of dizziness almost laid him low again, but he waited it out and when his eyes focused, he saw the dog was awake and on watch. They both rose to their feet, stretching to ease their aching and abused muscles.

Coffee and another dose of Mrs. Billings' headache powder got Eli moving. He saddled Henry and restored Mollie's pack, fed the dog and gave both horses a handful of grain. After stamping dirt over his small fire, they moved out again. Slower than before, taking care not to strain Henry's fetlock.

Easy in the saddle, his mind drifted to what he'd heard last night. What about the sea? And the girls? Had the man been talking about Zora and January? Thinking back, it almost seemed as though he'd imagined the voices until he found fresh tracks in the road, and after half a mile, saw where they'd camped. Smoke still rose from their abandoned fire, and he dismounted to finish putting it out. If there was anything he dreaded, it was to be caught in the mountains with fire raging through the timber. Thank God it wasn't summer and the big dry.

After a while, it seemed to him they were going in circles as they wound steadily upward on the steep road. The sun warmed, drawing out the scent of pine. A lark sang. A sudden drumming of wings announced the presence of a ruffled grouse, enticement to Pen who ran into the woods to investigate.

At least he hadn't found a body, nor even any blood. In his mind, this indicated Mrs. Billings was alive and, probably, well. Horse tracks on the trail could be deceptive. Could be she was trailing the outlaws the same as he. He had no proof she'd been taken. Or, his glance fell on the dog, only the fact her dog stayed with him.

Find her and he'd find his horse, or so he told himself.

With their pace slowed in order to save Henry, it was mid-morning when he came to a turn-off where many hooves had churned the soil into dust. Some of the tracks went forward, some returned. Eli couldn't discern which was which. He found one of Windswept's clear among them. And those of Mrs. Billings' horse, Hoot. From the beginning of the search, he'd noticed that Hoot's shoes cut a sharper print in the soil, as though he'd been freshly shod before starting out on this search.

Eli kept going, pausing often to listen. When they reached a break in the woods, he dismounted and, leaving the horses, walked silently ahead with Pen at heel until he spotted the house. Not a fine house, by any means. Small, mean, the porch sagging, green moss growing on the roof with its broken shingles. The few windows were dirty and tiny.

An outhouse squatted nearby, closer than a smart person ever dug their hole. A shed hardly worthy of being called a barn lay a hundred yards away, and Eli winced to think of a horse like Windswept or Hoot being kept there.

But the point was, he saw no horses. None at all, the empty corral indicating the place was deserted. What he did see was a small trickle of smoke rising from the chimney, as if from a dying fire.

Pen's cold nose as she thrust it into his fist almost caused him to yelp like a girl.

"What about it, dog? Is your woman in there?" Eli waited, as if expecting an answer, receiving only a whimper and a lick.

"Yeah. I hope not. I got a feeling," he said, "and it's telling me that house is not a good place." He sucked in air through his nose. "Well, let's go see what's what."

He dashed toward the front of the house, against all logic expecting a shot to fell him at any moment. Turned out he made it to the door unscathed, Pen stuck to his side as if nailed to his leg. Once there, Eli didn't pause. One kick and the door flew open, hinges screeching.

CHAPTER 13

"I'M HUNGRY," ZORA SAID AFTER A WHILE, HER VOICE CATCHING.

"I am too," January said, although she wasn't. Not really. It just seemed better to keep things normal for the girl. To sympathize without stirring her up. Although, thinking about it, nothing about the situation was normal. Better though, to think of hunger than of being sold like an animal.

Up until now, they'd been silent. Sitting in the dim room on what she knew must be a filthy floor. She thought it just as well they couldn't see how bad it really was.

The simple exchange sent Ruby into a rage. "How can either of you think of food at a time like this? Didn't you hear what that old biddy said? What Ike said? They said we're for sale. *For sale!* Just like that stupid horse."

If Ruby had been looking, she might've cringed at January's narrow-eyed glare, especially when Zora, almost bursting at the seams, said, "Windswept isn't stupid. Anyway, whose fault is all this? Yours, that's who. You and those awful men. You're nothing but thieves and killers. All of you."

"What? Me? Nonsense." Ruby, the whites of her eyes flashing in the feeble light, took instant umbrage. "You just shut your mouth, little girl, before I shut it for you."

January straightened, prompt to intervene. "If I'm not mistaken, Ruby, you are part of this gang. Even take it upon yourself to give orders to the men. If not your fault, then whose?"

"What was I to do? Lawson and Dent cooked up the whole plan." Ruby flounced, the effect lost as she huddled on the floor. "They didn't know what Ike was planning and I certainly didn't. Heavens, I didn't know he was *capable* of planning anything."

Zora stood and set her hands on slender hips. A horse-woman's hips, just like January's.

"Horse feathers," Zora insisted. "I heard you all talking at night when you thought I was sleeping. You're the one who found out about Windswept because of Mr. Pasco buying our ranch. And you told them. You were proud of it. You bragged."

Ruby darted a quick glance at January. "I may have talked about E...Mr. Pasco buying the ranch, but I never said anything about kidnapping or selling you. You may be sure of that. And I most certainly didn't brag."

E—Eli? If January had needed proof of there being something secret between Ruby and Pasco, the use of Pasco's first name was it. Hearing another half-truth out of all that mess, she snorted. The signs pointed to Ruby having some kind of vendetta against Pasco. Or maybe some kind of hold over him. One he didn't want to talk about, possibly with good reason. While the woman may not have said anything about a kidnapping, January suspected it was only because it hadn't occurred to her. How hard had Ruby protested the plan? Now she was on the wrong side of the sale, she'd had a change of mind. Not that it had done her any good since she was as much a prisoner in this room as January and Zora.

Ruby knew it, too. She went silent for a moment, then rose and trod over to the door, pounding a tattoo on it with her fists.

"Dent?" she called. "Dent, get me out of here. What is going on?" Pausing as though waiting for an answer, she received no such thing. There was only silence on the other side of the door.

And then a shuffling sound, men shouting and cursing, all followed by a single gunshot.

"Dent!" Ruby's outraged cry had enough volume to shake the dirty old window in its frame.

Something crashed against the wall outside, then a peculiar hollow-sounding thud. The door rattled, making Ruby step back, but it didn't open.

January had a sickening premonition. "Be quiet," she ordered, "before you get us all shot."

"Dent has to help us. He has to."

"I doubt he can."

"What do you mean?"

Zora answered, sounding small and distant. "Because somebody shot him. Because he's dead."

"No. We don't know that." Nevertheless, Ruby started crying. The only good thing is that the sobs shaking her were soft. Even those ended when she curled her arms around her middle and stepped back into the center of the room.

Which is when the floor fell out from beneath her and she disappeared.

Just like that.

Clapping her hands over her mouth, Zora stifled a shriek. Shocked, January's mouth dropped open. The two stood frozen as seconds ticked by.

"Stand back." Recovering enough to move, January grabbed the girl by the shoulders and pulled her away from where the floor had been. Zora had been closest, within inches of the opening.

"Ruby?" January called down. "Ruby, are you all right?"

She waited. Silence. "Answer me, Ruby."

But Ruby didn't.

Kneeling at the edge of the aperture, January peered in. It appeared to be empty down there. No sound. No hump in the shape of a woman. No light. Nothing but black at the bottom. Or, actually, she couldn't see the bottom. What she did discover was the piece of flooring hung downward, supported by hinges showing it could be raised again. So. No more than a drop-off.

"What happened?" Zora whispered. "Where did she go?"

"I don't know. This is a trap door," January said.

Evidently, Zora had read some history because she said, "You mean like to an underground railroad? Or where people used to hide from Indian attacks? Or..."

January held up her hand to stop the flow. "I don't know, Zora. Something like that. An escape hatch."

"Maybe Ruby got away. Maybe we can get away. Shall we jump down, too?"

"If we did, we could be in a worse fix. We don't know how far it drops. We don't know what's down there." The silence from below worried her.

Zora put her anxiety into words. "Or who. Or why Ruby doesn't say anything."

"Exactly. She may have gotten away. Or she could be hurt. Or she may just be ignoring us while she escapes. Either way, I doubt she's coming back for us."

"Good. I don't want her to come back."

January had to smile. "Not sure I do either."

Zora might be right, though. Daring the unknown might be their best chance to escape this awful place. On the other hand, going down into that hole could just as well be their doom. She was here to rescue this girl, not get her killed. But what was the right way to go about it? The rescue she meant. The other didn't bear thinking about.

Which is when January realized she wished Eli Pasco was here with her—with them. Except for a secret acquaintance with Ruby, he'd showed himself to be trustworthy and determined. So far. Not one to give up easily. As long as they hadn't killed him. Unlooked for, maybe even unwanted, a vision of Shay came into her mind. Her husband had been trustworthy, tough, determined. Not one to give up easily.

And he was dead.

Fear pounded her like a hammer on a nail.

* * *

THE FIRST THING TO STRIKE ELI AS HE AND PEN RUSHED INTO THE house was the stench. Blood, dirt, stale cooking. Maybe even fear-sweat. Some old, some recent, and all a leftover from previous visitors. It overpowered all of a man's common olfactory defenses.

The silence came next. A sense of waiting. Of emptiness.

He saw the blood splashed on the wall, then, and more on the floor where it blended with the dirt. Blood fresh, but mostly dried.

Pen, who'd thrust herself inside with him, growled long and low. He put his hand on her and found the longer hair of her ruff standing up like porcupine quills.

"Easy, girl." He didn't want to say it, but he must. "Is she here?"

The dog snuffled and, as if she'd understood him, began nosing around, seeming to follow a trail only she knew. Eli followed. Together they stopped in front of a closed door only inches to the left of the blood-splashed wall. Pen scratched at the door with a paw.

"Here?" Eli turned the knob and peered through the opening, his attention immediately caught on a square cut out of the floor. "What the..." Pen darted between his legs, almost upending him. He followed her into the room.

Mrs. Billings had been here, Eli knew. The way the old dog acted guaranteed that much. So January—he'd begun thinking of her by her name—was alive. Or had been when she'd been in the room. A prisoner. Kidnapped just like little Zora Winkler.

"Here, stand back," he told the dog as she stepped to the edge of a mysterious hole. When Eli lay on his belly and looked in, daylight glancing in through the open door allowed him to see to the bottom—not that there was much there of interest. A pile of dirt, where the crawl space under the opening had been deepened to a depth of maybe eight feet. Why anybody would've gone to the trouble of digging it, he had no idea. A rope hung from a floor joist. A getaway of some sort, he imagined, as he had some idea of the people who owned the place. An escape hatch to the outside. Had Mrs. Billings gotten away? Maybe with the Winkler girl?

But on further thought, he didn't think so as Pen had backed away and lost interest in whatever lay below. She'd already returned to the other room and headed into the farther reaches of the filthy house. Eli went after her.

They didn't find much. Together, he and Pen nosed through a room containing a rumpled bed and a half-full chamber pot. The dog sneezed and turned away. More than half-sickened by the stench, so did Eli.

The kitchen proved filthy, yet food on the table where several plates showed people had been eating. A couple mice darted away as he walked in. Shaking his head in disgust, he followed Pen past an empty pantry and out the back. The dog stopped, showing interest in an almost empty woodshed tacked onto the side of the house.

Almost empty, because aside from a few chunks of wood, all it contained was the body of a man sprawled flat on his face.

Jaw tightening, Eli hesitated before he went in and turned the body over. He recognized the dead man immediately, although it had been a long time since he'd seen him.

Dent Johnson. He'd been shot through the heart.

Before he'd become a horse thief, Dent had worked for Eli's dad and hung around the house hoping to get something on with the older Pasco's flirty young wife. Evidently, he'd succeeded in connecting with Ruby.

Once a thief, always a thief, Eli thought, whether women or horses. Dispassionately, Eli looked down on Dent's slack gray face and figured he'd probably had it coming. The main question remained. Who had done the deed? One of the gang? Whoever had lived here?

Eli backed out of the shed, his mind reeling. Another question surfaced.

Why would the outlaws be killing each other? The question didn't make sense, which made him wonder how long it would be before they began killing the women. Starting, he was certain, with Deputy January Billings.

"Come on, dog," he said roughly. "You've got a job to do."

A willing worker, Pen soon sniffed out where the horses had stood and people mounted. The dog kept wanting to head off into the woods, aggravating Eli until he finally gave in and followed her to a mound of dirt thrown up behind a boulder.

The reason for the mound soon became clear, being the soil scooped from the outlet for the hole in the house floor. Only one set of footprints showed in the loose dirt. Too big for Zora, and the wrong kind of boot for January. The prints belonged to Ruby, and though it appeared she'd tried to get away, a couple men had caught and brought her back. He saw where she'd struggled.

Eli didn't really need the dog to track the outlaws. So many riders left a clear trail. Mounting Henry and leading Mollie, he urged the horses into a gentle lope. Before long, they came to a fork in the road and the choices became more difficult.

"Whoa," he murmured, bringing the horses to a stop. He got down to study the tracks, frowning in concentration.

The outlaws had broken into two groups. In the one headed due north, towards Canada, tracks were clear for four horses. Windswept was one of them. The others headed in a more westerly direction. By Eli's count, this second party had gained a couple riders, even considering Dent laying dead in the woodshed. Hoot's tracks mixed with these.

It seemed obvious the gang had met someone at the house. More than one someone. Those men on the trail last night, what had they said? Something about uncooperative girls? Had this been where they'd been headed? He figured so. Got a cold chill just thinking about a youngster like Zora Winkler in the hands of men who'd buy and sell girls. January Billings, too. She might be strong and tough, but he had a notion she also had a certain innocence. As for Ruby, well, he figured Ruby had a lot of practice dealing with people like that. After all, wasn't she one of those people herself?

Just thinking of the girl's danger made Eli's head ache with strain. Which set of tracks should he follow? Windswept's, or the larger bunch with January's horse? As long as Zora Winkler was still with Windswept, she'd be the one January would urge him to get after.

She'd say Zora was just a child in need of protection, and that she could take care of herself.

But had she ever faced off against so many? And did he know for sure where Zora was? Or January?

Or did he just want to find his horse?

Pen sat in the middle of the trail, dusting a clear spot with her wagging tail.

"Well, dog? Which way?" Eli didn't know why he asked the dog unless it was because January had instructed her to track Windswept, not Hoot. He guessed Pen retained the memory. Most likely, she was as confused as he.

They went north, the old dog in the lead.

With Henry still not up to speed, Mollie shaking her head with annoyance of being on a lead shank, and Pen sitting every now and then for a little rest, Eli made camp earlier than he wanted. Worried about the waste of time, he figured they were falling behind.

But that, in a way, turned out not to be such a bad thing.

Awakened at the crack of dawn by the sound of nearby gunshots, Eli shot up out of his blanket. Pen, who'd spent the night stretched out beside him, had already risen. She stood, every muscle tense. Poised like a statue, she looked off to the west, nose up scenting the air.

Eli grumbled something under his breath, blinked sleep out of his eyes and said, more distinctly, "Now what?" Early morning gunfire couldn't mean anything good. One shot or two might've meant a hunter. This fusillade sounded more like a war. And—he listened more closely—there were at least four or five, maybe more, guns involved.

Figuring there was no time to waste, Eli pulled on his boots, secured his bedroll, saddled Henry and slapped the pack on Mollie. Consumed with worry about the shooting, he didn't bother with breakfast. There'd be time for coffee later. Or not. Only as he mounted did he realize his headache had finally gone.

A wry grin twisted his mouth. One good thing about having a hard head. He wished he could let his dad, who'd tried to tell him it was a flaw, know it had helped him survive. But then, that had always depended on which side of the fence he was standing on.

The gunfire died as he headed out on the trail. Whatever the cause, the fight seemed to have ended. Still, urgency drove him as he whistled to the dog and tightened his knees.

Henry broke into a trot.

CHAPTER 14

ALTHOUGH SHE'D MEANT TO STAY AWAKE AND KEEP WATCH, JANuary had fallen into a light doze while sitting on the floor, her back to the wall. Worry over their predicament, she'd discovered, wore one out. Alone in the dark, it had been easy to let her fears overcome determined fortitude. She'd hoped Eli Pasco would catch up by now, unless Ike's explosives really had stopped him. Stopped him permanently.

How much could just one man do, anyway? There were four outlaws. Three for sure since she didn't know whether Dent was out of the picture or not. On the other hand, she had to add in the old woman, a mean and tough old biddy if she'd ever met one. Maybe Ruby, too, for that matter. So yeah. Even if Pasco came riding in right now, the odds were not in his favor. Or hers. She still had her hide-out gun, but only five shots. It was there as a last resort, and to provide help if Pasco ever did appear.

And her dog. What had happened to Pen? Her heart clenched.

Sometime during the night Zora had settled in beside

her, finally slumping over with her head and shoulders in January's lap.

A chilly breeze blew up through the hole in the floor, smelling musty and grave-like, and the cold had crept into her bones. It came as a relief when, as daylight lifted the gloom to the point January started wishing for dark again, the door slammed open, and the witch stepped inside.

"Uppie, uppie," the old woman said. "Let's get moving."

Zora, blinking with sleep, popped upright, her head bumping into January's chin. "I'm hungry," she announced, not whining like a child, but in a simple statement of fact.

January had other things on her mind. After seeing the condition of the house, she didn't think she wanted to eat anything fixed in that kitchen. Food poisoning was not on her list of preferences. "Where's Ruby?" she demanded.

Mabel cackled. "Wouldn't you like to know?"

"Yes," January said. "I would. That's why I asked."

The woman glared. "Keep your smart mouth to yourself. You ain't in charge here, Mrs. Deputy. I am."

So, Mabel had learned who, or what, she was. January wondered who had told the old harridan. She hadn't announced her legal position, having left the outlaws to wonder why she was with Pasco. If they even gave her a thought beyond taking her hostage. Something else to blame on Ruby, she figured. Pasco had probably talked about her when the two spoke back in Claremont. And Ruby had probably told Dent. And Dent had probably told—

"Get up." Mabel prodded January with the toe of a scuffed boot. More than a gentle prod. More like a kick to the ribs.

January winced.

"Stop that." Zora, already up, shoved the woman away before January could move.

For which January was very sorry, as it didn't help alleviate the sharp pain in her abused hip and earned Zora a backhanded slap across her face. A slap that staggered the girl.

Zora's green eyes widened, and she went white, mewling faintly. January lunged to her feet, meeting Mabel's squint-eyed glare.

"No breakfast for you, girlie," the woman snarled. "No food at all until you learn to respect your elders."

Ike came in then. He loomed over January, openly eyeing her scar and grinning like an ape in a zoo. January had seen one once, when she and her dad had passed through Portland. She hadn't liked the creature or the way it fondled itself. The animal, as she remembered, hadn't smelled much worse than Ike.

"Take'em to the outhouse and let'em pee," Mabel instructed her son. "And no peekin', Ike. We ain't got time to waste on those kind of hijinks."

"Sure, Ma."

Ike's leer made January suspect there was a knothole in need of blocking. She thought it best not to mention it to Zora.

Putting her arm around the girl, she let Ike steer them outside and past a woodshed to the most loathsome privy she'd ever encountered.

"Best if you don't antagonize them," she whispered to the girl.

Zora touched what, had she known it, was the clear

imprint of a hand on her face, and nodded. "Ugh," she said then, gagging as January opened the outhouse door.

Advising the girl to hold her breath for as long as she could, and to breathe shallowly when necessary, January thought at least the odor helped the girl forget her abused face. "Try to ignore the fumes," she whispered. Meanwhile, a tiny spot in the wall where a crack in the dry boards allowed the sun to shine through suddenly turned dark, and she moved to stand in front of it. The rattle of Ike's heavy breathing faded.

"You go first," she told Zora, and after, had the girl stand in her place.

Zora knew the score. "I have brothers, you know," she said in a matter-of-fact tone.

When they returned from the outhouse, they found two men had joined the group. A group, January noted, that did not contain Dent Johnson. She'd seen the blood on the wall and floor as they left the house. Dent's blood?

Had to be.

The men, one tall and muscular, the other shorter and a bald head revealed when he removed his hat to fan away a fly, appeared at first glance to be more prosperous and respectable than the outlaws. An illusion. They proved no more decent or well-meaning. Far from it.

Before she had time to dwell on them, Zora nudged January and cocked her head toward the woods behind the house. "Look, Mrs. Billings," she said in a shocked whisper. "It's Ruby."

More than a little shocked herself, January at first thought Ruby might be dead. But no. As if she knew they were talking about her, Ruby raised her head and glared through a tangle of dark hair.

She stood with her back against the rough bark of a Douglas fir. Tied there with ropes wound about her torso and lower legs, her pose reminded January of an illustration in an old Leatherstocking tale. At first, January felt sorry for her, until she wondered if that's all it was. A pose. One meant to draw sympathy and perhaps, keep her and Zora cowed enough to go along with the outlaws without fuss.

If so, Ruby was on the wrong track.

January looked away. She'd seen no bruises. No blood. A little artfully applied dirt and a couple rips in her skirt, is all.

"I think she's all right," she said. "I doubt you need to worry about Ruby."

"Really?" Zora seemed doubtful. "But what about Dent? I don't see him."

Wondering how much to say, January settled for the truth. "No. I think he's gone."

"Gone? Gone where?"

"It's hard to say." *Heaven?* Doubtful. *Hell?* More likely.

Overhearing this exchange, Ike sniggered and left them to swagger over to where his mother was conferring with the two newcomers. Money changed from their hands to hers. It looked like quite a lot of money, and January noticed Mabel, grinning her satisfaction, took most of it and stuffed the bills in her bodice before handing the rest to Ike. Presently, Ike, self-important as an Arabian potentate, distributed a share to Shandy and Silas, the silent man.

"Let's get moving." The muscular one called out. "Get

those women on their horses. I've got a boat waiting over on the coast."

A boat? A tingle of dread coursed through January's veins. *A boat to where?*

Zora, as anyone might have expected, had a hissy fit when the other man took hold of Windswept's bridle and began to lead him away.

"No." Her scream echoed through the clearing and made even Hoot dance. "That's my horse. You can't have him. I won't let you."

Quick as a fish in water, she tackled the bald man. Taken by surprise, he overbalanced and went down, the pair of them wrestling right under Windswept's feet. Not that the man stayed down. He got up, red-faced and angry, and swatted her away. He never even lost hold of the reins though the horse stamped and pulled against him.

"Madame," the man shouted. He was speaking to Mabel. "Control this child before I..."

Mabel shrugged. "She ain't mine no more. Speak to him." She cocked a thumb at the muscular man. Turning her back, she climbed with surprising agility onto a showy, if thin, palomino.

January moved quickly, shoving between the man grabbing onto Zora with his fist raised. She spun the girl out of his reach. "I've got her," she said.

He appeared confused, but his hand dropped. "Keep her quiet," he said, as if she were a paid nanny working for a rich man. Or maybe the madam in charge of a house of ill-repute.

She hugged Zora to her whispering frantically. "Zora, no. Hush now. Sweetheart, they'll hurt you. Don't make a fuss."

"He's got Windswept!" Zora sobbed as if her heart were breaking—and January figured it truly was. "That man is stealing my horse."

The bald man mounted his own horse. Without a backward glance, he jerked the rein attached to Windswept's bridle and led him away. Shandy, having been paid off, rode with him. So, to January's amazement, did Ruby. The trio rode into the band of trees hiding the house from the road and disappeared from view.

January, aware of the man watching them, gave Zora a little shake. "I know. You'll have to let Windswept go, Zora. I'm sorry. There's nothing you can do. Nothing I can do." She bent closer, speaking directly into Zora's ear. "Nothing I can do for now. But I swear to you, when we get away from these people, we'll find Windswept and get him back. I'll do it if I have to steal him myself. You understand me?"

Zora managed a shivery nod, listening to her even as tears ran down her cheeks. "We'll never get away from them, Mrs. Billings. Don't you know that?"

"Yes, we will." January kept any of her own doubts from showing. Enough to fool Zora, at any rate.

"That's enough." The muscular man scowled as he walked toward them. "Quit your bawling, kid. If there's anything I can't abide it's a bawling female. Bad things happen when I'm around them."

His narrowed gaze landed on January like a ton of the rocks she'd been using to build her new house. "As for you," he added, "watch yourself. And keep her quiet before I stuff Ike's old socks in her mouth." Yelling over to Ike, he told the outlaw to tie her wrists. "No slack. I don't want her getting loose."

The clear threat in his cold voice warned January he meant it. She leaned protectively over Zora, muffling the sobs. "You have to calm yourself, Zora. Please. He'll hurt you otherwise. I don't want you hurt."

A certain desperation in January's voice must've gotten through to the girl. Taking a great shuddering breath, Zora pulled away and nodded.

Silas led Dent's horse over for Zora to ride, saying something as he tossed her into the saddle. January pulled herself aboard Hoot and they started off only a minute after the man who'd claimed Windswept.

With the muscular man hurrying them along, they soon caught up with the others. Ruby, January noted, was no longer a prisoner. At the fork in the road, the three of them soon turned onto the road north.

Riding behind her, Zora sniffled.

Their case, hers and Zora's, was very different from Ruby's. No doubt about whether they were prisoners. Silas led Zora's horse; Ike led Hoot. They went west, toward the coast.

Mind racing, January pondered. She had to make a plan. But what?

ELI DREW HENRY TO A HALT WHEN PEN, WHO'D BEEN SCOUTING the trail ahead of them, plopped down in the middle of the road. Her head tilted upward, her black nose worked furiously.

Simple curiosity made Eli do the same, although he smelled nothing. Nothing but dust, horse, and the forest around them, at any rate.

"What is it?" he said aloud.

January Billings' dog turned her head toward him and gave a short bark.

If Eli had thought Pen capable of such a thing, he'd have said she was warning him about something. And he wouldn't be surprised. This whole pursuit was a surprise from start to finish. If it ever finished. Finished satisfactorily, he meant. With the girl and January kidnapped, and Dent, leader of the outlaws, dead in the woodshed back at that ramshackle house, he figured a successful conclusion became more unlikely by the minute.

With a click of his tongue, he got Henry moving again, bypassing the dog to continue up the steepening trail. Several horses had passed this way not long ago, a few hours at most. One of the sets belonged to Windswept. He and Pen moved more slowly now, with Eli on the watch for movement ahead, for any change of sound, or shoot, for any difference in the still air.

He didn't need Pen to tell him to pull up as the road curved around a jumble of boulders just ahead. Whatever had the dog, and Eli himself, on edge was about to be revealed. Dismounting, he ground-hitched Henry, moved the holster with his Broomhandle Mauser to the middle of his chest and eased on around the bend. Pen stayed with him, slinking along with her tail tucked between her legs. Whatever awaited them, she didn't like it. Eli didn't figure he would, either.

His first warning, aside from the dog's far ranging one, consisted of a group of magpies fluttering between trees and strutting in the road. Their odd yodeling and raspy cries were loud, so irritating to the nerves that Pen darted forward, chasing the stubborn, carrion-eating birds into the air.

Eli had a sick feeling over what he figured to find. Turns out he wasn't wrong.

The first body lay on its side, arm outstretched, a man's hand still holding a Remington .44. The birds had begun their work on the side of his face, attracted first to his eye. Gritting his teeth against the gory sight, Eli chased them away. Kneeling, he turned the man over, relieved when he proved a stranger. A crackle of paper at the turning caused Eli to reach into the man's coat pocket, where he found a letter. Its address bore a name and address. Thomas Lighthouse, Cranbrook, British Columbia. The man's wallet lay in the dirt beside him. A wallet emptied of cash.

Eli got up and went toward the second body. Pen had beaten him there, snuffling about and barking at birds. No sign of Windswept. Just one damaged gelding, head hanging, standing alone.

He looked back down at the victim and nudged the dog away. "Easy, girl. Let me see."

This one was still alive, though not, Eli suspected, for much longer. And he knew him. He patted the man's face. Gently, so he wouldn't add to the harm already done. "Shandy. Shandy Hermann. Wake up."

Shandy's breathing was shallow, drawn in then out with a queer burbling sound. He'd been shot twice in the chest, and going by the powder burns in his shirt, whoever had done it had been standing right in front of him. It appeared he'd flung up an arm as if thinking it would protect him from the bullets, one of which had broken the arm bone before passing on. Adding to the damage, he'd been pistol whipped.

"Shandy, wake up."

Shandy's eyelids wiggled and he groaned. "Ssssst," he said, or something like. Blood bubbled from his lips. His revolver lay beside him and as he began to awaken, he patted the ground with his good hand, searching for it. Eli moved the gun out of reach though he figured the man too weak to lift it.

"You're hurt bad, Shandy. Don't look like you're going to make it." Eli sat back on his heels and waited for Shandy to open his eyes. "So tell me, who shot you? Where are Mrs. Billings and Zora Winkler?"

"Taken," Shandy said.

As if he didn't already know. "Who shot you?"

"She did. She shot me."

She? What she? The women were prisoners. Weren't they?

Shandy moaned. Tears leaked from behind closed lids. "Hurts. Head hurts."

Yeah. Eli knew all about getting hit on the head. In truth, it rattled a man's brain. Not that Shandy had ever had much of one.

Eli repeated the names. "Who did this? Who attacked you, Shandy, and took the horses? Where are they taking the women?"

Shandy's body shuddered with the effort to speak.

"Tom hired me. I'd care for the horse when we got to Cranbrook. But Windswept, they took him. All planned." Shandy uttered an odd sound. "Tom paid for a stolen horse and then got robbed himself. Funny." But he wasn't laughing.

"Who planned it? Who took Windswept? How many of them were there?" Anger built in Eli like a bonfire burning straight through his gut.

As though he hadn't heard Eli's questions, Shandy said, "Ruby went with them." And then, struggling to get the words out he added, "She planned it with them."

"Ruby planned this? The ambush?" Eli's frown could've done serve as a scarecrow to chase the magpies away. "Are you sure? Why? What..." He stopped. If he expected to get sense out of Shandy before the man finally died, he'd have to ask his questions one at a time.

He started over, watching as the dog nipped at a bird alighting too close to Lighthouse's body to suit her.

"Where are they headed?" he asked.

But Shandy was fading fast. Not that he'd been exactly lucid in the first place, but now his words became almost unintelligible.

"How many are there?" Eli asked grimly. How many would he have to face?

"Some..." The answer, if that's what it was, meant nothing.

Eli leaned in closer. "Mrs. Billings. Is she with them?"

"Ruby..."

That was it. Shandy's words died in his throat.

Leaving him, Eli thought bitterly, not one whit wiser. Or not much. When this all started, he'd figured Dent the leader and Ruby along for the thrill. Or there'd been Lawton, until between himself and January, he got taken out of the equation. But now Dent was dead, too, and from the little Eli knew or could guess, Ruby might be trying to run the show. Might be? Maybe she already was. Maybe she always had. But where did this new bunch of thieves and killers figure into it? And what about January Billings and Zora?

What had begun as the simple theft of a valuable horse by a runaway girl had not only turned into a wider crime, it had become a whole lot more deadly.

CHAPTER 15

THEY'D BEEN TRAVELING FOR A COUPLE HOURS BEFORE JANUARY learned the muscular man's name. She heard Ike call him Frank. The circumstances turned out to be fairly amusing. To her, if not to Ike. As it happened, Frank didn't appear to approve of Ike's familiarity.

"That's Mr. Peel to you, bud," the bald man snapped.

"Huh?"

Peel didn't even look at him. "My friends call me Frank. You aren't my friend."

"What?"

The bald man ignored him and spurred his horse to more speed. Ike stared after him with his shoulders slumped and a mean slant to his eyes.

Mabel, who'd been riding beside Peel, opened her mouth, then closed it without speaking. Her fierce scowl showed she hadn't much cared for the man's condescending tone either, but as he sped up and left her behind, she turned toward Ike and snapped out, "Listen to him, son. Do what he says."

At first January smiled, considering the Wilson

pair deserving of any kind of scorn dealt them. Until she reflected that if Mabel Wilson walked so carefully around Peel, he must be someone she and Zora best beware of, as well.

Carefully, she urged Hoot as close to Zora's horse as the tether between her and Ike allowed. "Zora," she murmured, hoping Ike, caught up in his own sense of insult, wouldn't hear.

The girl looked over at her with green eyes swollen and red from crying.

"Be careful around that man. Try not to draw attention to yourself." January nodded toward Peel. "He's dangerous."

"I know." Zora's mouth trembled. "Is he more dangerous than them?" She meant Mabel and Ike.

"I'm afraid so. I hope not, but—" She stopped. "Just be careful."

Silas overheard. Catching Zora's eye, he nodded. "A bad man." His mouth barely moved.

Having him break his silence to say so didn't exactly reassure January when it came to their odds of escaping. At some point they'd have to try. Be smart. Because one thing for certain, if they failed the first time, there'd never be a second chance. She would not be getting on any boat. And neither would Zora.

The day wore on. The horses plodded. They crossed streams and entered the high desert country of the middle of the state. A dry desert where sagebrush cast a musty scent into the air, and sage hens, almost the same color of the vegetation, fluttered at their passing. January didn't like this area with its knobs of boulders, some might call them monoliths, rising straight out of what appeared at first to be flat land. But there were deep gullies hidden until the trail cut off at the edge and veered abruptly in a different direction.

Looking over her shoulder, she saw that a strong breeze swept through and wiped out their tracks almost as quickly as they made them. If Eli was trying to catch up, how would he know how to find them? Unless Pen—

She stopped herself. Eli Pasco and Pen were probably dead. Both of them. If they weren't, why hadn't they caught up by now?

The riders rarely stopped as they made their way across this part of the trail. Only when, or if, a cluster of trees or brush hid them for brief minutes to modestly—more or less—relieve themselves. Or the hour Mabel demanded in the early afternoon while the horses grazed on the sparse bunchgrass and rested. The pause allowed the humans to stretch their legs and ease their behinds. The old woman brought out store-bought crackers and jerky for everyone to nibble as they sat by a small stream January figured the coming hot weather would dry to a trickle, if it survived at all.

They rode on through the afternoon, never seeing another traveler.

January, drowsing in the saddle after her sleepless night, came alert when Mabel steered her palomino closer.

"You and me, we should have a talk," Mabel said. But what she meant was for her to do the talking, ask questions, and then for January to answer them.

January, though it strained her self-control when what she wanted to do was to lash out, kept her mouth shut.

She'd had plenty of experience doing that, God knows, as a child when she and her dad were running from the law. Women, in particular, had wanted to know more about the handsome stranger with the scarred daughter, and figured the best way to find out was to question the daughter. January learned to play a mute. While theirs had been an unnecessary flight as it turned out, the same kind of silence was critical now, when Zora's safety was at stake as well as her own.

Mabel stared at her out of beady, almost lashless eyes, fixing on the scar. "Who done that to you?" she said. "Ought to be whipped. Spoiled your value. Some other woman?"

Several answers ran through January's head, none of them anything but uncouth. Eyes narrowed, she bit down on her tongue and remained silent.

"See, I figure you been used before," Mabel said. "You can wise the girl up when it comes to tricks. Let'er know what to expect."

January sucked air in through her nose until her lungs felt like overblown balloons. She knew her face was flaming. Her hands tingled with the urge to shred the old woman's face with her fingernails, no matter they were bound in back of her.

"Too bad you ain't got the looks of a woman like Ruby Pasco. Give'er a run for her money if the two sides of you was alike."

January barely heard most of this. Or if she did, it didn't register. She heard the Ruby Pasco part, though. Especially the *Pasco.* Did this mean Eli Pasco was part of the gang? Or a competing faction? What was the connection between him and Ruby? She'd known there was one. *Known it.*

Was she his wife?

But then, why would he have involved her?

Watching her, Mabel cackled. "Ho! You didn't know them two was related, did ya? Well, not blood related. In-laws." The cackle came again. "Or outlaws."

January didn't even try to explain the relief that came over her. For Zora's sake, of course.

The woman's laughter had the rest of the men staring around and trying to hear what amused her. All but Silas. He'd slowed his horse, and along with it, Zora's, until they'd dropped several yards behind the others. January took note.

"What's the joke, Ma?" Ike hinked around in his saddle, placing his hand on the horse's rump. He appeared hopeful it was something better than Frank Peel's sneer.

"This'un is the joke." Mabel leaned close enough to poke a gnarled fingernail into January's chest, like a stab with a stiletto knife. "She didn't even know about Ruby bein' high and mighty Mr. Eli Pasco's mother-in-law."

Unable to stop it, January's mouth gaped. *Mother-in-law?*

Mabel cackled again. "Look at her. Not until just now and I tole her. Ain't that a hoot? Ain't so bright for a deputy. A deputy." Her rot-tinged breath blew in January's face. "Did you think anybody'd believe you was a real deputy? We ain't stupid."

Even Peel had an opinion. He glanced around. "There's no such thing. Female deputies aren't allowed. Women are useless creatures, good for only one thing. As these two will soon find out if they don't already know."

Mabel glared, not liking his opinion, although the men's laughter signaled agreement from all but Silas.

"Aren't you? Stupid that is?" January, unwise though she knew it to be, spoke up.

The grating cackle came again. "Who you callin' stupid? I ain't the one bein' held prisoner."

"An impermanent condition, I assure you," January said.

"Huh? Fancy talk. But I'm the smart one. I'm the one let Ruby go. Figured Pasco would chase after her. Her and that horse. And I was right. He ain't showed up here, has he? That's if he ain't dead."

"Better be." Ike had to add his couple cents. "Lighthouse is gonna be plenty nettled if Pasco shows up out of nowhere."

January's heart gave a leap. Did that mean Eli was alive? And that he was on the right side?

Mabel shrugged. "Don't matter none to me. Anyways, Lighthouse ain't gonna live that long. Him nor Shandy either one."

"They ain't?" Ike asked.

Peel reined in his horse. Reined him in hard, so the animal, mouth open, rose a few inches on its hind legs in protest. "Shut up, old woman. Both of you," the man said. "Yak, yak, yak."

Her face resembling the witch in a Grimm fairytale, Mabel glared. "Shut up your own self. I ain't one of your gang. You'd better be glad me and my boy are ridin' along with you."

"Really?" Peel snorted. "Why is that?"

"Otherwise the deputy here might get loose and run off. Look at her. She wants to."

Peel snorted. "Deputy. Nonsense." But he looked and looked again.

January had to suppose her face revealed the desire to do just that. But only if Zora got away too.

Mabel was still giving reasons. "See, was it just you and the girl, the woman could run off and you, havin' to take care of the girl, might not be able to catch her. I hear she's a wily one. So you need us more'n we need you. Could be it's best if you keep a civil tongue in your head."

Wily one? January wondered who'd told the old crone that.

"Nonsense." Peel continued to stare at January. "I'd simply shoot her. A small enough loss."

January knew he meant it. She trembled with anger, with fear, until Hoot danced beneath her, sensing his rider's unquiet.

They rode on into the dusk, facing a darkening sky lit by streaks of red and pink. A pale moon rose, and at last they made camp. Everyone, including January and Zora and even the aloof Frank Peel, gathered around the fire Silas built.

Once again, Mabel unpacked jerky and crackers, and they made do to stop their bellies from grumbling. At least there was coffee. Even Zora drank a cup, her nose wrinkling at the bitter taste. Nobody talked much.

As for January, as much as she wished to learn their destination, she again fell mute. It struck her that if she heard the words, they'd become true. Unchangeable, planted in her mind like weeds. Well, she refused to let them take root. For her own sake, as much as for Zora.

The night was cold, and she was glad of the bedroll tied on the back of her saddle before she left home. Glad, too, she'd been able to keep riding Hoot, although it surprised her one of the men didn't take him. But that they hadn't made it possible to offer the blanket to Zora, who shivered in the night air. January herself had her coat to huddle into.

Mabel, the old harridan, kept the girl between her and Ike as they slept. January knew the reason. Mabel didn't want Zora talking to her. Oddly enough, Peel didn't seem to care, so certain was he of his power over the females he'd "bought".

In the morning, they stood around a small campfire and drank weak coffee. There was nothing to eat. Poor planning, as far as January was concerned, her stomach growling. Zora had already begun to look pinched.

As they moved on, the terrain changed, steepened, grew wilder. Trees grew bigger here, taller and more closed in, the blue of the sky seeming farther away. The road, no more than a trail, really, stretched out ahead. In late afternoon, after a good many mind-numbing miles fell behind them, they came to a rough log cabin sitting at the edge of a small mountain lake. A whiff of smoke puffed into the sky, a sign the cabin was occupied.

Peel rode up to the door and stopped. "We'll stay here for the night," he announced. "There'll be something to eat besides jerky. You—" He pointed at Silas. "There's mallards on the lake. Go shoot a mess for supper. And make sure to clean them well. I don't want to bite down on lead."

Silas, his dark face blank, handed the lead of Zora's horse to Mabel and, without a word, went.

A frown puckered Mabel's face. "I'm beginnin' to doubt that man," she said, plenty loud enough for Silas to hear as he rode away. "Ike, do you trust him?"

Ike, unconcerned, shrugged. "I suppose. He came in with Lawson, but he ain't caused no trouble. Don't talk much, does what he's told. Him and Shandy both."

She was still staring after the dark man. "Humph. I don't like him."

As far as January could tell, Mabel didn't like anybody. At least she was reliable in her lack of affections.

The door to the cabin banged open, and a man who might've been the reason for the Bigfoot legend ducked his head to clear the lintel. He had some age on him. Large, hairy, wearing dungaree's cut off at the knee, he went barefoot and bare-chested, his arms bulging with muscle and marked with scars. A gold hoop earring dangled from one ear, pirate style. His light-colored eyes raked the party, fixing first on Zora, then on January. The others he ignored.

"This all? Slim pickings." His deep voice struck January as more cultured than she expected. "We've got room for more."

Peel dismounted, throwing his reins over a hitching rail that leaned toward the lake. "The girl will sell for a high price. Got a buyer all lined up for her."

"See, Ma," Ike whined. "Tole you we shoulda sold'er ourselves."

"Hush. And I tole you, we ain't got the contacts."

"Well said, madam." Peel cast a sneer infused glance

at Ike. "Your son best listen to your wisdom. He won't live through trying to double-cross me."

"Us," Bigfoot put in, and truly, January thought he could crush even Ike with one smashing blow of a massive fist. But then his gaze fell on her and sharpened. "What about this one. She's damaged."

Peel barely spared her a glance. "This one is a special case."

"I don't like shelling out good money for a product we ca..." Bigfoot began, but Peel cut him off, even as he gestured the rest of them off their horses.

"You'll be relieved to hear I didn't pay anything for her. Don't worry," he said, and left it to Ike and Mabel to usher Zora and January into the cabin, closing the door just as a couple shots sounded from down by the lake.

January's heart leapt with hope for a moment, until Peel spoke.

"Dinner," he said at Bigfoot's questioning lift of an eyebrow the size of a hog-bristle hairbrush. "I sent a man to hunt."

Bigfoot made a sound that January construed as a chuckle. "Manfred is down there somewhere. I hope they don't run into each other. One of them might not survive."

"Manfred is here? Why?" But then Peel shrugged. "Doesn't matter. We don't need either of them now."

Bigfoot's bushy brows lowered. "That may be true, but he'll still need paid. You know how he can be."

"I do." Peel didn't take the reminder well. "Then he'd better make himself known soon."

January tried to ignore the persistent quake causing a disturbance in her innards. How many of these thugs were there, anyway? By her reckoning, the count went up with every passing day. She'd believed her little piece of the country, at least after the Hammel contingent had been dealt with, to be a peaceful, almost bucolic, spot to live. A place for hardworking people to make a living and raise a family.

But here was Zora. And herself. More than one dead man. And the missing Eli Pasco, along with her dog. The list grew longer every moment, pitting her and a small bore five-shot revolver against all these evil people.

Deputy January Billings. Most thought her a joke—except for those either dead or serving time at Walla Walla State Penitentiary. Doubts, along with a good dose of bitterness, filled her. Could be in this case that those doubters were right. Did she even stand a chance?

The scar on her cheek itched, the S etched there making itself known. A reminder telling her she couldn't give up. There must be some way to escape these people and to take Zora out of harm's way. Had to be.

The men milled around the small cabin while Bigfoot brought out a brown glass bottle January figured held whiskey, although she didn't see a label, Mabel made a trip out the back to an outhouse visible through a window that, unfortunately, held no glass.

"Watch the girl," Mabel shouted over her shoulder, but the men, occupied in passing the bottle, paid no attention.

January, whom Ike had shoved down on a cot with a smelly, rumpled blanket spread over it, ignored his demand to stay put. She got up and went over to join Zora, hunkering beside her and sitting arm to arm. The girl had sought the darkest corner of the room where she cowered as if hoping to disappear. Silent tears ran down her cheeks. January didn't blame her.

"Be brave," she whispered. "Try not to worry. We'll get out of this."

"Will we?" Zora shivered. "H...how? I wish I hadn't taken Windswept. I wish I'd stayed with mother, even if she didn't..." She broke off and looked away.

"Hindsight." January didn't know if the girl knew what that meant, but she suspected so.

"I love Windswept, but now he's gone forever. I bet...I bet Mr. Pasco would've taken good care of him. Do you think he's dead? I think he is." Zora wiped at her face as if she were angry.

"We don't know that. Somehow, I doubt it." January sighed. "Anyway, I'm sure he would, that he will, take good care of Windswept. You see, I don't think Pasco will stop until he finds him. You'll be glad of that, won't you?"

"Yes! Yes."

"Me too." But what January congratulated herself on was the excuse she'd made for Eli Pasco never showing up. An excuse not only to comfort Zora, but herself. Because when she came right down to it, she, too, figured Eli must be dead.

The shots they heard owed to Silas having killed a couple mallards coming in for a landing. He'd taken the time to thoroughly clean them. Feet still attached, he toted the carcasses into the cabin and handed them to Bigfoot.

He was alone.

January's stomach growled a welcome, just thinking about food. From the look on the others faces, she wasn't the only one.

"See anyone around down by the lake?" Peel asked.

Silas shook his head.

"Huh," Peel said. "Huh." He shot a glance at Bigfoot who shrugged.

"He'll be around," Bigfoot said to Peel. He pressed the birds back into Silas' hands. "Go ahead and get these birds on to cook."

Silas tried to argue. Overruled, he set to stoking the small stove and finding a pan. When Mabel returned from the outhouse wiping her hands on her filthy skirt, Silas tried to push the cooking chores onto her. The woman would have none of it.

Silas, by far cleaner in his habits than either Mabel or Ike—or Bigfoot, for that matter—scowled, but giving in to the inevitable, found a container of salt and sprinkled some on the birds. January heaved a sigh of relief.

Eyeing her, Mabel removed January's shackles and set her to peeling potatoes with a dull knife. She made biscuits, too, willingly and without argument. Zora needed food, and she wanted to be sure the girl got something edible.

It wasn't until morning that everything went to pot.

CHAPTER 16

Eli, impressed and grateful for January Billings' almost prophetic provisioning, pulled the short-handled shovel from the pack on the buckskin. Choosing a more-or-less level spot, he used it to scrape out a hole in the hard earth. Long enough and deep enough to keep the bodies from the hungry birds, it made for hard work. His headache returned to plague him before he finished. Sweat burned into his eyes.

Speaking of eyes, Sheriff Schlinger, as useless as he must be, needed to have a look at these two dead men at some point. And if Eli met the same fate as they had somewhere up the line, for now their bones could molder in the earth decently covered.

He repacked the shovel and mounted Henry before pointing down at Windswept's tracks and saying to the dog, "Seek," just like he'd heard January say. The dog, well-rested after her nap under the trees, barked a short note and set off at a trot.

After an hour or so, Eli began to worry. Unlike at the beginning, when he and Mrs. Billings first discovered the

Winkler girl had been taken, they'd found those hairs that belonged to her. Why wasn't he finding any now? And if not hair belonging to the girl, why not some of January's? Her hair was a pretty, brown color. Eli had noticed it in particular, thinking the shade was almost the color of Henry when the sun shone down on him, showing glints of deep red.

He'd feel better if he knew the woman the dog was trailing was January. Shandy had only spoken of Ruby.

"Fool!" His sharp exclamation startled Henry, causing the horse to toss his head and sidle like a colt. Pen, trotting ahead, stopped and looked back.

"Yeah, me." He scowled so ferociously it made his head hurt again.

What had he been thinking? Not what he should have his mind set on, that was certain. Furthermore, the woman had only been widowed since the fall. He figured she didn't entirely trust him. It hadn't taken her more than thirty seconds to surmise he knew Ruby, and that Ruby was part of the gang. He didn't guess he could blame the deputy for her caution in accepting him.

Deputy.

She was a woman who'd killed people, all in the name of law and order and self-preservation. Yeah, folks in town had been all too eager to tell him about her. About her history. About Shay Billings' murder and what Mrs. Billings did about it. But didn't that set her apart from the peaceable kind of woman a man would want, should want, for himself?

He pondered the question as he rode. No answer came to him.

Riding on into the afternoon, Eli sharpened his senses and kept his eyes peeled for what he suspected might be another trap set along the way. Windswept's tracks continued on, so he knew he hadn't lost the trail. Besides, January's dog still led the way. Slower now, as the old gal tired, but with her nose still down determined to do her duty.

Then, at some distance beyond the next crook in the trail, he heard a whistle. A melodious whistle that had to have a human source.

The dog stopped and sat down in the road, panting. Eli drew Henry in beside her and listened. Not only melodious, he discovered, but the whistler was tootling one of his favorite songs, issued with some expertise. While he'd heard of birds that could copy complex sounds, it seemed doubtful to find one in the middle of this wilderness.

Loosening the latch on the Broomhandle Mauser, he swung it forward into easier reach and rested his hand on the butt. His brain told him that whoever was whistling didn't pose a threat. Bad intentions would most likely rule out sounding a warning. But those bodies he'd buried earlier gave notice to pay attention to anybody he met along this lonely road.

A mule came into sight. First its ears above all else, then its nose. The animal rounded the corner at a plodding walk, head bobbing in time with the song. The rest of it came into sight, with a squat little man perched atop an English style saddle. The bay mule was a tall fellow. Eli had no idea how the short-legged man managed to mount without a stepladder.

The odd pair approached. When they got to where Eli waited, the music stopped. So did the mule.

"Howdy, friend," the little man said. "It's a fine day for a ride, isn't it?"

Eli, his attitude not so jaunty as the other's, hadn't noticed. But then, he didn't suppose this fellow's day had started off by burying two murdered men while on the trail of horse thieves and kidnappers.

Watching for any reaction, Eli studied the man. "Could be worse," he said. *Yes. It could've been January Billings and Zora Winkler he'd had to bury.* "It's better for hearing your tune. You're a fine whistler."

A grin split the man's bewhiskered face. "Why, thank you, sir. Glad you appreciate the music."

He appeared so tickled by Eli's compliment, Eli had to smile. "By the looks of things, so does your mule."

The mule in question got a hearty slap on the neck. "It does seem to soothe the savage beast. Who'd have thought a mule like Mountain would care for whistling."

"Savage?" Mountain looked big to Eli, but not savage.

The little man laughed, but a second later his grin faded. "Not everyone does, I've been told. Care for whistling, I mean to say."

Something about the reply got Eli's ears perked. "No?"

"No."

Eli thought a moment. "Somebody tell you that recently, did they?"

"Afraid so." The little man ducked his head. "Big fellow, rough around the edges. Had an Indian with him. Oh, and a woman and..."

Eli interrupted. "A woman?"

"Sure. A fine-looking woman, in fact, but she didn't appear any too happy. But more disgruntled than sad, if you catch my meaning."

Nerves prickling, Eli said, "I don't suppose there was a dark brown, almost black horse with them."

"There was. Prancing and dancing and sweating. I figure had anybody been trying to ride him, that rider would've landed on his behind in the road. Most definitely an unhappy horse. Nervous. Flighty, I would say."

"He's a racehorse. Might be a little high strung," Eli said. But he'd seen no sign of the horse being the prancing and sweating sort before. Plus the fact a young girl was accustomed to riding him. The report made him worry.

"Ah. That explains it. I'm Icarus Meadows, by the way."

Icarus? For real? Eli snorted. The name must be an alias.

"Who'er you?" Meadows continued, overlooking Eli's reaction to the name. "If you don't mind me asking? Tell me, if you know the horse, do you know the man? Is he your friend?" His genial attitude had cooled a degree or two in the last minute and a cagey attitude crept in.

"Whoever he is, he's no friend of mine." Eli lost no time in setting Icarus straight. "My name is Eli Pasco, and I own the horse. This is the third time he's been stolen since I bought him a couple weeks ago. That's what I'm doing here, getting him back." And January. He needed to get her back too. And the girl. "Did you introduce yourself to him by any chance?"

"I did. I don't believe he cared. In fact, he said so. Clearly."

"I don't suppose he told you his name."

"No, he did not." Meadows turned sunny again. "So he's a horse thief. Can't say as I'm surprised. I expect that explains why he didn't want to stop and talk. Aside from taking exception to Mountain as well as my whistling, anyhoo. He accused me and my mule of scaring the horse. It's my belief the only thing scaring that horse was him. Or the Indian. And I'd say he had the woman shaking in her boots, as well."

Shaking in her boots didn't sound like January Billings.

Eli ground his teeth together. Still, a murderer. Of course, he scared her. She'd be a fool if she weren't, and he didn't think Mrs. Billings was any kind of a fool. He leaned forward. "How long's it been since you saw them? How far back?"

Icarus Meadows stared at him, squinting against the sun. "Why? You aren't figuring on facing them down by yourself, are you? Best leave that to the law. Or are you the law? Either way, mister, those two are a pair a wise man doesn't want to tangle with by himself." He looked away as he made an admission. "I'm not too proud to say Mountain and I got some distance between us as quickly as we could. The Indian, he looked plenty fierce, too, you see." He shook his head and waggled his eyebrows. "You, alone? Best you leave it until there's a posse backing you, preferably a big posse."

Eli brushed the advice aside. "How long ago?" he repeated. "Where?"

"Why, twenty minutes ago, I'd say. Only a mile or so back. I think..." He stopped and gawked at Pen. "What's that dog doing?"

Pen had stood up. The hair on her back formed a ridge as she stared off toward the empty road behind Meadows. A soft snarl signaled a warning and she looked back at Eli.

"Mr. Meadows," Eli said softly, "Are you armed?" He didn't see a gun. Or a knife or, for that matter, even a club.

"Armed? No. I don't own a gun." Apparently, the little man faced the wilderness with a whistle and a smile.

"Then I suggest you take cover behind those trees. Looks like trouble is following you right around the bend."

Meadows' eyes widened, although he sat unmoving atop his tall mule. "Trouble? No. Why would it be? I have no enemies. And those horse thieves. They're headed the other way."

"You think you have no enemies, but you've seen some men on this road who'd rather not be identified. They'll not want anyone pointing out their direction."

"What?" The truth in Eli's warning finally seemed to strike him. "No, no. That doesn't make sense. If they've stolen your horse, then they must be looking for you. Best I beat it on down the road. Hup, Mountain."

But Eli turned Henry to bar the way. "Thing is, Mr. Meadows, they don't know I'm after them. But you, you've seen them with the woman and the horse. They've already murdered two men this morning. Could be their intent is to add you to the list."

"Murdered two men?" Meadows' mouth dropped open. "But... How do you know it's them? It might not be. That dog can't talk, can she? How would she even know?"

Eli had no time to waste in discussion. "Do you want to take the chance?"

Icarus Meadows shook his head, and Eli snapped, "Then take cover. Sitting on that tall mule makes you an easy target. If they get through me, they'll think you're running. If that happens, you high-tail it in the opposite direction."

Icarus gaped.

"Move," Eli said. "Now."

Startled realization of the truth of Eli's warning finally got Icarus moving. He slid from the mule like a child on a play toy and hustled into the thicket of trees Eli had indicated, using Mountain to force a way through. When Eli looked for them, he was surprised to see how well the mule blended with the tree trunks, almost disappearing from view as soon as the brush stopped moving. Except for the ears.

He couldn't see Meadows at all, and figured the little man had hunkered down, making himself into an even smaller target.

Smart. It made one less thing to worry about.

He heard horses then, hoofbeats thudding on the road. He let go of Mollie's lead and slapped her on the rear, urging her back the way they'd come. Getting her out of the way left more room for Henry to maneuver. As for Pen, the old dog stood her ground. Eli wished he could send her off to safety with a slap on the butt. Deputy Billings was depending on him to keep her dog safe.

Loosening the shotgun he kept in the saddle scabbard, he gigged Henry forward to meet the riders. Dust rose in a cloud visible above trees silent of birds or insects. He heard yipping, as though from a hunting coyote. The Indian Meadows had mentioned?

Pulling Henry to a halt, he situated the horse cross-wise in the trail and drew the Mauser. Easing back, he waited, but not for long.

Moving at a fast trot, three horses swept around the last bend of separation. Make that four horses. The big man who'd disturbed Meadows led the way with Windswept, riderless, on a rein behind him.

Next in line and riding parallel with the third rider, the Indian drummed his heels on a dun mare's flanks. Sure enough, the yipping noise rose from his throat.

The other rider, a woman, made Eli's heart race faster in shock, although when he had a second to think back on it, he shouldn't have been surprised. Anyway, her hands were bound and tied to the saddle horn. She looked tired, worn, scared, and scared wasn't a look that was natural to, or became her. Ashen of complexion, tears gleamed on her cheeks.

He knew when she looked up and recognized him. Her eyes widened. She reared erect in the oversized saddle that must previously have belonged to either Shandy or the man killed with him, since the stirrups, too long for her to reach, flapped as she rode.

"Stop right there," he shouted, poised for them to overrun him. Or try.

But they didn't. They stopped no more than six feet apart.

The woman's mouth rounded into an "O", surprised no doubt that he'd take matters into his own hands and face down this pair by himself.

"Hello, Ruby," he said, although his attention fixed on the man in front of him.

CHAPTER 17

JANUARY HADN'T SLEPT MUCH. NO MORE THAN A SPURT HERE AND there. She'd fall asleep only to awaken with a start, stretching her neck as far as possible in order to check on Zora. The neck stretching was necessary because of the manacle and chain around her ankle attaching her to the leg of the bed. A short chain, combined with hands bound behind her, didn't allow for much movement. As for her bound hands, well, after so many hours, she could scarcely bend the swollen fingers.

The manacle, in a size large enough to slip from her bare foot, had forced Peel to leave her boots on. A mistake she vowed he—they—all of them would pay for. But for now, she was helpless. All she could do is wait for an opportunity.

If one ever came. It was hard to push the thought out of her mind.

On every one of those awakenings, she had spotted the gleam of watching eyes. Twice it was Mabel, twice Bigfoot, once Peel. Ike simply snored, sounding like a bull elk in mating season.

Meanwhile, Zora slept on, restless and fretful. January worried the girl might be falling ill.

Morning, when it finally arrived, came as a relief. The outlaws got up, leaving January chained to the bed as they scratched at bug bites she figured came from lice or bed bugs or some other awful critter that thrived on filth. She wasn't immune. Zora either. Silas seemed to have come through best, which apparently elected him chief water drawer, wood chopper and breakfast cooker. Not an onerous job as it turned out. They had no time for such niceties as real food as they prepared to abandon the cabin, making do with whatever remained from last night's supper.

"We have to get moving. There's a boat in harbor just charging up docking fees," Peel said, his aggravation clear as he turned to Bigfoot. "If we're not at the meeting point tomorrow night, it'll have to leave without the cargo."

"Best not to keep the others around longer," Bigfoot said, nodding. "Loggers in those woods might get curious if they hear anything."

"Which means we need to get a move on." Peel scowled. "Tides don't wait for anyone. Where's Manfred? He should've been here by now. Are you sure he's around?"

Bigfoot chuckled. "He's around, all right. You can leave him his pay here in the cabin when we go."

"Leave his pay?" Peel frowned.

"Leave it anchored to the bed. He'll find it and catch up with us."

"Ah." Peel nodded understanding. "Yes. A good plan."

Zora crept closer to January to eat a dry biscuit and a

chunk of bacon that would've done better with a longer rendering. "What are they going to do now? Where are they taking us?" she whispered.

At Zora's begging, January's hands, numb from the too tight bonds around her wrists, had been loosed to pick up a biscuit. Choking a bite past the lump in her throat, she shook her head. "I don't know. Stay close to me, Zora. We can't let them separate us." Not that fighting any of them would do any good. Most probably, they'd be worse off for the struggle.

She'd heard some of Peel's and Bigfoot's discussion the night before. About Zora going one way and her another since Peel had no use for her. He considered her dangerous to his enterprise. *Enterprise.* The very word made her skin crawl. What kind of enterprise was it that dealt in the sale of young girls?

That wasn't a question. She knew.

Peel sent Silas out to saddle the horses, which Silas seemed relieved to do. He left, leaving the door open to the morning sun, and January heard him speaking to the horses. She caught a glimpse of Hoot, tossing his head as Silas tied him to the rail and lifted a saddle onto his back.

It wasn't, she noted, her saddle. A chill swept over her.

But then she lost track as Mabel and Ike began a long and loud complaint about coming up with the short end of the stick in this deal.

"What," Mabel demanded, "are we to do if the law comes around? What if they point a finger at me and my boy? You said you'd take care of us. See we got away."

"And so you have. You're free to go wherever you like." Peel's mouth curled in a sneer. "You see, I have no further need of your services. We made a deal. You've received your pay. I suggest you shut up and go while you can. I'm sick of listening to you and your idiot son chatter."

"Chatter? Idiot son?" Mabel screeched her outrage. She looked ready to rip into him. "You can't talk to me like that, like I'm a nobody."

"Yeah, we're somebody, and don't you forget it." Ike lumbered up, his face red with anger, his hand on the revolver at his side. "And I ain't no idiot."

Bigfoot intervened, pushing between the two men as Mabel jumped up and down like a grasshopper on a hot stove.

January's lips twitched and Zora giggled—until the doorway darkened and a man walked in. Everyone hushed. Even Peel.

A stranger, smallish of stature only when compared with Bigfoot, the man wore a black stove-pipe hat with a beaded band over long, blond hair. Fringed buckskins and moccasins completed his outfit, although a heavy beard denied any Indian blood. He had the look of a character from Buffalo Bill Cody's Wild West show. Or a clown, right down to his colorful, ornately beaded gloves. More amusing than alarming—at first.

But then, silent and almost as though he floated, he sort of "appeared" beside the quarrelers and held up a hand whose glove flashed bright red.

Blood red.

And January, along with everyone else except maybe Zora, realized it was blood.

A lot of it.

The sight of which held them all in thrall. Even Peel

wore a look of something that might've been dread.

For a few moments, at least, then he stepped back and said, "Manfred. It's about time you got here."

With a quick, warning motion, Bigfoot shook his shaggy head. A little late, as it happened.

Manfred's eyes narrowed. "I come, I go. I suit myself." Then he added, "Mr. Peel," and his simple saying of the name once again silenced the boss.

His gaze traveled around the room. It caught on Zora for a moment before losing interest and discarding her. His eyes were almost colorless, January saw, as if the irises had been dipped in bleach.

His gaze settled on her and stayed and when his tongue flicked from between lips almost obscured by the beard, her heart thudded with sudden fear.

"This her?" he said. He didn't look away, and for some reason, January couldn't.

"Yes," Peel said. "Are you pleased?"

He considered. The tongue flick came again. "Yes."

Bigfoot smiled.

She became aware of Zora tugging at her arm. "Missus Billings? What are they talking about?"

"I don't know." But she did. The real question in her mind concerned the blood on Manfred's gloves. And where was Silas? Because through the open door, the hitching rail was visible. Five horses were lined up there. One each for Peel, Bigfoot, Mabel, Ike and Zora. But none for January or Manfred or...or for Silas.

One of the saddled horses was Hoot.

It was Bigfoot who came over to collect Zora. Not that he had an easy task of it. The girl had taken to heart January's advice to stay close.

"Missus Billings!" Zora reached out with surprising strength, grabbing hold of January as Bigfoot lifted her away.

Tugged between the pair of them, January thought for a moment they'd dislocate her shoulder. "Leave go of her, you brute," she said, slapping and punching at the man. They'd neglected to replace the ropes to her hands after eating. Even so, she knew nothing she did would do any good. Zora was the reason he and Peel were here. Whether they believed her a deputy or not, her presence was no deterrent to anything they did. Indeed, Bigfoot laughed as he held the girl in one arm and stepped on the chain holding January to the bed. It snubbed so tightly she could barely move.

"I think not," he said. Then he stepped back and flipped a key to Manfred. "Here you go. This one is feisty. I believe you'll enjoy a little tussle."

Manfred caught the key. His pale eyes gleamed. "I will."

Zora had begun screaming. Wildly, but without tears. She fought Bigfoot with tooth and nail, her teeth drawing blood from his arm. Until he hit her, and all resistance ended on a gasp.

January struggled with the chain while Manfred laughed. Mabel and Ike hurried outside and, gaining prudence at last, found their horses. Clambering aboard, they rode off at a gallop, wise to be putting distance between them and Peel's men.

Meanwhile, Peel stared coldly at Bigfoot and Zora where the girl hung from the big man's arm in a daze.

"You'd better not have damaged her. If you have, the difference will come out of your share."

"She'll be all right. Just a little out of sorts. She needed taught a lesson." Bigfoot was unmoved by the threat. "She'll have worse than that little tap done to her before long."

Peel didn't deny it. "Get her out of here. I'll be right behind you." He looked back at Manfred, and at January.

She glared at him. "What kind of man are you?" The scorn in her voice sounded clearly.

Undisturbed, he had an answer ready. "A rich one. One with power over life and death, when it suits me."

"Go," Manfred said to him.

"Goodbye, Missus Deputy." He sighed once, in a facetious sort of way. "You see, this is why women aren't suited to law enforcement. Your kind is simply not strong enough.

"Catch up when you're done here," he added to Manfred. Without another glance, he walked out, shutting the door behind him. A few seconds later, January heard hoofbeats as he rode away.

Manfred had been listening for them too, because as they faded, he took a deep, shuddering breath as he shed his bloody gloves. "Now," he said, taking a step toward her. "Now."

It struck January that his action was anticipatory, as if deliberately stirring himself into a frenzy.

"What's the S stand for?" The fringe on the arm of his jacket wriggled as he pointed at the scar on January's cheek. His dirty forefinger nearly touched her.

He laughed at her furious expression, a peculiar

high-pitched sound for such a rough man, as she jerked her head away.

"Did it hurt?" He yanked her close, until their bodies touched. Deliberately, he raked a dirty fingernail across the scar's raised surface. "Who did it?"

January clamped her mouth shut. She flinched backward, trying to make herself small.

"Answer. You do, and maybe I'll give you this." He still held the key and he held it up, tantalizing but far out of her reach.

She knew he wouldn't.

"Or maybe..." He drew out the word, thinking, anticipating, planning. "Maybe I'll try my hand at carving your other cheek first. What about that?"

Then, so fast she had no way to prepare herself, he flung himself upon her pressing her all the way down to the grimy floor. Air gushed out of her lungs; her head bounced on the rough planks hard enough to make her vision blur. When she could see again, she felt him drawing a pattern on her good cheek. It took a moment for her to realize it was his finger digging at her and not a knife.

"Yes," he breathed. "Yes, yes. That's what I'll do. It'll be fun. It'll be pretty."

She twisted beneath him, bucking and jerking like an animal caught in a trap. Once he slid to the side.

"Yes," he shouted. "Yes." He caught at her unbound hands as she pushed against his chest, easily raising them above her head. "I like it."

Did that mean she should stop her struggles? That perhaps he'd lose interest and leave her be? Or just kill her quick? Because she knew he'd never leave her alive. Not even after he'd marked her. Especially after he'd marked her.

Besides, she couldn't *not* fight. Fighting was in her blood. But with one bound leg, she had no real freedom of movement. She couldn't roll as he lay flat on her, crushing her body and breathing his foul breath in her face. She knew when he hardened, knew his excitement, knew by the heat and wetness, what her fate would be.

"Why don't you cry?" he said once as he twisted her wrist. When that didn't work, his fist lashed out, smashing the side of her face like being struck by a board. "Cry. I like it when they cry."

But she didn't.

They, he'd said. They? But January Schutt Billings doesn't cry. She didn't speak out loud, though. Nor would she.

The fight went on forever. Or what seemed like forever. After a while, January realized she was weakening. That somehow this struggle had changed and become a race to the very end. She knew he was growing tired of wrestling with her, that his sense of fun had faded. Would he become serious about the carving next? Did he plan to ravish her first and then be done, riding off to join Peel and Bigfoot leaving her dead body for animals to devour?

Shook from the idea, she went slack.

Manfred, surprised by her sudden lack of resistance, reared back. Then he grinned, let go of her hands, and went to work on the buttons of her shirt, cutting the first one away with a wickedly sharp knife he drew from the beaded scabbard at his belt. He knelt above her, breathing hard in his excitement.

This was it. She had enough strength for one last try. January twisted hard beneath him.

Taken unaware, he flipped to the side. The knife slid out of his hand, stopping a yard to two away. Oh, he recovered fast, came at her again, but by this time she had her legs drawn up and when he moved to cover her, she lashed out. Her boots caught him squarely where no man wants to be caught.

Letting out a scream, he fell to the side. The kick she'd dealt him did more than just quell his impulses. Her little boot gun came loose from the holster. It dropped into her hand, and he howled his rage.

"No." He writhed across the floor toward the knife like a wounded snake.

"Yes." Glee rose in her. She had him cornered now, all right, and he knew it.

January took careful aim, taking her time.

"Oh. Because you asked..." Rising to her knees, she stared at him as his colorless eyes widened. "...the S is for shooter."

He was stretching for his knife when she shot him dead.

CHAPTER 18

SETTLED INTO HIS SADDLE LIKE AN IMMOVEABLE GRANITE BOULDER, Pasco blocked the road. Ruby, after a single surge of energy when she saw him, sort of deflated as the Indian drew her horse right up against his. The men faced each other.

Eli, taking another quick glance at her, noticed she sat her horse like a rag doll emptied of wadding. She seemed dazed, as if she'd been drugged, but still, she managed to lift her head. "So," she hissed, as though she were angry with him. "You're alive after all."

He didn't know what to make of her words. Best if he ignored them, he figured, as if he didn't know she'd been speaking to him.

The white man jerked around. "Shut up, woman," he snarled at her.

Pen growled at the tone and Eli noticed the way the Indian looked at the dog, cold as a beady-eyed hawk. Eli figured he'd better give a share of his attention to keeping the old gal safe, this being a situation certain to go sideways. Nerve and sinew told him so. And bluntly, he plain didn't want Deputy Billings displeased with him.

"You know this woman?" the white man said to him.

"I know her." He didn't see any way to deny it. Or any reason, either. But he didn't add anything, and they each took a breath, at an impasse. "I see you've got ropes on her. Mind telling me why?"

The Indian spoke. "Not your business."

"Well, now, that might be true," Eli said, mildly enough to fool most folks into thinking him about to back off. "But I do hate to see a woman mistreated or held against her will. And since I do know who she is, I guess I have to make her my business." While the two men were still deciphering that, he spoke to Ruby. "It is against your will, I take it."

"You know it is." But she agreed without hope of change.

This was a Ruby the like of which Eli had never seen. One he could hardly believe. Whoever this pair of men were, they had her cowed, and in his experience, that just didn't happen. Unless this was more of her trying to con him.

The white man spat a wad of tobacco juice onto the ground and wiped fleshy lips. "Let's just say I found her in the wrong place, and she poked her nose in where it don't belong."

Eli nodded. "That sounds about right. She's got a reputation for that."

Ruby managed a glare.

"But," Eli continued, inching his Mauser to where a tip of his hand would bring it in line with his first target's belly, "that doesn't mean I can let you haul her off anywhere in ropes."

Chuckling, the white man hawked out his wad of tobacco, the nastiness splashing his horse's front hoof. "Don't think you can stop us." He glanced at the Indian. "Two against one, mister, in case you forgot how to count."

"I can count." Congratulating himself on his excellent playacting, Eli shrugged. In truth, his guts had seized up like a gasoline engine drained of grease. Or oil. He'd forgotten which it should be and didn't much care.

"Helmer," the Indian cut in, "I think I know this man."

A clear warning, if Helmer, the white man, had been listening.

But he wasn't. He dropped the lead holding Windswept and grabbed for the low-slung revolver. He fumbled as both horse and holster moved under his hand. At that, Pen leapt forward, biting at his horse's rear foot. The animal hopped and reared a couple feet off the ground, nearly unseating Helmer who still groped blindly for his gun.

Eli's first shot took the Indian out of the saddle. The Indian's convulsive shot went wide, somewhere over Eli's head.

Helmer, his gun finally in hand, shouted his surprise and his rage, but by that time it was too late. Eli shot again. Helmer sagged. His gun dropped from his hand. A few seconds later, Helmer tumbled to the ground under his horse's pounding feet.

Meanwhile, Ruby shrieked Eli's name as the horse she was riding bolted. Windswept, already nervous and understanding he was free, followed before passed her running full out. Both horses raced back the way they'd come. Pen ran after them, losing ground, but game. The other two horses, the Indian's and the one Helmer had been riding, milled about, stopping only a short distance down the road.

The woods around them were silent, as if waiting for the next shot.

Until Icarus Meadows stepped from his hiding place in the bushes. The mule ambled behind him, long head hanging over Meadows' shoulder. "Well, well, well. That was something now, wasn't it?" Icarus said.

"Yeah. Something." Eli, reloading the spent cartridges in the Mauser's magazine, wasn't so sure that was admiration he saw on the whistling man's face.

A moan from Helmer drew their attention. Dismounting, Eli went to kick the outlaw's revolver into the brush. Icarus joined him, leaning over and studying the downed man. "Not a killing shot, as long as he don't bleed to death," he announced. "Or get an infection."

He looked up at Eli. "Was that your intention?"

Eli made a sound in his throat. "Mister, I just wanted to come out of the fracas alive."

His mind set on capturing Windswept before the horse got lost or broke a leg, Eli climbed aboard Henry. "I figure there's a reward on these two."

"The Indian is dead."

Eli nodded. "Mostly, rewards are for dead or alive. It's yours if you can get them into Claremont. The sheriff should be there about now. If not, you can wire him."

"Mine? Mister, why would you do that?" Meadows' mouth puckered into a whistle. "The Indian, he said he knew you. Are you an outlaw?" He frowned. "Or are you the law?"

Surprised, Eli laughed. "Mr. Meadows, that could be a dangerous question." He hesitated. "But I'm neither. The Indian, he probably knew me as a bounty hunter. I used to be one. Retired now."

Icarus seemed not to have heard the 'retired' part. "Bounty hunter? Then why are you giving this job to me? You have to be on hand to collect the bounty. If I..." He stopped, maybe unsure of his facts.

Eli shook his head. "Best you don't look a gift horse in the mouth, Mr. Meadows. Think you can handle them?"

"A dead man and another next door to it?" Icarus scoffed. "I'll handle them." He proceeded to prove it by gathering up the Indian's loose horse and, in a feat of strength surprising for such a small man, heaved the Indian's flaccid body over the saddle. He indicated Helmer. "I'll rig a travois for him. Mountain will haul it."

"That'll work." A quick salute, and Eli set off after Windswept and Ruby.

Ruby hadn't gotten more than a quarter mile down the road. The horse she rode had stopped as soon as he wore out his fear of the guns. She was waiting expectantly, a smile on her face, when Eli rounded the corner to find the horse, head down and nibbling the early green grass sprouting along the trail. Pen sat guarding them.

He wasted an extra moment in sitting apart and simply staring at her while Pen rested. Ruby had reacquired her usual aplomb, smiling at him with that flirty look in her eyes. Confident, shoulders back, head high, as if she knew he'd be along to save her and delighted to do it.

She was mistaken. Feeling everything she did was an act, Eli felt only impatience. Windswept hadn't stopped, which meant he had to delay capturing the horse in order to attend to the woman.

His insides tightened.

"I knew you'd get them. You always do." She held out her bound hands. She'd managed to get loose from the saddle horn, but not the ropes around her thin wrists. "Cut these, will you, darling? They're hurting me."

Darling. She spoke the endearment as though she had the right. Anger flushed through him. *Darling.* Without speaking, he unsheathed his knife and reached across to slice through the twisted rope. Yes. It most probably did hurt. The white skin of her wrists had been rubbed raw.

"Are they dead? I hope they're dead." Ruby wasn't paying much attention to him, shifting in the saddle and examining her wrists. There was a bruise on her cheek. "Helmer killed Shandy, and Kingfisher insisted on cutting up the man who bought the horse. That damn Indian wanted me, but I'm not sure if he wanted my body to have sex or to cut me up too. Eh!"

Eli's lips tightened. Ruby thought every man wanted her body and wasn't shy about saying so. She made a game of making every man desire her. Mostly, she succeeded. He understood why a man might want to cut her up.

He still hadn't spoken.

"Well?" she said, her tone sharpening. "Cat got your tongue? What took you so long? I was beginning to think you'd never catch up."

Eli reached down and caught up the reins trailing from her horse's bridle. He handed them to her, avoiding her clutching hands. "Helmer is alive. The Indian is dead."

"How much will you get for them? I deserve a share, don't you think? After all, I led you to them."

"Get for them?" Oh, he knew what she meant, all right.

"The bounty." Ruby waved her hands. "Helmer must have a large reward waiting for whoever brings him in. From what he admitted to me, he murdered himself right out of Missouri. That bounty would set us up good, somewhere. Maybe South America? I hear luxuries are cheap there. People with money can live like kings."

Greed had always been her middle name. If only his father had been able to see it before it was too late.

He frowned as what she'd said caught up with him. "Us? There is no us, Ruby. Never has been, never will be."

She gaped at him. "What are you saying? Of course, there was an us. There is an us. Why else..."

Shame caught at him. She had almost caught him in her trap once. Almost, but not quite.

But then she was laughing, gay as a little girl dancing around a maypole with flowers in her hair. "I understand. You can't admit you love me, can you? Well, that's all right. But I do need money, darling, and want my share."

But he laughed too, which made hers stop. "There is no bounty, Ruby. No share. I didn't bring him in. Him or the Indian either one."

"What? But you said the Indian is dead."

He hoped Meadows was a long way down the road toward town by now.

"So I did." And he flat out lied to her. "But the bounty isn't mine."

"Then whose is it?" she demanded.

He shrugged. "Some other fellow got there first."

Her jaw dropped and her eyes opened wide. "Liar. You lie."

Ignoring her, he gathered his reins, and whistled to Pen. Brushing past her, he continued on his way, ignoring the curses and shouts she sent after him.

Two hours later, when he backtracked with Windswept in tow, to Eli's relief he found she'd moved on. He hoped to God Icarus Meadows had gotten far enough ahead that she failed to catch up to the little procession. He'd hate to have his intended generosity subject an unarmed innocent like the whistling man to a hellcat like Ruby Pasco.

At the cut-off Icarus—and probably Ruby—took to lead them eventually to Claremont, Eli went the opposite direction. Passing the spot where he'd buried Shandy and the other man, he went directly to the cabin where the tracks for two parties had split. Flies buzzed in and out of the woodshed where Dent Johnson still lay. Nothing had changed.

Or perhaps one thing. The tracks, so clear the previous day were blurred now and quickly fading. Under Eli's command to seek, Pen took the scent and set off, her nose busy. But he could tell the old dog was near exhaustion. How long would it be before he had to lift her onto his horse and do all the tracking himself? Not that he begrudged her. And for now, the dog's loyalty to her owner was keeping her on the right trail, which meant he didn't have to lose time scouting the sign.

"Hup, Pen," he called to get the dog's attention. "Seek. Let's find January."

CHAPTER 19

THE NEAT ROUND HOLE JUST BELOW MANFRED'S LEFT EYE OOZED blood. Not a horrific amount. He'd died too quickly for that. It was the brain matter leaking from the exit wound in the back of his head that disturbed her. And while January knew he must be quite thoroughly dead, his body made sounds as muscles let go. Disgusting sounds. She hadn't realized that happened.

She made sounds too. Little squeaks and broken gasps, as though she'd been running a race.

And so, in fact, she had. A race where winning meant she got to live, and he didn't. She had no regrets about killing him. Not a single one.

Presently, she became aware she still held her pocket pistol aimed at Manfred's corpse as though she expected it to rise and attack her again. Hands shaking, she replaced the gun in her boot, defying her fear.

January had no idea how much time had passed as she fought Manfred. No idea whether Peel and Bigfoot—with poor little Zora—were still in earshot. If they were, would they return to see what had happened?

No. She didn't believe so. They'd expected her to die.

And, she thought, panic rising in her, she still might. Tethered by a manacle around her ankle to the heavy bedpost, survival depended on if she could find a way to slip free. Manfred had had a key to the lock. What had he done with it?

Her thoughts about to turn her into a jittering fool, she leaned back and closed her eyes. Hiding her surroundings behind closed eyelids even for a minute or two helped, and when she could bear to look again, her panic had faded. Oh, not entirely, but some. Enough for her to keep it from overwhelming her.

Not that the view was any better a second time around. The dead man was still dead, and the cabin still reeked of sulfur and blood, burned food, unwashed bodies and feces as Manfred's bowels gave way.

Dear Lord, but she was thirsty. And dirty right down into her deepest pore. She craved water like an opium addict craved dope, a thought that caused her to sit up and tell herself to stop acting the fool. Thirsty? Dirty? Then find a way to release her leg and she could have all the water she wanted. A whole lake lay only a couple hundred yards from where she sat bemoaning her fate and she could drink it dry if it pleased her. She could wash until the filth peeled from her skin.

All right. The key. I have to get the key.

The bullet's impact had knocked Manfred backward, almost, but not quite out of her reach. Stretching full length on the floor brought his foot near enough for her to grasp the buckskin thongs lacing his moccasin. Though she cringed at touching him, she grabbed hold and yanked. Once, twice, again and again. Without much leverage, she could only move him an inch or two at a time. Sliding his body left a streak of blood, body waste, and pale brain matter on the floor.

He'd fallen atop his knife. It screeched as she moved the body, catching on the rough planks.

Sweat ran down the sides of her face when she finally got him close enough to go through his pockets. The key was in the pocket of his jacket, along with a human ear. A fresh human ear, the blood still wet. A trophy?

She recoiled, dropping the object from nerveless fingers.

"Silas?" She whispered the word to herself. She knew who the ear belonged and that he was dead. Had to be.

January's hands shook. It took a long time to get the key in the lock and free herself. Legs unsteady, she got to her feet and lurched outside. Her face hurt, her arms hurt, in plain fact, she hurt all over. Thankful for the restorative components of sunlight, she circled around the cabin to the back where a corral held three horses. One was the bay Silas rode. He was already saddled and had evidently gone to be with the others on his own. Another was the small animal Zora had been riding after Windswept got taken away. The last one she'd never seen before. Manfred's, she assumed, and probably recently stolen as the animal not only looked of better breeding, but to be in better shape than what she'd expect of a man like him.

All three horses had gathered at the far end of the corral. It didn't take long to figure out why. They were avoiding the body lying at the gate, shying from the scent of blood. The blood, as she'd feared, came from Silas' cut throat. Blood had spewed in an arc several feet beyond him, an indication he'd been fighting and his heart pumping hard. His left ear had been sliced from his head, and since there was a lot of blood from that, January figured he must've been alive at the time.

With a whispered apology, she took Silas' revolver and gun belt from his body, leaving his body where it lay. Peel had spoken of catching a boat, with urgency in his voice. That meant they'd be headed for the coast as quickly as possible. Which also meant she had no time to delay.

Her own saddle had been dumped on the ground. Switching it onto Silas' bay, she put Manfred's mount on a leading rein. This chase would mean riding hard and catching up, switching from horse to horse if necessary. The third horse she turned loose.

Back in the cabin she went through Manfred's pockets in case she'd need money to buy or bribe Zora's freedom. Her hat had gotten shoved under the bed. Retrieving it, she jammed it on her head then, body aching more than ever, went out and mounted Silas' steady pony.

"Hya." She urged the bay into a lope and didn't look back.

The tracks were clear. Those of Mabel and Ike split off and headed north when they reached the main road. Those of Peel, Bigfoot and Zora went west, toward the coast. Since she knew Hoot's tracks like she knew her own hand, January had no trouble following. For now, at least. She couldn't help wishing for Pen's comforting presence, then pushed the thought of the dog out of her head. The distraction could prove dangerous.

It wasn't until she reached the next crossroad, the one where they'd headed up the mountain, that January switched horses. It was open here, where she could see the sky without the forest canopy overhead, and she discovered it was past noon.

Tomorrow night, Peel had said, they were slated to catch the boat.

There were a lot of miles to go.

Though hungry and weary, she didn't stop. Urgency drove her to the limit. Her's and the horses'.

* * *

THE GROUND STEEPENED THE FARTHER JANUARY RODE INTO THE mountains. Daylight faded, along with any hope she had of catching up to Zora before dark. The horses needed rest and so, she admitted to herself, did she. Even then, she went on longer than she should have, thinking that around the very next bend, beyond the next thick clump of old growth forest, she'd run right into them. What she'd do to stop them remained a question.

Shoot first. She'd have to.

The opportunity didn't arrive. She knew Peel and Bigfoot must be driving their horses hard, uncaring as to whether they ran them to death. Hoot. A strong, fast and well-fed horse, she figured if any could hold up under the pace, he could. Anger burned in her core. And what about Zora?

When she came to a fork in the road at dark, she knew she had to stop. When she'd taken the time to retrieve her own saddle, her forethought became clear. Her bedroll and saddlebags were intact and still attached to the cantle. She'd packed a little food in her bag when she started from home, knowing from experience the wisdom of being prepared. So now she had food and a blanket against the night. It would be cold at this higher elevation. Below freezing most likely, even though the day had been warm for the first of April. She hadn't forgotten that only a few days ago there'd been snow even down in the valley.

A thought of Eli Pasco tossing a canvas over his saddle to keep it dry and his horse warm rose in her mind. Where was he now, him and his horse? Dead? Hurt? Alive?

Prudence dictated she go without a fire when she stopped. Walking out a bit, she searched the darkness ahead to see if Peel might've started a fire, but not a flicker caught her eye. Except for the company of the horses, she was alone.

Sometime during the night, a scream like a woman in torment awakened her from an uneasy sleep. January leapt to her feet. The eerie scream caused the horses to throw up their heads and stand, ears pricked, looking off toward the northeast. Her heart pounded. Her limbs felt weak, as though the bones had been removed. Then she wished she hadn't had that particular thought. It reminded her too much of Manfred.

A second scream a half-minute later bounced from mountainside to mountainside. This time a glimmer of recognition told her it was the cry of a hunting cougar. Not that knowing it wasn't a woman in distress eased her mind. Truly, there was a woman in distress out there somewhere. A girl, anyway. And if there was anything she didn't need at present, it was a hungry cat on the prowl. The horses knew it too, fluttering their nostrils, stamping in place, squealing softly to each other.

"Easy," she told them, whispering first in the bay's ear, then the dun's. "It's all right. We're fine. You're fine." She stood between them, patting their necks, caressing velvety noses until they calmed. Then, from far off, she heard the crack of a rifle as someone fired three or four rounds in rapid succession. She flinched. Any shot was sure to be chancy in the dark. Of all things, she hoped the shooter hadn't wounded a big cat. Nothing in these mountains was as dangerous as a wounded cougar.

Unless you counted men as the ultimate predator. She slept again with Silas' pistol near to hand.

Daybreak found January already on the move. Those shots she'd heard last night hadn't been all that distant and she rode with caution. Sometimes it seemed as though she were stretching her eyesight beyond human capacity, straining to see ahead. Her only safety lie in the fact Peel and Bigfoot wouldn't be expecting her. They no doubt figured she was dead by now, possibly cut into unrecognizable bits by Manfred's knife, and safely buried.

Her lips twitched. She couldn't wait to see their faces when she disabused them of the idea. That would be when she took Zora from them. When she got her horse—Shay's horse—back. When every one of them were either incarcerated for the rest of their miserable lives or killed. Of the two choices, the latter struck her as the best solution.

Anger burned inside her, the flame white hot.

* * *

ELI MADE GOOD TIME FOR THE FIRST FEW HOURS. UNTIL JANUARY'S
dog began to lag. He'd been expecting it. Hardly needing
Pen to show him direction as the route seemed fairly
established, he took her up, laying her in front of him so
she could rest. They went on, wending every higher and
farther into the mountains.

After a while, when the tracks died out, he set Pen
down on the ground again. She followed the trail, ignoring the fresher hoof prints that showed where horses
had passed.

This morning, he figured. He wasn't more than a few
hours behind them. If he weren't such a careful man, he
would've turned Windswept and followed immediately,
but he hadn't become a renowned bounty hunter by
being careless.

Where had they been and why had they left? That's
what he needed to discover now.

"Seek," he said to Pen and, tongue lolling, she sought.

The dog smelled the stench before he did, lifting her
head and emitting a howl that sent a tingle up his spine.
He smelled it too, before they actually stopped in front
of the cabin, the door of which hung open. Sour meat.
There was no mistaking it.

"Rot."

Pen looked back at him and plunked her furry butt
down on the stoop, refusing to go inside.

Eli stiffened. Did the dog refuse because she knew the
smell came from her dead mistress, or because it didn't?

Only one way to find out. He slipped inside.

The room was dark, not being blessed with much in the way of windows. However, enough light came in that, as his eyes adjusted, Eli made out the general shape of the body sprawled about midway between the door and the bedstead taking up one corner.

The body belonged to a man. A held-back breath gusted out before he could stop it.

Eli had never seen the man before. He thought he might've heard of him though, as he'd been cautioned about a man who wore buckskin clothing and had flowing blond, though greasy and dirty hair. The buckskins bore both old and new bloodstains. He'd heard about that too. The man had been shot in the face with a small-bore bullet, judging by the smallish hole.

Grimly, he smiled. January's doing. Eli was sure of it. If it were indeed her, she'd left no real sign of her presence, and with a shrug, he retreated. Now what? Follow the dog, he guessed. But when he got outside, Pen had disappeared.

Eli's hand went to his Mauser. "Hey, dog," he said, not too loud, and waited.

Nothing.

"Pen," he called, a little more forcefully. Straining his ears, he heard something, A little whuff. A whine.

Following the sound, he went around the corner of the cabin and stopped. The dog was there, sniffing at yet another body. Another man. He didn't need to get closer to see as much. Yet dutifully, he walked over to see if he could identify the man. So. He'd seen this one before and recognized him. He didn't know the name, but the man had been one of the original horse thieves with Ruby, Dent, and Shandy.

Whoever he had been, he'd been slaughtered like a pig. The work of the man inside the cabin, Eli figured. The one January had killed.

He stood on the cusp of a serious decision. Some might say he had every justification to quit the trail right here. He wasn't claiming rewards for the dead men. He wasn't the law, in any shape or form. This wasn't his responsibility, or even his business anymore. He had his horse back. Unless she was still a prisoner, Deputy January Billings must be on the job. Her job.

The fact remained. The kind of people January was up against were of the worst kind. She needed help. His help.

A sense of urgency rose up, a sense that she needed that help fast.

"C'mon, dog." Eli whistled sharply. "Let's find your deputy."

Backing away from the body sprawled on the ground, Pen's tail dragged in the dust. It didn't rise to curl over her back until they'd gone a quarter mile and headed down the trail again.

Some hours later, Eli found where January had stopped the previous night. The credit belonged to Pen, mostly, as the only signs were minor. Some bark scraped from the trees where January had tethered her horses, an area of chewed down grass, a scuffing where she had probably spread a blanket. He felt better, knowing she had a blanket.

The dog seemed happy at catching the fresh scent, her eyes bright, her tail wagging.

Eli switched his saddle to Henry and continued on, faster now. In a short while, he found another camp. And blood. From what, he didn't know, until he found the giant paw prints of a large, wounded cat. After that, he rode more cautiously, respectful of a wounded cougar.

But what drew his real attention was that the two camps hadn't been all that far apart. January must be on the brink of catching up—if the cat didn't attack her.

With Pen on the saddle in front of him again, he urged his horse into a lope, slowed to a walk, then into a lope again. Hour after hour, so many minutes on Windswept, so many minutes on Henry. He didn't draw a real easy breath until he came down out of the mountains and discovered people and houses. A signpost said the little town of Canton was only a few miles away. The odor of the briny ocean swept landward on the breeze. Seabirds flew overhead, calling loudly and scaring Windswept who jumped and bucked and generally acted the fool. Pen, never having seen the like before, kept looking up and barking, no matter how he tried to hush her.

"How far to the port?" he asked the first man he met, a farmer, Eli figured, raising crops on the rich flat ground before the coast.

"A mile or so," the man replied, and almost before he knew it, Eli saw the waters of Puget Sound spreading toward the horizon.

CHAPTER 20

JANUARY HAD NEVER SEEN—NEVER EVEN IMAGINED AN EXPANSE OF water so huge. Hitching her horses to a convenient piece of driftwood, she picked a way on foot across a rock-strewn beach toward a pier jutting out into the water.

This is where the trail she'd been following ended. Right here at land's end.

A couple men were trundling boxes, kegs, crates and rolled up something or others down a wooden walkway from the ridge above them. She followed them.

Eyes wide and popping at the sight, she breathed deeply of salty air that felt heavy in her lungs and smelled vastly different from what she was used to. She wasn't sure she liked it, but the water—that was different. Emitting a sigh of awe, she stood rooted. A weathered-looking man working on the pier looked down at her and laughed. Dwarfed by the boat bobbing next to him, he was coiling the biggest rope she could even imagine.

"I reckon you for a landlubber," he said. "Seen you got horses. First time on the coast?" He wore a funny hat with a brim like an umbrella, a loose coat, and big, clompy boots.

She nodded and picked a way up a wooden ramp onto the pier.

"Well, this is only the sound," the man said. "Puget Sound. Wait till you reach the Pacific Ocean."

"Puget Sound?" She'd heard of it. "You mean this isn't the ocean?" January's wave indicated the distant horizon.

"Nope." He looked out over the water with a satisfied expression. "But it's a lot of water just the same, ain't it? And salty, too, seeing as how it's an inlet of the Pacific."

January, not quite sure of the explanation of all that, was willing to take his word for it.

"Move it, woman," a gruff voice spoke from behind her, causing her to skip to the edge of the pier. It put her only inches from the water, with no guard rail to keep folks from falling in. More men were wheeling big kegs of something she heard sloshing down from the port to the waiting boats.

"You going out again tonight, Jimmy?" the gruff fellow said to January's informant.

"On the tide," Jimmy replied. "You?"

"Oh, aye. Tonight."

Three boats, or maybe they were ships, she wasn't certain of the nomenclature, were tied, front and back, to the long pier. The water was cluttered with floating seaweed, garbage, and she was sure, dead bodies although she didn't actually see any. The air smelled of brine and fish, an odor not entirely pleasant to her senses. Her nose wrinkled.

Since he'd been eyeing the scar on her cheek, the talkative Jimmy noticed this reaction. "Aw, the smell ain't so bad today. It'd be better if we had a little breeze blowing the stink out to sea, I suppose. But you get used to it. Stay here long enough and you'll see."

She hoped she wouldn't be here for the length of time that would take. "And have you been here a long time?"

"Yes, ma'am. Got here in '67."

"Then you know everybody?" She figured he must. From what she'd seen, the place wasn't that big. Not much bigger than Claremont. Strangers, using herself as an example, were bound to stand out. And just maybe, Peel and Bigfoot, too.

A man with a crate holding leafy vegetables peeking through the slats pushed past, grumbling at having to move to avoid them. January ignored him.

"I wouldn't say everybody. Folks come and go." Jimmy's gaze sharpened. "But mostly I do. Why? You looking for somebody?"

She hesitated, then decided only the truth would do. "I am. Two men who have kidnapped a young girl. They will have gotten here a few hours ahead of me, I believe, and they intend on catching a boat."

He'd been friendly up to now, but as she watched, his expression changed. He didn't say anything for a full minute. Made uneasy, January chafed at the delay. Was the question that difficult to answer? Or no. The real question seemed to be, why wasn't he answering, period?

"Sir?" she said, hearing a note of command come into her voice.

"You say they kidnapped a young girl?" he said at last.

"Yes." Something else important occurred to her. "One of them is riding a grey gelding, which means they are not only kidnappers and procurers of girls, but horse thieves."

If a man ever looked uncomfortable, he did. He flicked a glance at her, then looked down. "Ma'am, are you sure about that?"

"I'm sure. The gray horse is mine, you see, and the girl..." Another important thought lit up her mind. The thing being, would he even believe her? As she watched, his lips puckered and, though it may have been her imagination, formed the letter P.

Eyes narrowed against the sun, she watched him as she said a name. "One man is known as Peel. Frank Peel. The kidnapped girl, Zora Winkler, is a twelve-year-old. She—and I—hail from eastern Washington. I've tracked her from there."

He jerked when she said the name. Peel's name, that is. "Guess I don't know why I should believe you," he said, not so very friendly now. "A woman alone? Women don't track men across the mountains. Women ain't got the guts, the strength, or the know-how."

January snorted her disdain.

"What's this girl to you, anyhow?" he demanded.

She had taken Silas' pistol, a single action army Colt revolver, from his body and was carrying it on her hip. Smiling slightly, aware that the man wasn't going to believe this next part either, she folded her coat away from her hip and revealed the firearm. "It's not what she is to me," she said. "It's what I am to her."

He eyed the gun. "What's that?"

"A Stevens County deputy sheriff. January Schutt Billings is my name, duly sworn to serve and protect the citizens of Stevens County and the State of Washington. For me, right now, little Miss Zora Winkler is the most important person in the state."

For a second, he didn't move. But when he did, it was to emit a false sounding laugh and blow a raucous raspberry in her direction. "You don't expect me to believe a wild tale like that, do you? A deputy sheriff? You? A female?"

She raised an eyebrow. "Actually, I do expect you to believe. It is the truth."

"Yeah?" A jeer. "Where's your badge?"

She'd been waiting for this. Smiling, she flipped the coat lapel back, revealing the silver-colored six-pointed star. "Right here."

"Stole it, most likely." He looked past her now and didn't do more than glance at the badge. It was as if he regretted ever speaking with her.

"No, sir. I assure you, I did not steal it." January had an itchy feeling he was dragging this conversation to the limit. As if he were waiting for someone with more authority to come along and relieve him of having to think.

The feeling became strong enough she looked over her shoulder then. Pure luck. Unless the man had meant to give her a few seconds of warning.

"Bigfoot."

"Bigfoot? No, that's Merle Hill," Jimmy was saying, but January barely heard him.

"You. What the hell?" Bigfoot recognized her about the same time as she did him, as before she could even gather herself, he broke into a run. Straight at her. He yowled something that included *Manfred* and that she was supposed to be dead. Then he launched himself into a flying tackle with what appeared to be the intention of smashing her flat.

If it hadn't been for the almost waist-high coil of rope Jimmy had just wound, January would've landed in the water at the very least. If she had, it would've been easy for Bigfoot to dispose of her. Push her head under in the guise of fishing her out. Shoot her dead if it didn't matter if anyone saw him—and she thought it might not. Stick a knife in her if she tried to climb out.

But it happened that she didn't fly off into the water. Instead, she dodged around the coiled rope and reached almost leisurely for her gun. Silas' gun, that is, that he'd kept cleaned and oiled, the action as smooth as her draw.

Before she had the pistol in hand, Jimmy had helpfully managed to put himself in front of Bigfoot and get in his way, an action which may have been accidental on his part. Or not. Impeded, the two played do-si-do just long enough for January to set herself for the onslaught. She pointed Silas' pistol at the middle of Bigfoot's chest. She could almost hear her dad saying, "Aim for the biggest target, Janny. In a man, that's his chest. Don't get fancy. No head shots, no hand shots."

In this case, Bigfoot's chest would be almost impossible to miss since less than a yard separated them.

"Stop," she said. "I will shoot you."

Jimmy stepped aside, clearing the target.

"Mr. Hill, you're under arrest." She knew how prim she sounded. Silly, even. She had no idea how the short mention of the man's name had come to her.

Bigfoot stopped. "Where is Manfred?" His eyes narrowed to slits.

"Back at the cabin where you left us. Dead."

"Dead? No. You're lying. He can't be."

January raised one fine eyebrow. "Can be and is."

"Who..."

God forgive her, but she enjoyed saying, "Me. I killed him."

"No, no."

January could barely believe her ears, the way he carried on. Out of character, puzzling. Who had Manfred been, that a man like Bigfoot seemed so broken at the death?

Or maybe not so broken as he took advantage of her distraction. Big feet, big hands, long arms. Arms long enough to reach out and swat at her gun. But not quite long enough to take it out of her hand. She kept her grip, spun the pistol back up and, just as he lunged past her guard, pulled the trigger.

Her dad was right. The biggest target on a man, his chest, was hard to miss. The pistol's roar, muted as it caught between them, faded into the backdrop of surging liquid waves, men's yells, and birds wheeling overhead.

But Bigfoot refused to fall. Sheer willpower kept him on his feet, surprise spreading across his features even as he lunged toward her. She pulled the trigger again, but still he kept coming. His hands stretched out in an effort to reach around her neck. Falling short, they came down on her shoulders instead. He collapsed finally, crushing her toward the rough wooden pier as he fell. She found it impossible to support his dead weight. Literally dead weight.

Strained to the limit, she fell onto her knees, pushing at him. He toppled to the side.

Jimmy bent over him, staring down in what looked like shock at Bigfoot's contorted face. "I'll be! I think he's dead. Merle Hill is actually dead. Didn't think he could be killed."

January took a shuddering breath. "If he isn't dead, he should be."

"If he isn't, he will be soon," he corrected her.

Men appeared out of nowhere. They called from one end of the pier to the other.

"Get the marshal," one yelled.

Footsteps pounded toward them. A nervous tremor swept through her. What if she had to fight them all?

She'd been a fool to let Hill get so close. Even as the thought struck her, she saw his chest rise. His eyelids flickered.

"Manny," he whispered. "My boy."

His boy? Manny. Manfred? Her thoughts raced.

"His boy? Huh," Jimmy said, evidently as astonished as she.

Well, if he wasn't dead, perhaps he could still serve some purpose. January took hold of his jaw and turned his face toward her, squeezing with all the strength of her fingers. His eyes opened again.

"Where is she? Where is Zora Winkler?" she said.

Blood foamed and bubbled from his mouth, his teeth stained red. Evidence of a lung shot. Bigfoot grinned, more of a grotesque grimace. "Peel's got her. You...too late."

She squeezed again and he groaned. She refused to

let the sound unsettle her. "Where? Where is Peel?"

"Gone," he said. And so was he, gone for good.

Another man, his laden cart abandoned in the middle of the pier, stood beside them, mouth gaping like the village idiot. He stared, and scratched his chin, never saying a word.

Jimmy stared down at Hill's body. "Didn't know he had a kid. Not one he'd admit to, anyways. Did you, Wilmer? Did you know Manfred is his?"

The man, Wilmer, shifted his gaze to Jimmy. "Manfred?" he said. "Yeah, I'd heard. And the other one."

"Well," Jimmy said. "Imagine that. Manfred, crazy as a monkey on opium."

January winced, thinking about him. "Not just crazy. Pure evil. Not anyone to be proud of, I can tell you that. But no different than his father, in the end."

Jimmy nodded. "A hard man. Him and his partner both."

"You know Peel?"

"Oh yeah. Seen him around town when he plays big man. Spreads a lot of cash around while his boat is tied up. I don't work on the *Fore Sail*. Won't work it. He stiffs his workers."

The other man, Wilmer, nodded his agreement. He didn't either, apparently.

For a moment, January couldn't figure what he meant, then almost slapped herself in the head. The boat Peel and Bigfoot intended to take was no doubt one of the three tied up here. Why else would Bigfoot even had been on this dock?

She drew a breath. "Which of these boats is his?"

Jimmy glanced down at Hill's body, then back up to January's set face. He turned and pointed. "That one. The squatty little tub named *Fore Sail*. It's the one the fellers are loading. They're off to San Francisco tonight. A few hours from now the tide will be going out. They'll be riding the tide."

He watched January as she cracked open the pistol and, ejecting the spent cartridges, refilled the chambers. "Peel ain't there now, though," he said. "I been working on the pier all afternoon and I ain't seen him. Him nor any little girl."

Wilmer spoke quietly. "He ain't been around."

This piece of news relieved her. She might be a landlubber, but even January knew about tides. Sort of. But impressive as this body of water was, she preferred dry land. Which meant she'd rather catch up with Peel before he got on board. Most definitely before he got Zora on the boat.

Peel hadn't struck her as the type of man to enjoy camping in the woods for the fun of it.

She'd bet he'd book himself the best hotel room in town as his due. But what about Zora? Was it possible he'd simply walk her in and hide her there until it was time to take ship? Or would he park her somewhere and drag her onto the boat at what he considered the proper time, depending on well-paid residents to close their eyes and pretend not to see.

She eyed Jimmy whom she surmised to be the counterpart of the town gossip. "Where does he stay when he's in town?"

Jimmy gave a start. "Who? Hill? Peel?"

"Either of them. Both. Do they stay together?" If not, it might take longer for her to find Zora. And she didn't really have 'longer'. She had no more than a few hours before the boat departed.

Sparing a last look at Bigfoot's body, looked up, toward the top of the bluff. "There's only one hotel. Don't think Hill ever stayed there though. He has...had a shack."

"Shack? Where?"

Wilmer jerked his head shoreward and pointed north.

"Yeah. Over beyond the bluff where it reaches into the trees," Jimmy agreed. "But Peel, he stays in the hotel when he comes to town."

"He doesn't live here?"

"No." His bristled face broke into a kind of grin. "Folks in this town ain't got the kind of class he prefers. He ain't a beer drinker. Likes his brandy. The hotel keeps a special bottle on hand just for him."

"The good Frenchy stuff," Wilmer said, licking his lips. "And champ-pag-nee."

The men who'd been hauling provisions to the other boats had crept forward, muttering among themselves. Some asked Jimmy questions without bothering to listen to the answers. Not a single one of them seemed particularly broken-hearted over Bigfoot's demise.

January eyed them warily. "How many men does Peel have working on his boat?"

"Me," a man acknowledged. A tough-looking customer, a baton and a sheathed knife in his belt.

Jimmy's eyes rolled back as if he was counting. "That's Tom Short. Then there's Tom Hill, George Peel. That's three. Where are they?" he added to Tom Short.

"Tom Hill and George?"

The man shrugged. "Sleeping it off."

January could count. It wasn't the number of names that struck her. "That's all?"

"That's it."

"Tom Hill, you said. George Peel. Those are the last names of him..." she nudged Bigfoot's body with the toe of her boot, "...and of Peel himself."

"Hill is a cousin. Peel, a brother. But lady, neither one of them is apt to give a...hoot... about somebody shootin' this'un. Not even Tom. I heard you say you killed Manfred. If that's true, there ain't a man here who won't want to shake your hand."

Wilmer had something to add. "Or give you a kiss, if you'd druther." Snaggle teeth showed in a wide grin to show he didn't mean that last part.

Or maybe he had meant it. Hard to tell. Could she believe him about the rest? About the others being glad or at least relieved Hill and his son were dead? Alone here, it would be helpful if she didn't have to keep constant watch for an ambush, she reflected, eyeing each of the men. What she needed was a...

The sound of a dog barking alerted her. A familiar sound. Her head jerked up, eyes widening.

CHAPTER 21

ELI SET PEN AFOOT SOMEWHERE OUTSIDE OF THE TOWN. HE FOUND the burg to be a closed-up little place, with narrow lots overlooking a single main street and a couple short secondary lanes. Located on a bluff rising above the Sound, the few stores catered mainly to the boat trade with a few nearby farmers added in. Heavy ropes, chains, anchors and pulleys, for the most part, plow shares and axes being less in demand. In a predominant show, a dry goods store selling groceries that would last a long time at sea sat across from the hotel.

From the top of the bluff, if he strained his eyesight, he could just make out a blur where a thin band of land separated the sound waters from the ocean. If he hadn't known it was there, he might not have discerned the divide. As it was, the vista was impressive.

He wondered if January had paid notice to the view, and if so, what she thought.

Speaking of noticing, he saw Pen sniffing a pile of fresh horse manure. Her tail wagged and she bounced on her hind legs, all eagerness and good will. She appeared to have found a prize. He hoped it was more than just being thrilled with horse turds in general.

"Good dog."

The praise drew a short bark out of her, and Eli laughed, certain they were not far behind either Deputy January Billings or the outlaws and little Miss Zora Winkler. One way or another, this situation had about reached its end.

Tugging Henry along on the lead, he nudged Windswept into motion, anxious to get below and find where the man who'd taken Zora had tied up his boat. January would've done the same. She must be frantic by now, searching for the girl she aimed to save.

Or maybe she'd found Zora already, but to what result? Brought to safety or both in trouble? The question ate at him.

At the base of the bluff, he steered Windswept around a tall, weathered gray building with wide doors that he surmised to be a warehouse of some sort. A team of horses hitched to a farm wagon stood out front. Also, a couple tired looking horses tied to a chunk of driftwood someone had lugged over from where it had washed up. One of those horses bore a saddle he thought he recognized. Eli's heart lurched.

As for Pen, the dog went over to the horse wearing Deputy Billings' saddle, tail wagging, nose working. Eli would swear she was grinning.

"I see it," he said to her.

Dismounting, a little stiff from sitting a saddle all day, he tethered Windswept and Henry beside the other horses.

A pier jutted out into the water. Three boats, none particularly large or impressive were moored there with ramps leading onto their decks. A group of people had gathered next to the boat nearest to shore. They all seemed to be looking down at a body laid out on the dock. Whoever it was did not appear to be taking a nap. From the sprawl, Eli figured he was dead.

No violence going on at present, he noted. The men were talking amiably, and no weapons were drawn. Nevertheless, as Pen lifted her head and dashed forward barking, he wasn't far behind.

The gathering of men split apart to let the dog run through. The gap revealed the woman in the center of the group. Eli saw the smile on her face as she sank to her knees and received the joyful dog into her arms. Pen made funny little puppy sounds and January murmured to the tired old gal as if she were a child.

Eli realized his face wore a smile just as big. Even the men, a batch of hardcases if he'd ever seen the like, grinned at the reunion. They didn't ignore him, either. Some glances showed distrust, others simple curiosity mixed in with a certain amount of caution.

"I'm guessing you know this feller," one older fellow in a floppy hat said. Eli couldn't tell if he meant him or the dog.

"I do." January's hand rested on Pen's black head, calming her, as she rose. "Both of them."

"Deputy Billings," Eli said, watching her face, "I'm glad to see you alive. I found some evidence to make that outcome doubtful." Formal words, cool, he denied the urge to gather her into his arms the way she'd gathered her dog. Pure relief at finding her in one piece, he told himself.

"Mr. Pasco, I'm glad to be alive. Lucky and glad. I am relieved to see you are the same."

"Yeah," he said. "It was nip and tuck for a time. Have you found the girl?"

She shook her head gravely. "Not yet, but I think we're getting close. These gentlemen are going to help me." January leveled a piercing gaze on the rough group of men. "Aren't you?"

Deputy Billings didn't seem to expect anyone to say no. A couple nods from Jimmy and another proved her correct.

Eli fought back a smile.

"What about you? Did you catch up with Shandy and the man who took Windswept?" she asked in turn.

"I did. A safe recovery." For the horse, he meant, even if not for the thieves. None of them. "You'll be interested in the details, I think."

He discovered he wanted to get her alone, somewhere they could talk without these men hanging on every word. Maybe talk about something other than this.

"You came anyway. I thought—I thought you might not."

He smiled down on her. Her hair was mussed, he noticed. Windblown into tangles. Eli had thought her face dirty until he examined it. But those dark areas weren't smudges. They were bruises, deep and dark and almost hiding the scar on her cheek. She'd been knocked around good—or maybe he meant badly. His smile faded.

"Yes, I came. Figured you might need some help." He

felt like a snot-nosed kid with all these hardened men listening to every word, making him skirt around what he wanted to say. He settled for, "Besides, I had to see you got your dog back."

January's smile flashed brilliant. "Yes. Thank you," she said.

A rotund fellow sporting a marshal's badge, his face flushed with excitement, arrived just then, his town shoes pounding on the dock as he rushed toward them.

"Who is this?" he asked, the question at large to whoever might answer. "What's happened?"

Jimmy took it upon himself to answer. "The dead man is Merle Hill. The lady who shot him is a deputy sheriff sent out to arrest him. The fool seemed bound to resist." He winked at January. "Ma'am, I'm sorry to say I plumb forgot what you said when you told me your name. Excuse me. I reckon I'm too flabbergasted at learning you are a certified deputy sheriff. Go on. Show him your badge."

Eli, watching, may have been the only one to notice her embarrassment. Not to mention her irritation at the wrinkled brows and signs of disbelief regarding her authority. The men needed convincing, proof. She flipped her lapel to give them all a brief look at the badge before hiding it again.

"Billings," she said, cold as ice. "Deputy January Billings is my name. I'm from Stevens County." She turned to Eli and lifted her brows.

He tilted his head. Agreement.

"And this is my colleague, Mr. Eli Pasco. He's had a separate group of outlaws to contain. A successful operation, I believe."

"Yes. A success." Eli offered his hand to the marshal, who took it in a clammy, soft grasp. Clever, he thought, calling him a colleague. Maybe that made him semi-legal when it came to shooting people, whether or not they'd been trying to kill him at the time.

The fat marshal seemed a bit bewildered by what he was hearing. That suited Eli fine. If all went well, it might keep him from interfering.

January took over the conversation again. "A certain Mr. Peel is here in your town. He has a young girl with him. A girl he "bought" from her kidnappers. But not with the intention of returning her to her home. His intention is to put her on one of these boats and take her to San Francisco where he'll sell her to the highest bidder for what I'm told is a great deal of money. I heard mention of a Chinese consortium. I am here to effect her rescue and return her to her family. I will arrest him and take him back to Stevens County to stand trial." Her glance shifted to Hill's body. "Without more violence by preference, but I'll do whatever it takes. If we can keep this action contained it will be helpful."

The men exchanged glances, some disbelieving, others wary. It crossed Eli's mind to wonder which part they didn't believe. That Peel was a white slaver or that she could do anything to stop him.

Eli didn't think she meant the part about lack of violence. He had the feeling she'd as soon shoot Peel dead as not. But the part about keep news of this action contained? Yes. Better if Peel didn't learn his partner had been taken down until they had Zora out of danger.

If that proved possible. Doubtful.

He eyed the men on the dock. The marshal, the sail-ors, a kid who'd appeared out of nowhere and showed signs of ghoulish delight. They might nod agreement but having the lot of them keep their mouths shut for five minutes, let alone the time it would take to find Peel and arrest him struck Eli as unlikely.

January knew it, too. She'd already begun questioning them, probing their memories for any information as to where Peel would confine Zora until it was time to sail. The men here had worked for him. They must know something of value.

Eli hoped he wouldn't have to beat it out of them. He flexed his fingers. If he could. Sailors were known for their rough and tumble ways.

He hadn't counted on January having different methods of interrogation. His first impulse was to beat information out of them. She used a softer approach, but under the velvet, the metal was no less than steel.

* * *

JANUARY, TRUSTING SHE ALREADY HAD AN ALLY IN JIMMY, TURNED her attentions on the man he'd introduced as Tom Short. He didn't seem to feel any loss over the man lying dead at his feet. They may have worked on the boat together but must not have been friends. That didn't necessarily mean he knew where Bigfoot holed up when he was in port. So, appealing to any better nature he might have, she asked him. Politely.

"Am I mistaken, Mr. Short, or were you and..." she hesitated, having almost called the dead man Bigfoot, "...Mr. Hill at odds with one another?"

He thought this over. "If you mean was we enemies, then no. Not exactly. But we wasn't friends, either. You might say I had enough brains to stay out of his way. And then," he didn't seem to be bragging, "I be big enough he didn't want to take me on. Knew I wouldn't stand for his shenanigans. See, he was a bully, born mean, and that Manfred was just like him. Maybe worse. Just ask any of the whor—" He stopped and blushed.

January was not so delicate as to misunderstand. "Manfred beat up the prostitutes?"

Her understanding visibly relieved him. "Yeah. Took a knife to one. Damn near scalped her. Thought it was funny, right up until the marshal," he paused, then went on, "the previous marshal, that is, stuck him in the hoosegow for a couple months. Manfred came out worse than he went in, and the marshal, he was kilt along about then. Never caught who done it." He cast a scornful look at the present marshal, who feigned not to see it.

"But it wasn't long 'til Manfred took to the woods," Short went on. "Good riddance, I say. And so says just about everybody else in this here town. There'll be a lot of folks happy to hear they're dead. Both of them."

He seemed glad to have gotten this much off his chest.

"Do you know where Hill lived?"

Tom Short shrugged. "Sure. Least I know where he stayed when he's in town. He had another place about ten miles from here, but I only went there once to pick up a..." He stopped, swallowed, and continued. "Many a time it made him late getting to work, but he didn't care. The rest of us had to take over to get his job done. Caused hard feelings, I don't mind saying. Peel, though, he was fine with it."

January saw Eli, aware of the man omitting useful information, open his mouth as though to ask his own question. She cut him off. The sailor was having too good of a time showing off his knowledge and educating her, a mere female, of the vagaries of male competition. A little discord might work to her advantage. To Zora's advantage.

"Why did Peel keep him on? How did he manage to keep his job if he was often tardy? Jimmy told me about how sailors have to 'catch the tide'. That means close timekeeping, doesn't it?"

She saw Eli's frown and quirked a half-smile. She knew that part didn't really matter.

Short nodded. "Yeah. See, Hill and Peel was partners, of a sort. But Hill did a lot of special work for Mr. Peel. I asked George once why he didn't do it seeing as how him and Peel are related. He just hung his head and said it was all right with him. He didn't like their dirty work."

"Huh. He should've put a stop to it," Eli said.

"Hard to stop Frank Peel when he's got his mind set," Short said. "He's a force."

Excitement rose in January, almost like pins and needles poking into her nerves. They were getting close. Tom Short was on the verge of revealing what she needed to know to find Zora.

Now she asked the most pressing question. "Can you tell me where to find Hill's place?"

"The one outside of town," Eli said, and January nodded.

"Both of them," she added.

Even dangerous characters like Peel would think twice before openly revealing his white slavery operation. Wouldn't he? Which didn't mean any of these men were to be trusted. They'd worked on Peel's boat and had to know its cargo. Had they ever protested? Not as far as she could tell. Up until now, anyhow.

Shifty-eyed, the sailor glanced around. January had no idea whether the expression meant he was leery of his fellow deck hands or if the look was meant for her and Eli.

Tom Short lowered his voice to a deep stage whisper. "I'll do better than that. I'll show you."

Could she trust him? Not likely.

Eli had arrived just in time to back her play.

As for the marshal, his head swiveled from speaker to speaker throughout the entire discussion. The strange thing? He didn't say a word. Not one word. Not even as his florid complexion turned a sickly pale.

* * *

THE LITTLE TOWN MARSHAL, WHEN ALL HAD BEEN EXPLAINED TO him another two or three times, reminded January a little of Deputy Dabney back home. He did a lot of talking and fluttered about like a robin drunk on worm wine in the springtime. But, unlike Dabney, he had stiffer stuffing in his make-up. Once he made up his mind to a thing, it became locked in.

First off, he studiously ignored everything that Tom Short had said. It was as if everything had passed over his head and he hadn't heard a word. And that, she knew, provided an answer, if there'd been any doubt, as to whether he was an honest lawman on the side of law and order, or one of Peel's men set up in a position of authority to make certain his real boss' activities were never questioned.

Which meant she and Eli were on their own.

The marshal had ushered her over to his office, a tiny cubbyhole building in the tiny town. Seating himself behind an oak desk that dwarfed him, he laboriously wrote notes regarding, as he referred to it, *the trouble on the pier*.

"I'll take care of this," he said. "Send the undertaker after Hill's body. As for what you're saying about a kidnapping, well, I'll talk to Mr. Peel myself. You've got no authority here, Deputy Billings, even if you're even a real deputy. If Mr. Peel is holding a woman against her will, providing she presses charges, I'll have him under arrest quick as you can shake a stick."

"Zora Winkler is not a woman. She is a twelve-year-old girl who has been kidnapped from her family and is in need of rescue." January choked back a scream of pure frustration. *Mr. Peel*, he'd said, in a tone of utmost respect. The marshal was going to ignore every accusation against Peel. In which case, he'd better ignore the fighting when it started, too.

"I seen Mr. Peel in town earlier." The marshal shook his head as if negating every word she'd just said. "Told him howdy, he said howdy back. Didn't seem worried at meeting me."

Who would? she wondered. A man not especially fierce, and more than a little stupid? A toady.

The marshal's mouth continued flapping. "I didn't see any sign of a girl. Matter of fact, I got only your word there is a missing girl and I don't know you. Could be you're accusing an innocent man. He's got money. Might it be you're just trying to get some of it and hookwinking us with that badge? I'm doing you a big favor in bringing this up to Mr. Peel at all. Matter of fact, could be I ought to run you in for killing Merle Hill. Would, except Jimmy and the other men from his own boat say he charged you yelling he was gonna kill you. I reckon it was self-defense."

January, eyes narrowing, remained silent, teeth clamped on her outrage.

He preened. "See? Even a stranger gets treated fair in this town."

"Follow the law, that's all we ask," she said tightly, including Eli in that *we*. He needed a reminder that she wasn't alone here. "And I urge you act with all due speed while investigating."

"Well, sure." He pouted and pointed to her face. "Say, what happened to you? How'd you get that scar? And them bruises. Kind of suspicious if you ask me."

"Nobody did ask you. My scars are none of your business." Plain speaking, although the marshal didn't appear to take offense. Proof that he wasn't paying attention to what she had to say anyhow. Not to the tone and not to the words. No one would ever have guessed her to be on the verge of exploding. She'd had a lot of practice over the years ignoring questions about the scar. As for the bruises, she'd keep her own counsel. For now.

Meanwhile, time was wasting.

The marshal patted his badge. He stood up and clamped his hat on his head. "You wait right here, Missus Billings, while I go along and have that talk with Mr. Peel. The sooner I hear what he has to say, the sooner we can put this all behind us." His trust in Peel seemed assured.

"Deputy Billings," she reminded him.

He refused her the courtesy of inviting her to the meeting. A toady and a toad, all rolled into one. She was certain he was another in Peel's employ. Bought and paid for.

"Wait here? What you mean?" She put astonishment into her question. "I certainly will no sit here and wait. I have my own questions to ask."

"Not with me, you don't," he said, and started rummaging through some papers scattered over his desk. Busy work, to keep from meeting her eyes.

Through the window behind him, January saw Eli walking with Tom Short as they brought up the horses. Not only his own Henry and the mighty Windswept, but the two she'd taken from Silas and Manfred. Pen ambled along with them, calm at Eli's side. Her heart eased at the sight.

As soon as they rescued Zora and Peel was taken down, she'd track Hoot and get him back. Mollie, too, wherever her old buckskin might be. Maybe Eli knew where to find her. Then she'd feel complete again.

CHAPTER 22

"ACCORDING TO THIS SHORT FELLOW, SHE...ZORA...IS BEING HELD somewhere close to town," Eli said. He'd moved January away from where Tom Short was tightening his cinch so they could speak out of his earshot. "He says before, when they had a "passenger"—that's what they called the girls—to load on board, it only took a couple hours there and back from wherever Peel had them stashed. Which makes sense. If they intend on leaving tonight, he'll want her somewhere nearby."

He hesitated and sort of chewed his tongue for a moment. "I was afraid they'd kill you."

If his eyes moved over her possessively, January wasn't going to complain. "They tried," she said. "Peel and Bigfoot left me in Manfred's hands with that intention."

"Bigfoot?" His eyebrows quirked upward. "Manfred?"

"Bigfoot equaling Hill. The man I just shot. I didn't know his name at first, but he reminded me of the Bigfoot, that mythical creature. Big, ugly, and dangerous." January embarrassed herself, admitting it, but Eli, who opened his mouth to say something, changed his mind and only nodded.

"Mount up. I'll tell you about Manfred as we go." When she wouldn't have to look at him and see him judge as they rode. Setting words to action, January climbed on Silas' mount, a chestnut gelding in better shape than the beast that had belonged to Manfred. "Mr. Short," she called out, "if you'd take the lead, I'd be grateful."

"Yes, ma'am."

Considering the awkward way he mounted, Short was not a man much at home on a horse. Once aboard, he headed inland, toward a distant belt of evergreens. January and Eli followed, not talking much no matter what she'd said about filling Eli in on Manfred. Bare essentials—that's all January could bring herself to share. The struggle with Manfred. The look in his eyes. The knowledge he'd just killed Silas who was supposed to be a valued member of the gang.

And his touch on her cheek, on the scars. The smell of him. She'd spent every hour of the time since then trying to put him...it...out of her mind. Not, she admitted, very successfully.

Last night? Worrying about wounded cougar had been an almost welcome diversion.

She didn't miss the look Eli gave her when she finished though. As if he could guess at the things she omitted.

January forced a smile. "It's over. He's dead. No more Manfred."

Eli nodded, but January didn't think he believed her. The part about it being over, she meant.

Pen ran out in front of them. Short had turned his back to fill his canteen at a spigot before they started off, and January had dug out the blanket she'd wrapped around Zora when they'd been in the cabin. She offered it to Pen to sniff. It helped prove Short wasn't leading them wrong when Pen set her nose to the ground and seemed to be on the same track.

"Do you trust him?" Eli asked, after a while, watching as Short leaned over his horse and spat a stream of tobacco to the ground. It barely missed Pen. Eli's expression hardened, as if Short's action had settled something within him.

The spitting struck January as a deliberate, if silent insult, making her hiss like a tea kettle at the boil. "Not a bit, but I'm afraid we don't have any choice but to follow him. For now. We'll see when we catch up to Peel." She raised her voice above the sounds of the horses' hooves on dry ground. "How much farther is it to this cabin, Mr. Short?"

They'd been riding almost three-quarters of an hour by then and had entered the fringes of the forest.

"Not much. We're close, if I remember right." Short pointed to where smoke rose into the sky above the verdant, dark green spread of the woods. "His shack is over that way. I wouldn't be surprised if we don't meet Peel on the way back."

"On the way...oh, you mean he'll be bringing her soon. Exactly when is high tide?"

Short squinted as he looked westward, into the sun. "It'll start rising in a couple hours. Mr. Peel'll want to be on hand to leave right quick when he gets there. He always is. While the boat can still pass over the reef."

"Reef?"

"A stone shelf that can rip the bottom out of a boat if there's not enough water under it to clear."

Cords in Short's neck stood out and he brushed at a trickle of sweat running down his jaw. His horse picked up on his nerves, tossing its head. A chipmunk ran across the path and the horse shied. Not enough to unseat the rider, although Short let out a shout as his butt flapped down hard into the saddle. Odd though, as neither January's nor Eli's horse took notice of the small scamperer. Which begged the question, why was Short so nervous?

Had Eli noticed?

He had. They shared a glance. January suspected they headed into a trap. Did Peel have extra men paid to protect his interests? A possibility. And was Tom Short one of them, no matter his assertion of distaste for Peel's enterprises?

January took noticed when Eli shifted his underarm holster lower and unsnapped the latch holding his bulky Broomhandle Mauser. The gun always looked awkward and heavy to her. Still, Eli must carry it for a reason.

His action encouraged her own surreptitious release of her holster's tie-down.

They were into the trees, riding beneath a thick canopy of towering spruce when Short looked around and pulled up. He cocked his head. "Do you hear that?"

January had been hearing distant voices calling to one another for a while now. "Men talking. Yes."

Eli nodded.

"Do you think it's him? Peel?" she said.

"Doubtful." Short tipped back the cap on his head, then jerked it back down. A nervous gesture, January realized.

"More than likely it's a logging crew," Short said. "There's plenty of them around here. You smelled the smoke from the fires, didn't you? That's just loggers burning slash. I recommend we keep a sharp look-out from here on. I ain't just exactly sure which, but Peel's cabin is set off along one of these trails through the woods. As I remember, there'll be a signpost. That's what George told me. George Peel. He said to look for a board on a stump that orders folks to keep out." The man was chattering like the guest of honor at a birthday party.

January almost snickered. Why was she not surprised at that? It only made sense for Peel to keep his procuring secret. Most men, even hardened outlaws, wouldn't approve of kidnapping young girls and selling them to the highest bidder like cattle.

But what she really did was keep a close eye on Pen. The dog was still working, tracking Zora. Eli watched the old dog, too. He must have learned to do that when he followed her here.

They wound around a blind corner just then. A place where a stone embankment rose higher than their heads. Partly natural, it appeared as if some time in the not too distant past, men had taken a hand. Made it into a levee to protect loggers from a flooded road during the wet season. Or it might've been an extra safeguard to help Peel keep his secret enclave safe. Whatever, she didn't like the way it loomed over her, and even Silas' horse she was riding tossed its head.

Eli's horse, Henry, didn't like it either. Didn't like something, anyway, but it was hard telling what disturbed them. And Pen.

Abruptly, Pen stopped in the middle of the trail. Legs stiff, the hair on her back rose while her tail drooped as she pointed her nose toward a sign nailed to a stump. "Keep out." This was it.

Still following the embankment, Short rode past the dog, directing them onto a narrow path that led them through some overgrown bushes bearing pink-colored blooms. The smell of greenery surrounded them as leaves were bruised by their passing. Signs of recent travel were marked by broken twigs, a pile of fresh horse manure and the hoof prints of several horses.

Several horses. How many men did Peel have with him? How many did it take to confine one small girl?

Most importantly, was Short leading them into a trap? Every sense she had shouted *yes*.

Glancing over at Eli, she wondered if he felt the same sense of waiting for something to happen. As if feeling her gaze, he looked at her and winked.

The sound of January's own breathing rasped into a silence broken only by the plodding of hooves. The muscles in her back tightened.

Tom Short's left hand twitched toward his holster, until he jerked it back.

So, she wasn't the only one who felt the tension.

Then, somewhere ahead, a girl screamed in a paroxysm of fear, of warning, of courage. Her cry echoed among the trees.

January drew in her horse at the same instant a bunch of white birds exploded into the sky on a rush of flapping wings. Barking, Pen bounded forward into the underbrush.

"Pen," she yelled out, but by then it was too late. Gunfire rattled through the bushes, blowing bark and leaves into the air, and she knew this was what she'd been expecting.

The next thing she knew, Eli, on his feet on the offside of Henry, grabbed her by the leg and without ceremony, yanked her off the horse. She tumbled to the ground. With more haste than grace, Eli pushing her from behind, she scooted into the shelter of a tree trunk as bullets whizzed past. Eli crowded in next to her, their shoulders touching. His Mauser was in his hand, but so far, he hadn't fired it.

Brush shots, considering a kidnapped girl was somewhere around, were entirely too dangerous. Besides, Peel was just the sort of man to use the girl as a shield.

Tom Short, arms flapping, heels drumming his horse's flanks, headed up the trail toward the small cabin they could see now from between trees. "I brung'em, boss," he was yelling. "I got'em here."

"Guess that settles that, doesn't it?"

A lift of January's eyebrow asked a silent question.

"Settles who Short is working for. Off hand, I'd say it isn't us. Or little Zora Winkler."

So far, January hadn't had a chance to be afraid, but it was growing in her. "Off hand, I'd say you're right."

Movement to her right—Eli's right, too—caught her attention. A man had stepped into the open for an instant before disappearing at the rear of the stone embankment that had worried her. He carried a long-barreled rifle and seemed intent on taking a position on the higher ground. Though out of sight, a scattering of rock fell to the ground as he climbed, marking his progress. If he found just the right spot, she and Eli would be the proverbial sitting ducks. Not, she decided, a position she wanted to be in.

She nudged Eli. "Look over there. There's a man climbing the ridge."

"I see him." Eli grunted. "He's got what looks like a sniper rifle. I got a taste of those in the Philippines. With a gun like that, if he's any kind of shot at all, he'll have no trouble picking us off when he gets higher. Best chance to stop him is before he settles into place." He turned to look at her, the muscle in his jaw working. "I'm going after him, January. Will you be all right?"

What was he asking? Did he think she would be too frightened to shoot back if he left her alone? Hadn't he learned better than that at the livery in Claremont? Or at what he'd found at Peel's cabin in the woods?

A faint smile crossed her face. "If you think back, it's not my first time being shot at, Mr. Pasco. Not even my first time being shot." A twinge of satisfaction went through her when his dark eyes opened wide. "You go on. I'll take care of the ones out front."

There were three of them, she thought, settled in at various spots where cover was the thickest. Plus, a fourth now, Short having ridden off to join them. They were lying as low as she and Eli. Maybe they even thought they'd killed them since there'd been no return fire. Could be Peel had sent the man with the sniper rifle up top for a better view to check for bodies. A surprise when he found otherwise.

The only problem January foresaw was her lack of ammunition. A glance back showed their horses, smarter than a lot of folks gave them credit for, had skedaddled out of the line of fire. Too far for her to reach her saddle bags and renew her supply of cartridges. Her—Silas'— holster belt held thirty cartridges when filled. Except a full third of those, she discovered, had been used. In a pitched battle against three or more antagonists, that was not enough. Not nearly.

January swiped at a trickle of sweat running down her cheek, the raised scar changing the damp course of flow. An errant thought struck saying she must smell like she hadn't had a bath in a week. To her surprise, a reckoning agreed that she hadn't. Her nose wrinkled.

Eli still hesitated. Until she said, "Well, go ahead then. As soon as you're away, I'll fire a few rounds to divert their attention."

He nodded. Said, "Take care. Keep your head down." He took off sliding on his belly and dragging himself by the arms until he reached the base of the outcropping and rose up. He'd have a couple strides until he found more cover. That's when she had to make Peel and his men look at her.

A flash of a brown canvas pant-leg stuck out a few inches beyond a boulder near the shed, and she took the shot. Blood spurted. A man bellowed. Good. That was good, aside from the renewed fusillade of bullets passing overhead. Her intention had been to draw their fire, allowing Eli to slip away behind her. Not fair to complain when it worked better than expected. Much better. It became obvious Peel's men had no shortage of ammunition.

She rued having to almost bury her head in the dirt. On the other hand, nobody would care how badly she smelled if she were dead. It was, after all, the natural order of death.

* * *

BEFORE THE SHOOTING BEGAN, ELI HAD NOTICED A CREVICE CUT into the side of the embankment as they passed. He crawled toward it, counting on January's return fire to hold Peel's attention. Her first shot worked a treat. When he reached the crack, one he figured had been caused by prodigious amounts of rainwater having poured down from the top of the scarp, he found plenty of handholds. Footholds was another story, his boot soles slipping on the rocks and leaving him dangling by his fingertips more than once.

He had time to worry about the length of time between January's shots, as well, as the space between them grew. He heard no more shouts indicating she hit anything. Both sides seemed to have dug in, Peel's men no doubt waiting for the sniper to find his position.

Well, that wasn't going to happen. Not if he had anything to say about it.

Eli renewed his efforts, breath coming short and sweat running into his eyes before he finally breasted the embankment. He made enough noise to alert a deaf man, or so he figured.

And must've been right as the sniper was waiting for him at the top.

The sniper's first hurried shot kicked sand and splintered tree bark into Eli's eyes. But it did not blow a hole in his head which, if the man had been any kind of gun hand would've put a period to Eli Pasco's life. Peel had sent the wrong man with the sniper rifle after him.

Slow on the uptake, as well.

The barrel of the rifle followed him as Eli scrambled over the lip of the embankment. Moving as fast as he'd ever moved in his life, although it felt slow, he rolled over and over into the shelter of some rocks. More bullets followed him and as he made a last dive for cover, fire burned across the top of his shoulder. He let out a yelp and saw the man, a swarthy foreign-looking character in short, wide-legged britches respond with a grin.

Partially blunted by the strong leather of his holster harness, the graze wasn't enough to stop him from drawing the Mauser. He was bleeding like a stuck hog, his blood already had made the leather slick.

The fool must've thought he'd hit Eli hard enough to stop him from returning fire because he stood up in plain sight and walked forward. "You landlubbers ain't a match for a mariner, horse boy," he said. Then, taking his time, he raised the rifle for the killing shot.

Idiot. All he'd done was cause Eli a little pain and a lot of aggravation, and now he was going to die.

At this close range, Eli couldn't miss if he tried. Gently, he squeezed the Mauser's trigger. The bullet took the mariner in the chest, spinning him around and dropping him several feet back from where he'd stood. The dead man didn't even have time to yell.

Eli lurched forward and grabbed up the sniper rifle, figuring it might come in handy. Down below, he heard January pop off another shot. Assured that she was still in the fight, he duck-walked across the embankment to where the sniper had climbed up. From here, he could see through the woods to where not a cabin, but a low, windowless shed sat in the shade of some tall firs. Even at this distance, the sun glinting off a padlock on the door indicated where Peel had Zora confined. Would there be other girls in there? A possibility.

Several nearby horses were tied to whatever was handy, tree limbs, brush, one short rail. Unhappy with the noise of gunfire, a lot of head-tossing and agitated shifting of feet signaled their distress.

The most anxious of the horses belonged to Tom Short. No doubt because of Short's body lying practically under the horse's feet, his eyes open to the sky.

Dead, by glory, and Eli had a notion he'd been killed by his own crew. Scanning the area, he spotted a dark-colored wet spot near a boulder. Narrowing his eyes, he saw a man slumped there, leaning in a position that showed he just might be another dead man. Credit due to Mrs. Billings, he supposed. He smiled grimly. Best never count out the serious way she took her deputying responsibilities. It had been the first lesson he learned about her.

It struck him that he didn't know which of these men was Peel. He'd heard him talk once, late at night in the dark, but had never seen him in the light of day. He's the one to go for, Eli told himself. The one that needed killed.

His job. One he was good at, even if it meant ripping through every single man here.

CHAPTER 23

WHERE WAS ZORA? THE QUESTION PLAGUED JANUARY, CAUSING something that felt almost like an itch. The girl had let out that one cry of warning all those minutes ago as they first approached. Minutes now beginning to seem as long as hours. There hadn't been a sound from her since. What had Peel done? Killed her? Knocked her out? Gagged her?

Lord, she hoped it was only a gag. *Only a gag.*

The thought made her blood boil. If there was anybody in the world who understood the shock of what the girl was going through it was January Schutt Billings. Her own childhood experiences had formed her into an independent woman who could take care of herself. Her scarred face had made it hard for her to make friends or trust in anybody, but it had also made her able to do things. Things like build a bridge or protect herself or others. No matter what it took.

Except she wasn't doing such a great job of protecting Zora Winkler at this moment.

From long habit, January refrained from sinking all the way into these uncomfortable thoughts and sorrowful memories. A part of her kept careful watch, tracing the source of shots and the outlaws' movements as Eli climbed the embankment.

She'd caught a good glimpse of one of the men. He turned out to be the other Tom, the one related to Bigfoot.

Another man, young, quick on his feet, and unseen until now, moved so fast he gave her an eerie feeling. he reminded her entirely too much of—she hesitated to even say the name—Manfred.

The man she'd shot in the leg slumped behind a boulder, either dead or unconscious—or maybe playing possum—visible enough to see part of his face. Enough to recognize it, too. George Peel, boss man Peel's cousin. So every man, excepting maybe Jimmy, who'd been on the pier had been biding their time, their loyalty all bound to Peel no matter how degrading his crimes. And now they'd die for it.

That left only Peel, himself. The one she needed to stop. Take him down and his men were sure to give up. Followers always did, didn't they? Look at those hired guns Mrs. Hammel had paid to go after her last year. They wafted into the yonder like chaff in a breeze the moment, helped by the bullet January put in her, the Hammel woman fell over a log.

But she wasn't rid of Peel yet, let alone his men.

A lull and its uneasy quiet settled in. Everyone sat back, caught their breath and regrouped. Outlaws as well as January. The man with the resemblance to—Manfred. The likeness struck at her like a fist—shifted position, gaining ground and drawing him another couple of paces nearer to her. He'd done that more than once, she realized. Best not allow him another opportunity, or he'd be right on her.

Most troubling, she'd spent six more of her cartridges. Extracting fresh cartridges from her gun belt, she fed them into the revolver's cylinder. Only a few remained. When they were gone, she'd have to rely on her boot gun. *Five shots there. Or no. Four. She killed Manfred with one bullet.*

Eli. Where was he, anyway? She hadn't heard anything from him beyond his Mauser's one shot sounding almost in tandem with the sniper rifle. Was he atop the embankment lying wounded? Or dead? Worry roiled in her stomach.

"Deputy Billings—" Peel calling her name brought her back her wandering thoughts, "I must say I was surprised when I heard you were alive. Congratulations. I expected Manfred to have taken care of you back at the cabin. That was his job."

Was. Peel said was. So that meant someone had told him what happened.

She shouted her reply. "I am aware. It is my pleasure to have killed him before he succeeded." He'd never know her satisfaction at saying that, although a little of it may have crept into her voice. "I suspect you are annoyed at his failure."

"Me? No, no, but..."

A pistol's report interrupted whatever he meant to say. A bullet pinged against a rock a few yards away. Then another. Trying to spot the shooter's target, she eased her head around the edge of her stone bulwark. She gasped. Her heart almost stopped.

"Pen. No, no. Pen."

The old black dog had chosen the lull to make her way back to January. She was a dog. Not a mind reader. Already hard of hearing, she must've figured the quiet equaled safety.

Without stopping to think, January stood up. From there she could see it was the Manfred look-alike, standing behind a tree whilst firing at her dog.

Too rushed to take aim, her first shot went high over his head. She didn't care. All that mattered was to get his attention off Pen.

"Pen, run Pen! Come." She called to Pen at the top of her lungs. The dog wasn't stupid, already running to get away from the bullets winging past her, at January's frantic scream, she flattened out like a border collie chasing stampeding cows.

January, taking better aim, fired again. And again. She saw his buckskin-clad shoulder wince away as the bullet plucked at the fringe dangling from the arm seam. Shot again, just as Pen flew over the rocks, where she knocked into January. They fell to the ground together. Pen, panting, excited, and not much bothered by her close call, wagged her tail. January, cursing herself for being careless and stupid and wondering how it happened she was still alive. Standing in plain sight? What was wrong with her?

She grabbed Pen and hugged the old dog around the neck.

Motioning Pen to stay down, she reloaded her weapon, emptying her ammunition belt.

"That was just for fun." Peel was laughing loudly. "If

my man had been aiming to kill the animal, it would be dead. But enough foolishness, Mrs. Deputy Billings. Come out where I can talk to you. We'll all hold our fire. Settle this."

She didn't even have to think. "Not likely, Mr. Peel. There's nothing to settle. Your only choice is to give up and deliver the girl to me unharmed. The only person I want to see up close is Zora Winkler, alive and well. She needs to get home to her mother. Send her out and stop this debacle. The law will go easier on you when you do."

"I see. An 'or-else' situation. We'll talk about it. Maybe make a deal—if you'll come out from that hole you're hiding in."

She forced a laugh. "You first, then we'll see."

He didn't answer.

She still hadn't gotten a glimpse of Peel. He'd found some good—from his perspective—spot to hide while letting his men take the brunt of her gunfire. And what about Zora? Where was she? A dilapidated shed squatted among the trees. Was she in there?

What about Eli? Where was he?

A moment later she had another thought. Why did Peel bother to talk? But then she knew. A delaying tactic while his two remaining men worked their way around her.

"You realize, sir, that this situation can only end one way." She risked a look behind her as she spoke. No sign of them. *Yet.* "I either arrest you or kill you," she went on. "It's your choice. Send Zora to me, safe and sound. Wouldn't you rather be arrested than killed?"

The bravado of her threat made him laugh. His merriment also allowed her to discover where he'd taken cover. A woodpile beside the shed where peepholes in the stack left him an uninterrupted view, while successfully hiding him.

She stretched her neck for another look around the boulder shielding her. Last time, she'd been able to spot the buckskin jacket of the Manfred lookalike. Not now. He must be making his move.

A shot from the left proved her right. She ducked back into shelter. At the same time, she discovered Zora's whereabouts. There were no windows in the shed but, with what must've been from a hefty kick, a piece of the siding went flying into the yard. It was followed a moment later by another, and after that, a small girl squeezed out of the opening. She dashed beneath the horses' noses and darted into the woods. All faster than it takes to tell.

January was the one laughing now. Zora saving herself. The girl was tough. Maybe as tough as January.

"Get the girl," Peel roared, himself popping upright at the edge of the woodpile. After a second, he seemed to think better of going after her himself and jumped backward. "After her," he yelled, which is when January spotted Eli as he leapt from the edge of the escarpment in a long drop. He had his Mauser in hand and a fierce look on his face.

That was all January had a chance to see, because just then a stinking buckskin jacket dropped over her head. Grabbed from behind, an arm around her neck shut off her wind. She heard Pen growling, then the sound of a blow and the dog cried out. But the arm fell away for that brief moment and sucking air, she fought out of the jacket's folds.

She spun, lashing out with her fist and slamming it into the side of her attacker's face. Her leg came up with unerring aim in a repeat of her battle with Manfred. Her stunned senses declared the attacker *was* Manfred. Identical, even though she knew he was dead. Had felt his hot blood pour over her. Suffered the weight as his dead body fell on her.

And yet, here he was. Yelling at her. Slapping her face, punching her ribs, her belly. Pain coursed through her body. At first, she couldn't make anything of it. Then she did, even as his hands settled around her throat and clenched. He was cursing at her—no surprise—the words garbled through gaps where teeth were missing. Garbled or not, she understood enough to know he was railing at her over the other Manfred's death. His twin. His brother.

Black spots flickered behind her eyes. He hadn't known his twin was dead until she told him herself just now. And he raged.

She twisted, rolled, tucked her face away. Her shoulder ground into a fist-sized rock. Pins and needles prickled in her arm, but it didn't matter. Here was a weapon. Her hand flailed, gripped the stone. She'd have only one possible chance. This had to go right, her aim true, before he choked the strength, the life out of her.

Once again it was Pen who saved her. The dog, limping after being flung into the rocks, joined the fray. Powerful jaws clamped down on the twin's ankle, biting through the moccasins he wore in lieu of boots.

The twin kicked out, but Pen had a good grip. Manfred II let out a bellow, releasing January's throat long enough to take a swipe at the dog. Time enough for January to roll and free her arm. With every bit of oomph she had left in her, she slammed the stone into the side of the man's head.

It was enough. The bone at his temple gave way. He collapsed across her body just as his brother had done and lay still.

"Well done, Pen," she said. Her throat hurt and she spoke with a peculiar rasp. "Enough."

Pen, no doubt feeling her ills, obeyed.

As the thunder of her heartbeat in her ears ebbed to a reasonable level, January met only silence. Pushing herself out from under Manfred II and sitting up, she looked first to Pen, finding the dog panting and with a lame leg, but otherwise all right. At least the dog licked January's hand and wagged her tail, seeming pleased with herself.

"Good girl." January ruffled the dog's ears. "You're a good old girl."

Her next step meant gathering in the outlaws, laying out the dead and placing the others under arrest, even though it was hard telling how much jurisdiction she had in this county. Probably none.

Didn't matter.

All to do, as soon as she felt able to rise.

That was first. Second was holding Zora under her wing and easing her fears. If she could.

And third, although it chafed that she couldn't do everything at once, she had to check on Eli Pasco. She'd seen blood on him as he took that leap to the ground. Hopefully, it wasn't his.

January stepped from behind the rocks into the open.

* * *

ELI THUDDED TO THE GROUND, HIS ANKLE TWISTING BENEATH HIM. Grunting at the pain, he had no time to worry about whether the dang thing was broken or just zinging. His target stood in front of him. The man shouting out orders must be Peel. The boss. Kidnapper, murderer, and all-around perverter of children. Time to end his game.

Caught in the act of trying to recapture Zora Winkler, the man's eyes bugged at Eli's sudden appearance.

"I'll be taking you in on charges," Eli announced. He'd dropped the sniper rifle as he fell but held his Broomhandle Mauser pointed at Peel. It tickled him when no one answered the man's call to find Zora. Not one of his men was able to go after her. Between the two of them, he and January Billings had done well at wiping out this gang.

For his part, Peel eyed the weapon leveled at his gut. The pistol was an oddity. Not many semi-automatic handguns were seen in these parts, and this one had a lethal appearance. Still, he had a bit of bravado left in him. "Does that thing even shoot?"

Eli smiled. "You want to try running, I'll show you." He wished the man would. In his business he'd found it easier to take in a dead man than one alive and doing his best to thwart you. He had a notion Peel would be less than cooperative.

"Turn around," he said. "Put your hands behind your back, crossed at the wrists."

Peel did it, turning away, the movement of his arms seeming obedient. Eli holstered the Mauser and leaned forward with one of the pigging strings he used in lieu of heavy metal handcuffs when Peel spun and came at him. Like he'd conjured it up, the outlaw held a Bowie knife and slashed out at Eli, the blade glinting with wicked intent.

Eli leaped back, the knife whipping past his gut. Pigging string forgotten, clumsy with the jump, he wrestled the Mauser out of the holster. "Stand back," he said.

Peel ignored him. The man came at him again, wearing a smile and sure of himself, probably knowing that most people had a horror of being disemboweled, their guts dangling. And he was fast.

But not fast enough.

Eli shot him. Shot him once in the shoulder and once, deliberately, in the elbow of his knife-carrying arm.

That's all it took. Flopping onto the ground, Peel screamed loudly enough to shatter a man's eardrums. Then he fainted.

Eli's heart was thumping to beat the band as January walked out into the sunshine. Bleeding, but strong. They eyed each other.

"Got him," he said, as if she didn't know.

"Zora is free," she said, which he knew too.

He smiled. "Job is done."

She nodded, then raised her voice. "Zora," she called out, "it's Mrs. Billings. Come on out. You're safe. This is over."

A rustling noise in the bushes answered. They waited, and after a minute the girl emerged. Her face was dirty, tear-stained, her clothing in tatters. She approached like a wild cat circling her prey to make certain it was dead.

"I thought you were dead," she said to January, stopping her slow pace around the unconscious Peel and staring down at him. "He said you were. He said Manfred killed you."

"That was the intention. But as you see, here I am."

"Yes." With that, Zora swung back her leg, probably the same one she'd used to kick through the shed and slammed her boot into Peel's ribs. Not once, but several times, with enough force he groaned even through his blackout.

Eli figured what with all she'd been though, she'd earned the right. He made no move to stop her.

Neither did January.

CHAPTER 24

THE PUNY LITTLE MARSHAL MET THEM AT THE EDGE OF TOWN, walking out into the street to greet them with his thumbs hooked in his belt. They made quite the procession, what with horses laden with the other Tom, Peel and George, both wounded, and several various bodies. In addition to Zora, a girl of maybe ten years, a beauty of about sixteen, and another not quite so beautiful fourteen-year-old added to the show. They'd been recovered from the shack.

Most of the Canton residents came out to observe the spectacle.

The marshal's jaw dropped. "What is this? You people can't do this." He looked to Peel who, pale and bleeding, slumped on his horse. Not a good rider at best, Eli had tied him on. "My God, woman, what you done to Mr. Peel?"

January stopped her horse in front of him. "I have arrested a very bad man and his gang of outlaws."

"Nonsense," he said.

He was interrupted by a woman rushing down the street shrieking loud enough to awaken one of the corpses. "Esamin! Esamin Johansson, is that you? Where have you been?"

The not so beautiful girl slipped from the back of the horse she was riding and sped to meet the woman. "Mrs. Houk, I must see my mother. I must tell my mother that I am saved. This lady and this man saved me. They saved Miranda, and Jane and this other girl."

"Praise the Lord!" The woman rushed up to the girl and hugged her tight. "We thought you were dead. We thought you drowned. Oh, your poor mother."

The girl, Esmin, stood up straight. "No, Mrs. Houk," she announced in a loud, carrying voice. "I was kidnapped. We all were kidnapped." She whirled and pointed a forefinger at Peel, then one by one at his men. "By them. He is the leader." Her finger went back to Peel. "He was going to take us to San Francisco and sell us."

Blood drained from the marshal's face. His eyes bulged.

"Sell you?" Mrs. Houk stared wildly at Peel, then at the marshal. "Girls can't be sold."

January snorted. "My thoughts exactly."

"Who are these girls? Do they tell the truth?" The marshal, disgruntled perhaps over his poor character judgement and the way he'd earlier denied Peel's part in this, made a try at weaseling out of responsibility.

"Are you asking for introductions?" Eli dismounted, stalked over to the girls on horseback and lifted the smallest one down. "Tell the folks your name, sweetheart," he said to her, his voice so gentle January hardly recognized it.

The little girl clung to him. "Jane. I'm Jane Smith."

"That's a pretty name, Jane," he said and went on to the beauty. She fell willingly into his arms. "Your name?"

"Miranda Pugh. My father is the mayor of..."

"I heard about her," someone said loudly. "About Miranda Pugh. Her picture was in the newspaper a few days ago. Said she'd gone missing."

"And here she is. Do any of you know Jane?" Eli eyed faces in the crowd.

No one did, but Jane knew where she was from. She mentioned a little town up toward the Canadian border.

"I'll send a telegram," the marshal said, and off he went, all officious haste to hand off the prisoners to the county sheriff.

January figured his abrupt change of heart due to a yen to avoid the condemnation he saw—and heard—emanating from the folks. He'd most probably served his last term.

As for her, she was happy to hand off her part of it, too, giving them Sheriff Schlinger's name and telling the sheriff here, when he arrived an hour later, to check her credentials with him. The least Schlinger could do, she figured, was handle the paperwork. Wedding or no wedding.

As for Eli Pasco, the sheriff called him into the office for a private meeting. January was a bit concerned, but when the office door opened a while later and he and the sheriff shook hands, something within her eased. She still didn't know what he was. Bounty hunter? Pinkerton man? Another like Ford Tervo? She intended on finding out, and soon.

The next morning, she, Eli, and Zora caught a train headed east over the mountains.

Hoot, discovered and recovered from the town livery,

picked his way up a plank ramp into a stock car, Windswept and Henry following him. Over the conductor's protests, Pen took a seat with the passengers. By far better behaved than two young boys who raced up and down the aisles, as January pointed out proudly. Even the conductor finally admitted it was so.

Besides, Zora spoke up on Pen's behalf, so forcefully the conductor had to back down. "This dog is a hero," she stated without taking into account Pen was actually a heroine, "who saved my life."

"And mine," January agreed, smiling a little.

"Mine too," Eli said.

* * *

JOHNNY JOHNSON SHOWED UP EARLY ON THE MORNING OF THE Schlinger and Inman wedding. January, schlepping around in her old clothes preparatory to feeding livestock, milking the cow, and gathering eggs while the bath water heated, was surprised to see him, this not being one of the days he was scheduled to help her out.

"Bo sent me over," he said. "He says ladies got to get all gussied up for doings like weddings and such, and he figures you're gonna want to make a good impression."

January, who'd been thinking along these same lines before she went to answer the door—loathe though she'd be to admit as much—gaped at Johnny. Then she frowned. Gussied up, yes, as much as she was able. But the other? "Bo said that? I don't know why. I don't have to make a good impression. It's not me getting married."

"Yep. He kind of surprised me, too. Didn't think he knew anything about women. Anyways, I'm gonna do your chores so's you can get ready. He says it takes a woman hours for a special occasion."

It wasn't as if she were the bride, January thought. She didn't really know the tricks of making herself pretty, anyway, as if that were even possible. Besides, who cared?

A vision of Eli Pasco floated in front of her face, but she waved it off. He might not even attend, although a shindig like this meant everyone in the surrounding countryside was invited. Rebecca and her sister better have a huge cake ready to serve the horde. Or maybe even two or three big cakes. And plenty of good strong punch.

Anticipation—or maybe a kind of fear—swarmed through her. She told herself she didn't care about her scar anymore. People who were her friends didn't notice, and those who weren't her friends were welcome to fly a kite in a lightning storm. For the ones who were neither, well, they could wonder all they liked. Shay had set her free of all that. Ford Tervo helped further the process. And now Eli Pasco, who had traced the scar on her cheek once, his touch gentle, and never seemed to see it again.

"Anyways, Bo says it's because you're going to declare for the sheriff position today, January. You know, when Schlinger officially resigns?"

It had taken her weeks to get him to call her by her first name. Congratulating herself on having finally gotten him trained, it took a moment for his question to catch up to her.

Her brows arched up, then lowered down. "What did you say?"

"Ain't you?" His sincere young face lifted toward her. "You'll be twice the sheriff Schlinger has been. Look at what you did with the Hammels. And now this feller who kidnapped the Winkler girl and stole Windswept."

"Johnny, I had help. Anyway, I can't be a sheriff. I'm too busy with the ranch and building my new house."

"Well, yeah. But see, that's what deputies are for." His eyes widened and he grinned. "What do you say about making me a deputy? Bet I'd be better at it than Dabney."

"I'm sure you would, but Johnny, I have no intention of running for sheriff. Folks wouldn't vote for me, a woman. They barely tolerate me as a sometime deputy."

"Huh," he said. "We'll see."

She waved her hands as if trying to shoo him away. "No, we won't, because I'm not running. Now scoot on outa here. If I'm supposed to make myself beautiful, I'd better get started. It's apt to take a while."

She laughed to show she didn't mean the beautiful part. But it would be gratifying to show people— some people—she didn't always appear to have come straight from the barn.

"Aw." Johnny turned red. "You're already beautiful, January."

Her heart—how could it help it—melted.

Eli Pasco wouldn't have missed this wedding for the world. In plain fact, he considered the occasion a time to make himself known to his neighbors once and for all. He felt certain his presence would be more accepted if they met him before they learned he'd been a bounty hunter in the past. While he was still revered for helping January Billings save young Zora Winkler and those other girls. He'd say he was retired now, but then, that's what he'd said when he bought the Winkler place. And Windswept.

Folks didn't always like having a bounty hunter living in their midst. They were prone to drawing men bent on revenge to the area, resulting in more killing no matter who got in the way.

Zora Winkler, resigned to losing her horse, had gone to live with some grandparents, her family having left her behind. Otherwise, he wouldn't have been riding Windswept today. The horse was showing off a little amongst the crowd gathering outside the little church where Schlinger's wedding was to take place. The building, he figured, would be packed to overflowing when everyone got inside.

He slipped Windswept's bit and tied him off by himself in the shade of a few maple trees. Bo Cobb was already there, spiffed up in a suit fit to rival Eli's own dress clothes. Bo rode a fine grey mare Eli figured must be a relative of January's Hoot. Bent Langley and his wife drove up in a buckboard, their two sons riding alongside.

Eli recognized a few others, received a few handshakes and slaps on the back. Even Schlinger, who stopped beside him and said, "There's an envelope with your name on it at the office. Drop in and ask Dabney for it. He'll give it to you."

So, Eli figured. It was true. Schlinger had resigned. Dabney was the law here for now. He hoped to hell nothing happened between now and the election.

But he didn't see January.

Not until the ceremony was over and Schlinger and the blonde woman he married beamed out over the crowd. Eli turned to watch them walk back down the aisle and there she was, standing just inside the door.

January Billings as he'd never seen her before. She wore a pretty, green dress with a squared off neckline that showed her collarbones. The dress had lace sleeves to the elbows, and a swinging skirt. Her hair was piled on top of her head and, he noticed, smiling a little, that a few strands had already escaped and lay along her neck.

The scar on her cheek stood out like it'd been painted on, but she tilted her head back and flaunted it even as some folks stared.

Eli headed toward her.

Bo Cobb beat him to her side. Then Bent Langley and a couple other men she greeted.

Eli stopped at the edges of the group, aware of her watching him. Watching for him. The corners of her mouth quirked up and she drew a breath like she'd speak.

Cobb spoke first. "Well, January? Have you made up your mind? You gonna declare? Fish or cut bait, woman."

What, Eli wondered, were they talking about?

She shook her head. "A waste of time, Bo. Mine and everybody else's. Why don't you do it?"

"Not me. I've got a ranch to run."

"As do I. As well as a house to finish building."

"Yeah, but..." Cobb trailed off.

Next, Bent took up the argument, if argument it was. Eli couldn't make heads nor tails of whatever they were talking about.

"You're the best candidate, January. You know you are," Bent said and his wife, Pinky, nodded right along with him.

"You've proved that time after time," Pinky said. "You proved it again when you saved Zora Winkler."

January stared around at each of them in turn, ending up with him. "I wasn't alone, you know. Not once. I didn't do anything by myself. If it hadn't been for Eli..."

"You're the catalyst." Interrupting, the oldest Langley boy spoke up.

Eli put random pieces of the conversation together and got a glimmer of direction.

"What should I do, Eli?"

Her question jolted him, but ignoring a sudden wave of cold fear, he had an answer. The kind of answer a woman like January Billings would understand. "Follow your conscience."

Quirking a smile, she pushed between Cobb and the Bentley boy straight toward him. "Well then," she said. "I guess I need to have a talk with my conscience. But not now. This is a wedding." Reaching out, she took his arm and started walking him toward an improvised dance floor where couples were beginning to swirl around. "Is that music I hear? I've never learned how to dance. Will you teach me?"

The music was a waltz. Heart beating hard, Eli gathered her closer. "You bet."

A LOOK AT: LIAR'S TRAIL BY C.K. CRIGGER

YOUNG GINCY TATE'S FATHER is murdered before he can fulfill a contract to supply the Army with remounts. In order to pay his debts and save the ranch, she must make the sale in his place. Afraid the lien-holder, whom she suspects of being the murderer, will foreclose before June 7, 1883, she tells no one Morris Tate is dead. Instead, she says he is here, there, or elsewhere. Gincy hires two cowboys to help trail the herd to Fort Spokane. One is on the murderer's payroll, but Sawyer Kennett hires on because he has decided Gincy is the woman for him. With an old Indian, who is her shirttail relative, the group battles storm, stampede, and sabotage to win their way to the fort and sell the herd. Then Gincy must make it home in time to beat the foreclosure and confront her father's murderer - but only if Sawyer is the man she prays he is.

AVAILABLE ON AMAZON

ABOUT THE AUTHOR

C.K. CRIGGER was born and raised in North Idaho on the Coeur d'Alene Indian Reservation, and currently lives with her husband, three feisty little dogs and an uppity Persian cat in Spokane Valley, Washington.

Imbued with an abiding love of western traditions and wide-open spaces, Crigger writes of free-spirited people who break from their standard roles.

Her western novel, The Woman Who Built a Bridge was a 2019 Spur Award winner. Her short story, Aldy Neal's Ghost, was a 2007 Spur finalist. Black Crossing won the 2008 EPIC Award in the historical/western category. Letter of the Law was a 2009 Spur finalist in the audio category.

CPSIA information can be obtained
at www.ICGtesting.com
Printed in the USA
LVHW041034191021
700836LV00009B/344

9 781639 770458